TRAIL OF A MISSING DAMSEL

ABHIJEET SINGH

INDIA • SINGAPORE • MALAYSIA

ISBN

Paperback 979-8-89777-697-9
Hardcase 979-8-89906-603-0

Gratitude

Writing a book is a journey filled with countless revisions, doubts, and moments of inspiration. But no writer walks this path alone.

I owe a deep debt of gratitude to my closest confidants who took the time to read this book and lend a hand with editing. Your keen eyes, honest critiques, and endless encouragement shaped this story into what it is today. You wrestled with early drafts, celebrated breakthroughs, and offered the exact tweaks this story needed. This book exists in its final form because of you, and for that, I am endlessly grateful.

And to you, the reader holding this book right now—thank you. Whether you picked it up on a whim or sought it out, you've become part of its journey. You may not realize it, but by turning these pages, you are making a difference in the life of someone publishing their first novel. This journey from idea to page has been a wild one, and knowing you've chosen to come along for the ride fills me with gratitude. You've given this book a home, and for that, I am deeply humbled.

Thank you for giving this story a chance.

Prologue

"So, this is why we are here?" one of the soldiers muttered under his breath, his voice carrying a hint of anticipation.

Akram did not look at him immediately. Instead, his sharp gaze remained locked onto the distant figures below. Then with a slow, steady nod he finally spoke.

"Do you see them?", he asked, his tone harsh and commanding as he pointed his sword toward the horsemen at a distance below. "We will make our move and crush those men to the ground."

The dawn was barely breaking, the first light of day creeping over the horizon, painting the sky with faint streaks of gold and crimson. A cold wind whispered across the elevated plain where Akram stood, carrying the scent of damp earth and the distant crackle of burning wood from a hut nearby. His face was sharp and angular, his piercing gaze holding an unshakable intensity. A thin scar traced his brow, hinting at past battles. Broad-shouldered and impeccably poised, he carried himself with quiet authority. His neat uniform, adorned with intricate gold embroidery, gleamed in the dim light, while a crimson-lined cape cascaded behind him. The polished insignia on his chest marked his rank, its presence undeniable. At his waist, a ceremonial sword rested in an ornate scabbard, its hilt wrapped in black leather. Every detail—from his measured stance to the gleam of his adornments—spoke of a man shaped by duty and command. His name alone struck fear into the hearts of many—he was an unstoppable force.

Behind him, around thirty soldiers sat astride their horses, silent and poised. Their unwavering stillness only intensified the tension in the air. The rhythmic clinking of horse tack, the occasional snort of an animal, and the distant echo of hooves painted an ominous scene.

From their elevated vantage point, Akram and his men observed the distant horsemen moving across the landscape, unaware of the fate that was about to befall them. Clad in jet-black cloaks, the riders moved with eerie, measured precision. They circled something—no, someone! A group of people trudging along on foot, shackled together. The prisoners' chains clinked in the still morning air, each step a reminder of their helplessness.

Akram's fingers curled around the hilt of his sword as his gaze locked onto the leader of the group, a flicker of disdain crossed his face. His face had a resentment. Without thinking he spat on the ground, his contempt for the man evident. This was no mere enemy—this was a man he had crossed paths with before. A man who had betrayed everything he stood for.

"Traitor!", Akram whispered, his voice laced with venom.

He took a deep breath, with steady calm he turned to face his men, his voice cutting through the stillness of the morning. "Not a single one of those horsemen will leave here alive. They are to be slaughtered without mercy. But remember this", he said, his eyes burning with cold intensity, "There's one among them I want alive. The man who leads them. He's mine."

The soldiers, recognizing the vehemence in their commander's voice, nodded in silent understanding. They knew this would be no ordinary fight, it was personal. The hatred Akram bore for the leader of that group was ancient, a wound that had never healed.

He turned back to face his men, "We'll take those hostages. Not a single one shall be harmed, but the men who stand with him... they will fall." His voice dropped to a near-whisper yet it carried the weight of an unshakable promise. "I repeat, the man who leads them... he is mine to kill."

The soldiers remained still atop their horses, the sound of hooves breaking the stillness of the dawn. Akram gave a sharp nod, his expression as cold and unforgiving as the morning air. Without another word he turned his horse and the group of riders surged forward, the earth beneath them trembling as they charged.

As the sounds of galloping hooves filled the air, a silent promise hung between Akram and his men: this was the beginning of the end. A battle was coming, one that would not only change the fate of the hostages below but also shape the course of vengeance and justice alike.

Chapter 1

"Stay still. Don't make a sound."

"Stay still. Don't make a sound."

The boy curled into himself, pressing his trembling body against the cold, unforgiving log. His breath came in ragged, silent gasps. Outside, the world was collapsing in chaos. "Run, Rana, run!" The screams pierced the night, laden with desperation and fear. Feet pounded against the earth, the metallic clash of swords rang through the air, and the acrid scent of burning wood clawed at his senses.

But he must not move. He must not breathe too loud. The shadows were hunting.

"Run, Rana, run!"

"Run, Rana, run!"

The voices rose again—pleading, commanding, fading.

Rana jolted awake, the echoes of the screams still ringing in his ears. His breath came in ragged gasps, his body drenched in sweat. The ghosts of the past still whispered in his ears, still clung to his skin. The nightmare had never left him. It never would.

The Ganga whispers its secrets under the pale light of the crescent moon, its dark waters flowing past the small village of Devran, nestled between a dense, foreboding forest and the eternal river. The Mughal Empire's shadow loomed over the land, its grandeur and tyranny seeping into even the most remote corners of life. But in Devran, the whispers weren't about emperors or battles. They were about the forest—a place both feared and revered, where the line between myth and reality blurred.

Devran was a village caught between tradition and survival. Its people lived simply, tilling the fertile soil by the river and hunting the forest's fringes. The men spoke of ancient spirits guarding the woods, and the women whispered of shadows that moved even in daylight. Outsiders rarely ventured here, and those who did seldom stayed. Life in Devran was quiet, predictable, and steeped in apprehension.

Rana was the exception.

A man of few words, he carried the weight of the village's survival on his broad shoulders. His sharp eyes missed nothing—whether it was the faint tracks of a stag in the forest or the subtle shift in the wind that warned of a storm. At thirty, he had earned the respect of the elders and the envy of the younger men. But Rana's stoicism masked a deeper solitude, forged by loss and hardened by years of isolation.

The villagers trusted him, but they didn't understand him. They saw a hunter who brought food when famine loomed, a protector who kept the forest's dangers at bay. What they didn't see was the man who spent sleepless nights staring into the dark trees, searching for something even he couldn't name.

It was on one such night that Rana first felt it—a change in the air, subtle but undeniable. The forest seemed to pulse with an energy that set his teeth on edge. He stood at the edge of the trees, his spear in hand, listening to the unnerving silence. The usual chorus of crickets and distant howls was absent, replaced by a heavy stillness that made his skin crawl.

The next morning, the village awoke to news of a missing child. Ten-year-old Pari had wandered too close to the forest and vanished without a trace. Her friend's wails echoed through the village as the men gathered to form a search party.

"The forest has taken her," one of the elders muttered, his voice heavy with resignation.

"Nonsense," Rana snapped, his tone sharper than intended. He shouldered his spear and fixed the elder with a hard stare. "We'll find her."

But even as he spoke the words, a sliver of doubt crept into his mind. He had hunted these woods for years, knew their trails and secrets better than anyone. Yet lately, there were signs he couldn't explain: deep claw marks on tree trunks, strange symbols etched into the earth, and the distinct feeling of being watched.

The search party combed the forest for hours, their torches flickering in the dim undergrowth. Rana led the way, his senses heightened, every snap of a twig putting him on edge. They found nothing—no footprints, no scraps of clothing, no sign of Pari.

Humans have a peculiar way of conjuring compassion for those they would otherwise overlook. Until yesterday, Pari was just another face in the crowd—a child some knew by name, others barely noticed, and most ignored entirely as they trudged through their own lives. But now that she was gone, they would rally to find her. It was a strange comfort, this sudden urgency to do good, as if their efforts could absolve them of the guilt of indifference. For some, it was about the child; for others, it was about the illusion of virtue, a balm to help them sleep at night.

As the sun dipped below the horizon, casting long shadows through the trees, the men began to mutter about returning to the village. Rana ignored them, pushing deeper into the forest until he reached a clearing. There, in the fading light, he saw it: a circle of stones arranged with unnerving precision, each marked with symbols that glowed faintly in the twilight. At the centre lay a single red ribbon, the kind Pari had worn in her hair.

The men behind him gasped, their fear palpable. "We shouldn't be here," one whispered. "This place is cursed."

Rana stepped into the circle, his eyes scanning every detail. The symbols were unlike anything he'd seen before, their shapes jagged and foreign. He picked up the ribbon, his molars pressing together. Pari had been here. But where was she now?

As Rana trudged through the forest, the flickering torchlight barely piercing the dense gloom, memories of Pari swirled unbidden in his mind. She had been more than just another child in the village; she had been his shadow, his constant companion. No matter how much he tried to keep his distance, she always found a way to wriggle into his world.

He remembered the day she had first followed him into the forest. He had been skinning a rabbit by the riverbank when her small, inquisitive face appeared from behind a tree. "Rana bhaiya, what are you doing?" she had asked, her tone filled with wonder rather than fear.

"You shouldn't be here, Pari," he had said sternly, his hands never stopping their work.

But Pari was undeterred. She had crouched beside him, her eyes wide as she watched him work. "Does it hurt the rabbit?" she had asked, her voice soft with concern.

"No," he replied. "The forest gives us life, and we take only what we need. It's how it has always been."

She had seemed to consider this for a moment before nodding solemnly, as though she truly understood the weight of his words. From that day on, she had been a constant presence during his hunts, though he never let her stray far from the village edge.

Rana blinked, the dense shadows of the forest pressing around him like a suffocating shroud. His grip on the spear tightened as he forced himself to focus, his sharp eyes scanning the dimly lit undergrowth for any sign of movement. The silence was unnerving, each step echoing louder in his mind than it should. A flicker of doubt crept in, an unwelcome companion to the edginess that had settled in his chest.

He shook his head, willing himself back to the task at hand. Yet, no matter how hard he tried, the memories of Pari kept clawing their way to the surface. Her laughter, her questions, her trust in him—they filled the empty spaces the forest left behind.

Another memory surfaced, this one of a summer evening when Pari had dragged him to the river to show him something she'd found. It was a cluster of wildflowers growing in a small clearing, their vivid colours shimmering in the golden light of dusk. "They're just like the ones Amma used to wear in her hair," she had said, twirling a flower between her fingers. "Don't you think they're pretty, Rana bhaiya?"

He had nodded, watching her as she gathered a handful of the flowers and wove them into a garland. She had insisted on placing it around his neck, laughing at how out of place it looked against his rugged appearance. "Now you look like a king," she had declared with a grin. For the first time in years, he had laughed—a deep, unrestrained sound that startled even himself.

Pari had a way of bringing light to his otherwise sombre existence. She was fearless, inquisitive, and endlessly optimistic, a combination that both exasperated and endeared her to him. She had a knack for finding beauty in the mundane, for turning even the darkest days into adventures.

And now, she was gone.

Rana's grip tightened on his spear as the memories faded, replaced by the suffocating reality of the present. He couldn't let her become another casualty of the forest; another name whispered in fearful tales around the village fires. She had trusted him, believed in him, and he would not fail her.

He pushed forward, his throat bobbed, his eyes scanning the shadows for any sign of her. The forest seemed to mock him with its silence, its secrets just out of reach. But he would find her. He had to.

That night, the village was gripped by fright. The men spoke of ancient curses, the women lit lamps and muttered prayers, and the children were kept indoors. Rana sat outside his hut, the ribbon clutched in his hand, his thoughts racing. The forest had always been dangerous, but this was something else—something older, darker.

He didn't sleep. Instead, he watched the treeline, waiting for a sign, a clue, anything that might lead him to Pari. The hours dragged on, the silence oppressive, until just before dawn, he saw it: a figure emerging from the shadows of the forest.

At first, he thought it was Pari, her small frame stumbling toward the village. But as the figure drew closer, he realized it wasn't a child. It was a woman, her movements slow and unsteady, her crimson dupatta catching the faint light of the approaching dawn. She carried a small, worn bag slung over her shoulder, its contents hidden but seemingly light, as though it held nothing but air—or perhaps something far more valuable. She collapsed before she reached the edge of the village, her body crumpling into the dirt.

Rana didn't move at first, his mind struggling to process what he was seeing. Then, instinct took over. He grabbed his spear and ran to her, his heart pounding as he knelt beside her. She was unconscious, her face pale and streaked with dirt, her breathing shallow. And yet, even in her weakened state, there was something about her that made his skin prickle—a sense of danger he couldn't explain.

A group of boys who had been collecting firewood nearby saw the figure collapse and came rushing over, their youthful faces pale with a mix of fear and curiosity. One of the older boys, Amar, hesitated before bending down to check if she was breathing.

"She's alive," he said, his voice shaking. "We need to take her to the village."

The others exchanged nervous glances, but with a few hurried nods, they worked together to lift her frail body. Her crimson dupatta trailed behind as they carried her through the uneven path, their murmurs drowned by the rustle of the forest. None of them spoke of the strange unease that seemed to cling to her, or the way her arrival felt like the forest's warning come to life.

Rana stayed by her side as the boys carefully lifted her, his grip tightening around his spear. His mind raced—he didn't know who she was or where she had come from, but something about her presence unsettled him. As they carried her toward the village, he walked alongside them, his gaze never leaving her face. One thing was certain—the forest hadn't finished with them yet.

The boys placed the woman on a charpoy outside the headman's hut, their hands trembling as they backed away. Dharamdas, the village headman, emerged from his home, his face stern as his weathered eyes fell upon the stranger. He knelt beside her, placing a cautious hand on her forehead.

"She has a fever," Dharamdas said grimly, gesturing for his son to bring water. "We must tend to her wounds, but the forest's curse has followed her here. Mark my words."

The crowd that had gathered murmured uneasily, their gazes darting between the unconscious woman and the forest beyond.

Rana stepped forward, his voice cutting through their whispers. "She's injured, not cursed. We'll treat her first. Superstitions can wait."

Dharamdas raised an eyebrow but said nothing, allowing Rana to take charge. As the villagers dispersed reluctantly, Rana crouched beside the charpoy, studying her face. Dirt and blood streaked her features, but beneath it, she was striking—a mixture of vulnerability and defiance, even in her unconscious state. The small bag she carried lay beside her, its worn leather hinting at secrets it refused to reveal.

"Who are you?" he muttered under his breath. But there was no answer, only the faint rustle of the wind carrying whispers from the forest.

Chapter 2

The city of Allahabad gleamed faintly under the same moonlight that cast shadows over Devran. Its bustling streets lay silent, the grand domes and spires of Mughal palaces silhouetted against the night sky. Inside one such palace, a figure moved with quiet purpose.

A man dressed in fine robes embroidered with gold stood by a latticed window, staring into the dark courtyard below. Zahir Khan, a trusted officer in the Mughal court, wielded power and ruthlessness that matched no other. Tasked with governing central India from his seat in Allahabad, he ruled under the banner of Emperor Qasim Khan in Dilli, ensuring the empire's hold remained unchallenged. Known for his ruthlessness, he had an uncanny ability to crush rebellion before it even sparked. Tonight, however, his mind was elsewhere.

"She escaped," he said, his voice cold and even.

Another man, cloaked in black, knelt before him, head bowed. "Yes, my lord. We were following her. She climbed the hill, but then… she vanished."

Zahir's hand tightened around the hilt of his sword. "Vanished? How do you lose a mere girl?"

The man hesitated, his voice tense with fear. "We searched everywhere, my lord. If she had fallen from the cliffs, she could not have survived."

Zahir turned slowly, his dark eyes glinting in the dim light of the oil lamps. "Then bring me her body. I do not work on assumptions. If she is dead, I need proof of it."

The kneeling man swallowed hard and nodded. "Yes, my lord."

Zahir studied him for a long moment, his expression unreadable. Then, dismissing him with a slight tilt of his head, he returned his gaze to the horizon. Somewhere out there, in the shadow of the Yamuna and the cursed forest, the threads of his carefully woven plans were unravelling. And Zahir Khan did not tolerate loose ends.

As he stood by the latticed window, memories of his past uncoiled in his mind, as vivid and sharp as the night he first tasted betrayal. He had not always been Zahir Khan, the emperor's trusted officer. Years ago, he had been no more than a simple merchant's son, an innocent boy named Nasir, with dreams far humbler than the ambitions that now drove him.

***

Nasir had grown up in the bustling lanes of Agra, his days spent working in his father's small silk shop. His life had been simple, predictable, until the day he met Afsana. She was the daughter of a wealthy jeweller, her beauty as intoxicating as the jasmine perfume she wore. For months, Nasir had courted her, their stolen glances turning into whispered promises beneath moonlit skies. He had loved her with a fervour that blinded him to the truths of the world.

Nasir's memories of Afsana were a garden of bittersweet moments, filled with the scent of jasmine and the glow of lantern-lit evenings. He could still recall the first time he had seen her, standing by her father's jewellery stall in Agra's bustling marketplace. She had been selecting gemstones, her fingers gliding over emeralds and rubies as though they were petals of a flower. He had been mesmerized, his heart thundering in his chest as her laughter rang out, bright and clear above the cacophony of the bazaar. She noticed his gaze upon her and lowered her lashes, a shy gesture. Yet, after a moment, she glanced back at him and smiled.

It had taken weeks of stolen glances before he worked up the courage to approach her. One fateful evening, as she wandered away from the crowd to admire the silk shops, he had stepped forward.

"The silk suits you," he had said, his voice steady despite the chaos in his chest.

She had turned to him, her dark eyes narrowing in playful suspicion. "And you, a merchant's son, are now an expert in women's attire?"

He had smiled then, a rare and unguarded expression. "Perhaps not an expert, but I know beauty when I see it."

From that day, their paths seemed to cross as though fate wove its threads around them. She would visit his father's silk shop under the pretence of buying fabric, though her eyes lingered more on Nasir than the wares. He would wait by the spice stalls, knowing she passed by them every Friday evening on her way home. Their conversations grew from teasing remarks to heartfelt confessions, and soon, they found themselves meeting in secret beneath the moonlit arches of the old city bridge.

One such evening, as the city slept and the stars shimmered above, Nasir brought her a small wooden carving—a delicate bird with outstretched wings. "For you," he said, his voice soft. "It's a nightingale. They say it sings only for love."

Afsana took the carving, her fingers brushing against his. "It's beautiful," she whispered, her eyes shining. "I didn't know you could do carvings. "But why a nightingale?"

"Because," he said, his gaze steady, "like the nightingale only sings for love, I would do carvings only for you."

She laughed; a sound so pure it made his chest ache. "You're a poet, Nasir. Who knew?"

"Only for you," he replied, his voice low. "Only ever for you."

Their love grew in stolen moments, each one a treasure Nasir carried in his heart. One afternoon, as the sun dipped low and painted the sky in hues of gold, Afsana led him to a hidden courtyard behind her father's house. Vines climbed the walls, and a single pomegranate tree stood in the centre, its branches heavy with fruit.

"This is my secret place," she said, her voice tinged with excitement. "No one knows about it. Not even my father."

Nasir looked around, marvelling at the tranquillity. "It's perfect," he said. "Like you."

She rolled her eyes but couldn't hide her smile. "You're impossible."

"Only when I'm with you," he teased, plucking a pomegranate from the tree. He split it open, the ruby-red seeds glistening in the fading light. "Here," he said, offering her a handful. "A gift from your secret garden."

She took the seeds, her fingers brushing against his. "You know," she said, her tone turning serious, "sometimes I feel like this—us—is too good to be true. Like it's a dream I'll wake up from."

Nasir stepped closer, his voice firm. "It's not a dream, Afsana. And I won't let anyone take it away from us."

She looked up at him, her eyes searching his. "Promise me, Nasir. Promise me we'll always find a way."

"I promise," he said, his hand reaching for hers. "No matter what happens, I'll always find you."

Their love flourished in the shadows, growing stronger with each stolen moment. She would weave jasmine flowers into her hair, knowing they were his favourite, and he would bring her small trinkets he carved himself, each one an expression of the depth of his feelings. One evening, as they sat by the Yamuna River, the water reflecting the moonlight like liquid silver, Afsana turned to him with a mischievous glint in her eye.

"Do you remember the first time we met?" she asked, her voice playful.

"How could I forget?" Nasir replied, smiling. "You were standing there, surrounded by jewels, and all I could think was how out of place I felt."

She laughed, the sound like music. "And now look at us. You're the only thing that feels right in my life."

Nasir's chest tightened at her words. He reached for her hand, his thumb brushing over her knuckles. "One day, I will marry you," he said, his voice steady. "I will give you a life of silk and jewels, but more than that, I will give you love. No one will ever hurt you."

Afsana's smile softened, her eyes glistening with unshed tears. "And I will be yours, Nasir. Only yours."

Their love was a flame that burned brighter with each passing day, but it was also a secret they guarded fiercely. One night, as they sat beneath the old banyan tree on the outskirts of the city, Afsana leaned her head against his shoulder. "Do you ever think about the future?" she asked, her voice barely above a whisper.

"All the time," Nasir admitted. "I think about a home where we don't have to hide. A life where we can be together without fear."

She lifted her head to look at him, her expression serious. "What if it's not possible? What if my father—"

"Don't," Nasir interrupted, his voice firm. "We'll find a way. I'll find a way. No matter what it takes."

Afsana searched his face, her eyes filled with a mixture of hope and fear. "I believe you," she said finally. "But sometimes I'm afraid."

"Of what?" he asked, his voice gentle.

"Of losing you," she admitted, her voice breaking. "Of losing this."

Nasir pulled her into his arms, holding her tightly. "You won't lose me," he vowed. "Not ever. And even if you do, I'll make sure to find you again"

But the world beyond their fragile bubble was unkind. Afsana's father, a man of ambition and pride, had noticed her absences, the glow in her cheeks that spoke of something forbidden. Nasir's warnings about being careful fell on deaf ears as Afsana, ever fearless, assured him that nothing could separate them.

The day her father confronted her; their world began to unravel. Afsana was confined to her home, her movements restricted. Still, she found ways to send Nasir messages—a flower left at their meeting spot, a scrap of fabric with her initials embroidered on it. Each token became a lifeline, a reminder that their love still burned bright.

One such message arrived late in the evening, carried by a young servant who hurriedly slipped a folded piece of parchment into Nasir's hand before disappearing into the crowded streets. Nasir unfolded the letter with trembling fingers, his heart pounding with anticipation and fear.

The letter was written in Afsana's delicate hand, each word carefully chosen:

Nasir,

My heart aches with the weight of the walls around me. I long for the nights beneath the stars, for your voice and the safety I feel in your arms. Father watches my every move, but

I cannot let this be the end of us. There is a way, but you must come to me.

Tonight, after the last call of the muezzin, meet me at the old banyan tree near the outskirts of the city. It will be dark, and you must not be seen. I will wait for you there. No matter what happens, I will always be yours.

Afsana

Nasir read the letter twice, his chest tightening with a mixture of hope and dread. He folded it carefully and tucked it inside his tunic, the words seared into his mind. The old banyan tree was a secluded spot, far from prying eyes, but the risks were immense. Yet, for Afsana, there was no hesitation. He would go, no matter the danger.

Love is the great paradox of existence—both the simplest and the most complex of human emotions. It defies logic, transcends reason, and bends the will of even the strongest souls. It is the unseen force that binds two strangers, weaving their fates together in ways neither can explain. It is an act of surrender, a rebellion against everything once held sacred-be it family, friends, rules of society or sometimes even each other. Love demands sacrifice, often pitting the heart against the blood ties that once defined a person's world. It is both a gentle whisper and a raging storm, a guiding light and an unrelenting abyss. Some are fortunate enough to hold onto it, while others are left chasing shadows, haunted by what was or what could have been. Yet, despite its uncertainty, its risks, and its inevitable pain, love remains the one force that no soul can truly resist. It is both the question and the answer to life's deepest mysteries.

Nasir arrived at the old banyan tree just as the final echoes of the muezzin's call faded into the night. The massive, gnarled roots twisted into the earth like ancient sentinels, their shadows dancing under the moonlight. The air was heavy with the scent of damp earth and night jasmine, and the stillness felt both serene and foreboding.

He stood beneath the tree's sprawling canopy, his breath shallow as he scanned the darkness. His heart pounded with a mixture of anticipation and foreboding. Then he heard it—a faint rustle of fabric, followed by the soft sound of footsteps.

"Afsana," he whispered.

She emerged from the shadows, her dupatta slipping off her shoulder, revealing a face etched with equal parts fear and longing. Her dark hair framed her delicate features, and her eyes glistened with unshed tears. Without a word, she ran to him, her arms encircling his waist as she buried her face in his chest.

"You came," she breathed, her voice trembling.

"Always," he replied, his arms tightening around her. "I told you I would never let anything keep us apart."

For a moment, they stood in silence, the world around them forgotten. Nasir tilted her chin up, his fingers brushing against her soft skin. "Tell me what's happening," he urged gently. "Why did you send for me?"

Afsana pulled back slightly, her brows knitting together. "Father has made arrangements for my engagement. It will happen in three days, Nasir. I… I couldn't let this end. I think we should run away!"

A muscle flickered in Nasir's face as a storm of emotions passed through him—anger, desperation, and an overwhelming need to protect her. "Then we'll leave," he said firmly. "Tonight. We'll go far away, Afsana. Somewhere your father's reach cannot find us."

She hesitated, fear warring with hope in her eyes. "How? Where would we go?"

"Anywhere," Nasir said, cupping her face. "As long as we're together, it doesn't matter. We'll cross the river, disappear

into the countryside. I have some savings hidden away—
we'll survive."

Afsana searched his face, her tears falling freely now. "You'd give up everything for me?"

"For you? Always."

A soft, broken laugh escaped her lips as she pressed her forehead to his. "Then let's go."

The night was their ally as they made their way through the outskirts of the city, careful to avoid the lantern-lit streets. Nasir held her hand tightly, his senses on high alert. Every rustle of leaves, every distant bark of a dog set his nerves on edge. They moved swiftly, the urgency of their escape driving them forward.

By the time they reached the riverbank, the moon was high in the sky, casting a silvery glow on the water. A small boat lay tethered to a post, its worn wood creaking softly as the current lapped against it. Nasir helped Afsana into the boat before untying the rope and pushing them off the shore. The oars sliced through the water with steady rhythm as he guided them toward the opposite bank.

When they finally reached the far side, the forest loomed before them, dark and imposing. Nasir led her through the dense undergrowth, his familiarity with the terrain keeping them on a safe path. After what felt like hours, they found a small cave nestled between two large boulders. It was dry and sheltered, a temporary haven.

Inside, Afsana sank onto the cool ground, her shoulders slumping with exhaustion. Nasir knelt beside her, brushing a strand of hair from her face. "Are you all right?"

She nodded, though her eyes were heavy with worry. "I'm just tired."

Nasir sat beside her, pulling her into his arms. The tension in her body melted away as she rested her head against his chest. For a while, they said nothing, the silence between them filled with unspoken fears and unshakable love.

"I never imagined we'd end up like this," Afsana murmured. "Hiding in the dark, running from everything we know."

Nasir kissed the top of her head. "We're not running, Afsana. We're starting over. Together."

Her hand found his, their fingers intertwining. "You make it sound so simple."

"It is," he said, his voice steady. "Because no matter where we go, as long as I have you, I have everything."

Afsana tilted her head up, her gaze meeting his. The love and trust in her eyes made his chest ache, a bittersweet reminder of all they had risked and all they stood to lose. Slowly, he leaned down, his lips brushing against hers in a kiss that was both tender and desperate. It was a kiss that spoke of stolen moments and unspoken promises, of a love that had flourished in the shadows and now burned brighter than ever.

The kiss deepened, their fears and uncertainties melting away in the warmth of each other's embrace. Afsana's hands found their way to his face, her fingers tracing the lines of his jaw as though memorizing every detail. Nasir's arms tightened around her, pulling her closer until there was no space left between them. The world outside the cave ceased to exist—there was only the two of them, their breaths mingling, their hearts beating in unison.

When they finally pulled apart, Afsana rested her forehead against his, her eyes closed as she tried to steady her breathing. "Nasir," she whispered, her voice trembling. "I'm scared."

He cupped her face in his hands, his thumbs brushing away the tears that had begun to spill down her cheeks. "I know," he said softly. "But we're together. That's all that matters."

She opened her eyes, searching his face for reassurance. "What if they find us? What if we can't escape?"

Nasir's brow furrowed, but his voice remained steady. "Then we'll face them together. I won't let anything happen to you, Afsana. Not now, not ever."

The cave became their sanctuary that night, the world outside forgotten as they shared whispers, laughter, and promises. Nasir held her close, his touch gentle yet filled with a passion that spoke of years of suppressed longing. In that moment, they weren't fugitives—they were two souls bound by a love that defied the odds.

But the morning brought reality crashing down.

The faint sound of voices reached Nasir's ears first. He bolted upright, his heart hammering in his chest. Afsana stirred beside him, her eyes widening as she registered the noise.

"Nasir," she whispered, her voice trembling.

"Stay here," he said, grabbing a makeshift weapon—a sturdy branch he had picked up during their trek. He moved toward the cave's entrance, his body tense as he peered outside.

A group of men, their torches flickering in the dawn light, were combing through the forest. At the centre of them stood Afsana's father, his face twisted with fury.

"They've found us," Nasir said grimly, turning back to Afsana.

Her face paled, and she clutched his arm. "What do we do?"

"We fight if we have to," he said, his voice low. "But I won't let them take you."

The men's voices grew louder, their footsteps crunching on the underbrush. Nasir positioned himself at the cave's entrance, ready to defend the woman he loved. But there were too many. The first man to approach swung a club, and though Nasir blocked the blow, another struck him from behind. He fell to his knees, blood trickling down his temple.

"Nasir!" Afsana cried, rushing toward him, but her father's men grabbed her, pulling her away.

"Take her," her father commanded, his voice cold and unyielding. "And make sure he never comes near her again."

Nasir struggled against the men holding him, his vision swimming. "Afsana!" he shouted, his voice raw with desperation.

She fought against her captors, tears streaming down her face. "I love you, Nasir!" she cried. "I'll always love you!"

Her words were the last thing he heard before a sharp blow to the back of his head plunged him into darkness.

Chapter 3

That evening, the woman stirred. Her eyelids fluttered open, and she winced as the light from the oil lamp near the charpoy touched her face. She struggled to sit up, her movements weak and unsteady.

"Easy," Rana said, stepping into view. He had been sitting nearby, sharpening his spear, but now he set it aside and crouched beside her. "You're safe here."

Her dark eyes widened as they focused on him, fear flickering in their depths. "Where… where am I?" she rasped, her voice hoarse. "My bag… where is it?" Her voice trembled with urgency and worry.

"Devran," Rana replied. "A village near the river. We found you at the forest's edge. You were unconscious." He pushed the bag toward her and added, "It was with you when we found you. It's safe."

She grabbed the bag and then clutched the edge of the blanket, her hands shaking. "The forest…" Her voice broke, and she shuddered. "I was running. They'll come for me."

"Who?" Rana asked, his tone sharp. "Who's after you?"

Her gaze darted around the room, as though expecting danger to emerge from the shadows. "Men," she whispered. "Sent by… by someone powerful. I can't stay here. If they find me, your village will suffer."

Rana frowned, his instincts bristling. "You're in no condition to leave. Tell me who's chasing you."

She hesitated, her lips pressing into a thin line. Then, as if surrendering to exhaustion, she murmured, "Zahir Khan."

The name fell like a stone in the quiet room. Rana's expression darkened. It was a name he knew all too well, whispered in passing tales of a ruthless Mughal officer, notorious for his unyielding quest for power.

"What does he want from you?" Rana asked.

She shook her head, tears glistening in her eyes. "It's not me he wants. It's what I know."

Before Rana could press further, Dharamdas entered the hut, carrying a bowl of herbal medicine. "She needs rest," the headman said firmly, his gaze flicking to Rana. "We'll get no answers tonight."

Rana stood; his jaw tight. "This isn't over." He turned to the woman. "If you want to survive, you'll have to trust us."

She remained silent, her eyes burdened with the guilt of bringing trouble to the village and the weight of knowing she couldn't give him the answers he sought.

Later that night, as the village settled into uneasy sleep, Rana sat outside the hut, his spear resting across his lap. His mind raced with questions about the stranger and the danger she had brought with her. The forest seemed quieter than usual, its shadows darker and more menacing.

From within the hut, he heard her murmuring in her sleep, her voice strained with fear. He didn't know what secrets she carried, but he could feel their weight pressing down on the village like a storm waiting to break.

In the distance, the forest rustled, as if the trees themselves whispered warnings. Ever watchful, Rana tightened his grip on his spear, prepared for whatever the night might bring.

***

The first light of dawn broke through the dense canopy, bathing Devran's dirt paths in a soft, golden glow. The village was alive with murmurs, but an unusual tension hung in the air—a rift between its people had begun to form. Outside the headman's hut, a group of villagers had gathered, their voices low but growing in intensity as they debated the fate of the woman who had appeared among them.

"Do we really want to keep her here?" Rajan, the village's blacksmith, asked sharply. His broad arms were crossed, his face as hard as iron. "She's brought nothing but trouble. The forest's curse is real, and I've seen enough to know that trouble follows those who defy its will. If we shelter her, we might as well be signing our death warrants."

"I agree," said Gopal, a farmer whose hands were weathered from years of tilling the land. "This village is small, isolated. The Mughals, especially Zahir Khan, won't hesitate to burn it to the ground if they think we're hiding someone important. We should send her away before it's too late."

Rana, who had stepped out of the hut, stood silently in the background, listening. His gaze was fixed on the ground as he weighed the words of the villagers. Tension simmered, but he knew this moment was inevitable—the village was always divided when faced with the unknown.

"But she's hurt," said Pooja, a widow with two children, her voice trembling but firm. "I saw her with my own eyes. She's not a threat—she's been through something terrible. If we cast her out, how will we answer for our cruelty when the Mughals come?"

"It's easy for you to say that," Rajan snapped. "You don't have to face the consequences. If the Mughals come, they'll burn everything. Our children, our homes—all gone. You think they'll care about a single woman's plight? They'll hang us all."

"Enough!" Dharamdas, the headman, stepped forward, raising his hand for silence. His voice was steady, but his eyes carried the weight of years spent making difficult decisions. "We are not the Mughals, Rajan. We must do what is right, not what is easy. If we refuse to help her, we tarnish the very heart of this village. What happened to the Devran I remember, where we took care of each other?"

"The Devran you remember is gone," Rajan muttered, his voice low but bitter. "This is a new world, Dharamdas. The Mughals are no longer just stories. They are here, watching. What are we supposed to do when they come for us? Tell them we've been keeping a fugitive?"

"You speak of survival, Rajan," Rana said, his tone filled with resolve. "But what is survival without honour? Without humanity? This woman, whoever she is, needs our help. And that means we stand together, not turn on each other."

Gopal shook his head, his face clouded with doubt. "You think we can fight the Mughals? They'll destroy us. We're not warriors, Rana. We're farmers, traders, craftsmen. What do we have to offer against their armies?"

Rana's eyes narrowed. "We have our strength. We have each other."

"And what if that's not enough?" Gopal challenged, stepping closer. "What if their strength is too much? What do you want us to do then? Stand and die for a stranger who's only brought trouble?"

Pooja stepped forward; her eyes wet with unshed tears. "You speak of death, but what about life? If we turn her away, we lose our souls. The Mughals may be powerful, but they cannot take that from us."

The group fell silent at her words. There was something in the quiet strength of her plea that made the villagers pause and reconsider their stance. But before anyone could speak, Rajan's voice rose again, laden with doubt.

"I don't care about souls, Pooja. I care about my children. I care about keeping them alive, keeping them safe." His voice trembled, but his conviction was unwavering. "We don't know who this woman is, or what she's running from.

I say we send her away, let her fend for herself. Let the forest decide her fate."

"You don't understand, Rajan," Rana said, his tone firm with unyielding resolve. "The forest isn't the enemy here. The enemy is outside—waiting for any excuse to invade our peace. The woman doesn't bring the trouble; she's caught in it."

Rajan scowled, his lips curling into a sneer. "So, you plan to fight the Mughals yourself then? How heroic."

Rana didn't flinch. "If I have to, yes."

Dharamdas stepped forward again, his face stern but calm. "Enough. We are a community, and we will act as one. I will not have our villagers turn on one another in fear. The question is not whether to help this woman, but how we can protect this village while doing so. I will not turn my back on someone in need, but I will also not put us in unnecessary danger."

A heavy silence settled over the group. No one spoke for a long moment until Raghunath, a young man who had been silent until now, finally spoke up.

"We cannot run from what's coming," he said, his voice calm but firm. "But perhaps we can help her and send her far from here, where she'll be safe. We need to form a group to protect her, lead her out of the village, away from the Mughals' reach. Let her disappear into the hills, where she won't bring danger to us. We'll make sure she's safe, and then we return to protect Devran."

His words struck a chord with the villagers, and for the first time in hours, they began to nod in agreement. There was still fear, still doubt, but something had shifted. The idea of taking action—of not simply waiting for the inevitable— gave them a new sense of purpose.

Dharamdas looked around the group, his eyes lingering on Rana. "I think Raghunath is right. We help her, but we don't bring danger to the village. We protect her and take her out of harm's way. Rana, I trust you to lead this group. Take her to the hills, to the safety of the higher ground. We'll be counting on you."

Rana stood tall, the weight of the decision settling on his shoulders. "I'll do whatever it takes to keep her safe," he said, his voice firm.

The villagers murmured in agreement, some with relief, others with lingering worry. But for now, they had made their choice. They would help the woman and ensure her safety, while also keeping the village protected from the dangerous forces that threatened them.

Compassion among humans is fragile. Just yesterday, on what seemed like any other day, a few had gathered with enough kindness to search for Pari, a girl from the village. Their minimum efforts were enough to convince themselves of their own virtue. But today, when fear has taken root, most have already forgotten her. Most—except for Rana. His mind still clings to her, and while he has taken it upon himself to protect the stranger, he also sees it as an opportunity to keep watch, his search for Pari never ceasing.

As the group began to form, preparing to leave the village and guide the woman to safety, Rana stood at the edge, his eyes focused on the distant forest. His thoughts were divided—one part focused on the stranger, the other still driven by the search for the missing girl who had once been inseparable from him. His heart told him he couldn't stop searching for Pari, no matter what else the world threw his way.

With that resolve, he turned toward the hut, ready to lead the way.

Chapter 4

Zahir Khan stood at the edge of his private chamber, staring out over the expanse of the palace courtyard. The moon hung low in the sky, its silvery light spilling over the stone and casting a soft, luminous glow across the earth below, but it was not the beauty of the night that captured his attention. His thoughts were consumed by one thing: Vishakha.

The news had come to him like a whisper at first, a murmur from one of his most trusted spies, Danish. She had escaped.

He could feel the weight of her disappearance settling like a stone in his chest. Vishakha—the woman who had somehow slipped from his grasp. She held the answers he didn't want the world to know, answers that would ensure his position within the Mughal Empire was unshakeable. She knew things. Dangerous things.

Zahir's fingers tightened around the hilt of his sword as he turned to face his lieutenant, standing rigidly by the door. "Tell me what you know," Zahir's voice was a low growl, filled with the quiet rage he had long since learned to control.

The lieutenant bowed slightly; his face drawn tight with concern. "We tracked her movements through the forest, my lord. But when we reached the village near Devran, the trail went cold. She is no longer there, and the villagers claim no knowledge of her whereabouts. We believe she is headed into the hills."

Zahir's shoulders tensed subtly and for a moment, the room seemed to close in around him. The frustration was overwhelming. Vishakha was a fugitive, but unlike others who would have hidden themselves, she was elusive in a way that made her far more dangerous. She had abandoned him once before, and now she was running again—this time with a head start.

His thoughts flashed back to their last encounter. He had not anticipated her departure, nor had he expected her to be on his tail after leaving. In their earlier meetings, he had seen a strength in her—a resilience that had both intrigued and maddened him. But now, as she disappeared into the wilds of the hills, her mystery was no longer just an intrigue—it was a threat.

He turned his gaze toward the lieutenant, his eyes cold as ice. "Gather the men. We are going after her. Leave no stone unturned. I want every man in the surrounding villages to report her movements immediately. She will not evade us again. If she seeks refuge in the hills, we will burn them down if we must."

The lieutenant nodded and quickly exited the chamber. Zahir's mind raced with strategy. The hills were a vast network of dense forest and hidden paths, making the search difficult. But he had no choice. He could not allow Vishakha to stay free. She knew too much, and her disappearance was a threat not just to him, but to the very foundation he has laid for his present and future.

Zahir walked to a table near the wall, where maps of the surrounding territories were spread out. He traced his fingers over the paths that led to the hills. The terrain was difficult, but his men were capable. If it meant tracking her for days, or even weeks, he would see it done.

She will regret this, he thought.

But it wasn't just the secrets that gnawed at him. As she slipped away, Zahir felt a familiar, unsettling ache—one that he had thought buried, one he had tried so hard to suppress. It reminded him of the moment Afsana was taken from him—the feeling of helplessness, of losing something precious to forces beyond his control.

Vishakha's escape wasn't just a blow to his ambitions—it was a reminder of his vulnerability, of the part of him that could still be touched by loss. Afsana's disappearance had torn him apart, but that pain had only fuelled his rise to power. And now, as Vishakha vanished into the hills, that same sense of loss stirred once more, unsettling the cold, calculating walls he had so carefully built around himself.

And he would not allow her to slip from his grasp.

The darkness in Zahir's chamber deepened as the moon climbed higher in the sky. The lieutenant's departure left the room in an oppressive silence, but Zahir's thoughts were far from still. Vishakha's escape had stirred a part of him he had long buried, reopening the wounds of a life he had tried to forget.

He sank into a chair near the window, the faint scent of night jasmine wafting in on the breeze. It reminded him of Afsana and the morning she was taken from him. The memory was sharp, vivid, and relentless—a scar that had shaped the man he had become.

Zahir's fingers tapped lightly against the arm of the chair; the rhythm uneven as his thoughts drifted back to that day. The loss of Afsana had been the first crack in the fragile foundation of the man he once was, and the events that followed had shattered him entirely.

***

He remembered waking up on the cold riverbank, his body battered and bruised. The morning sun had been merciless, its light illuminating the trail of blood and broken leaves where Afsana had been dragged away. Her voice still echoed in his ears, her cries of his name like a haunting melody that refused to fade. He had stumbled back to the village, desperate and half-mad, only to be met with closed doors and silence. No one dared to help him. His own family turned their backs on him. His father's words were harsh:

"You've ensured we can never look anyone in the eye again. Leave, and don't return." With that, he shut the door firmly in his face.

No one dared to challenge the might of Afsana's father, a man whose wealth and power loomed over them all like an unyielding shadow.

Days turned into weeks as Nasir scoured the city, following whispers and rumours, chasing any lead that might bring him to her. Nasir, with his eyes scanning every corner, approached another local at the bustling market. "Please, have you seen her? The one with the jasmine in her hair?"

The man, busy sorting his wares, didn't even look up. "Haven't seen her, boy. Now move along, you're scaring off my customers."

Disheartened, Nasir moved on, his steps echoing his diminishing hope. He found an old woman selling spices, her eyes sharp with wisdom. "Mother, I seek a girl, her name is—"

"Many girls come through here," she interrupted, grinding her spices. "You're not the first to chase shadows in this city."

Each rejection was like a stone thrown at his resolve, but it only made him more determined. Weeks passed like this, his questions a constant hum in the city's daily symphony.

Finally, a whisper from a beggar at the city's edge, his voice raspy with disuse, "Word is, she's married now. To a nobleman in Dilli."

Nasir felt as if the ground beneath him gave way. "Dilli?" His voice was barely a whisper.

The beggar nodded; his eyes full of pity. "Yes, Dilli."

That night, under the starless sky, Nasir sat alone, the news washing over him like a cold wave. "So, she's gone," he murmured to himself, the reality sinking in. He had no family, no friends. The life he knew, the man he was— everything was gone.

"From this moment, Nasir, son of a silk merchant, is no more," he spoke to the darkness, his voice steady with a new, hardened resolve. "I will never be powerless again."

And with those words, a new man began to form, one shaped by loss, driven by a fierce determination to change his fate. He left Agra without a word to his family, driven by a singular purpose: to rise above the world that had crushed him. Power became his obsession, his armour against the pain that threatened to consume him. The path was neither easy nor clean, but Nasir had shed his innocence long before he took his first steps toward the Mughal courts.

***

Zahir closed his eyes, the memories of those early years flashing before him like the fragments of a shattered mirror.

***

He had started at the very bottom, toiling as a lowly scribe in the Mughal court. At first, no one noticed him, just another unremarkable figure in a sea of faces. But Zahir's sharp mind caught nuances others ignored. He spent his days quietly studying the court's workings—the alliances, the rivalries, the unspoken rules of survival.

He learned to listen more than he spoke, memorizing which nobleman owed debts, which generals harboured ambitions, and which courtiers whispered secrets. When an opportunity came to provide crucial intelligence to a superior—a plot to siphon imperial funds—Zahir acted swiftly. He first overheard fragments of a conversation between two clerks in the palace archives late one evening, their voices hushed but their words incriminating.

"Keep your voice down, you fool," one of them muttered, his eyes darting toward the doorway. He glanced over his shoulder, as if sensing unseen eyes in the darkness.

"I'm not the one who's going to get caught," the other hissed, his tone sharp with frustration. "It's you who's risking everything by altering those records. The merchant is paying good money for this, but there are… risks involved."

The first clerk exhaled, shaking his head. "You think I don't know that?" His voice lowered further, almost a growl. "But you don't understand the stakes, how much money we can make. If we keep this quiet, no one will ever notice. We've been doing it for months now."

The second clerk hesitated, his fingers gripping the edges of a ledger. "And the officials?" he asked, doubt creeping into his voice. "They'll start to wonder why trade revenue is falling short. What if someone starts asking questions?"

The first clerk scoffed. "Who will question it? The merchants? The officials? They're all in on it. The money's already changing hands. We're just making sure it keeps flowing, quietly, and that we make some for ourselves in the process."

In the darkness beyond the lamplight, Zahir remained still, his presence unnoticed. His narrowed eyes followed every movement, his sharp ears catching every word. A merchant bribing official to falsify trade records… Imperial revenue siphoned into private hands.

His fingers twitched at his side as he edged forward, careful to keep his steps silent against the stone floor.

"But what if someone finds out?" the second clerk asked, his voice edged with qualms. He glanced toward the open doorway, as if the walls themselves could betray him. "What if someone finds the records and puts the pieces together?"

The first clerk let out a short laugh, filled with arrogance. "No one's going to find anything. We're careful, aren't we? Besides, it's only a few discrepancies in the ledgers. Who's going to notice? The emperor's eyes are on a hundred other things."

Zahir tilted his head slightly, his mind already working through the implications. This was more than just petty corruption—this was an opening. A single thread that, if pulled, could unravel something much larger. But information alone was not enough. He needed proof. He needed the right allies.

Silently, he stepped back, retreating into the darkness. The conversation was far from over, but for now, he had heard enough.

It seemed that an influential merchant had been bribing officials to falsify trade records, diverting a significant portion of imperial revenue into private coffers.

Zahir spent the next several nights piecing together evidence. He cross-referenced trade manifests, payment ledgers, and supply orders, identifying discrepancies that others had overlooked. It was a meticulous process, but Zahir's sharp mind and patience served him well. When he was certain of the scheme's scope, he knew he needed a powerful ally to act on it.

The opportunity came in the form of Malik Aslam, a senior administrator known for his strict adherence to imperial law. Zahir approached Malik with calculated deceit, masking his true intentions behind a veil of loyalty. He carefully staged their meeting, ensuring it appeared as though the information had come to him by accident—a fortunate discovery from his late-night work in the archives. He presented the evidence as if he had stumbled upon it while performing his duties, his tone humble yet persuasive.

"My lord," Zahir began, bowing deeply as he entered Malik's private chamber. "While reviewing trade ledgers for discrepancies, I noticed something unusual. At first, I thought it was a clerical error, but as I dug deeper, a pattern emerged."

He laid the documents on Malik's desk, carefully arranging them to lead Malik through the scheme step by step. Zahir's explanations were precise, guiding Malik to the conclusion without making it seem rehearsed. He even feigned hesitation at moments, as though reluctant to implicate the powerful figures involved.

"It's not my place to accuse anyone, my lord," Zahir said, his voice laced with deference. "But I felt it my duty to bring this to your attention. The empire cannot afford such betrayals."

Malik studied the documents intently, his expression hardening as he connected the threads. What Zahir didn't reveal was how he had planted subtle hints in the ledger's weeks earlier, ensuring that the trail would lead directly to the guilty parties. He had anticipated Malik's reaction and tailored his approach to appeal to the administrator's sense of justice.

By the time Malik looked up, his eyes were filled with a mix of anger and admiration. "You've done well, boy," he said, his voice firm. "This is the kind of diligence the empire needs. Leave this matter with me, tell me your name and you will be rewarded."

"Zahir Khan!" said Zahir.

This was the moment that Nasir died and Zahir Khan was born. Even he didn't know how he suddenly came up with that name and why he didn't say "Nasir" when Malik asked for his name. Probably he didn't want any remains of his old life. Maybe Nasir reminded him of the times when he was weak and helpless. But Zahir Khan would never be weak again.

Malik nodded and left with his guards.

Zahir bowed again, concealing the triumph that burned in his chest. He had played his part perfectly, ensuring that Malik believed the discovery was entirely his own. The arrests that followed cemented Malik's trust in Zahir, earning him not only recognition but also his first promotion. It was a modest position, overseeing minor logistics, but it was the foothold Zahir needed to begin his ascent.

More importantly, it cemented a lesson that would define his path forward: power was built not just on strength, but on knowledge, patience, and the ability to strike at the right moment.

As he rose to oversee minor logistics, Zahir's cunning only grew. He began cultivating alliances with merchants and bureaucrats, rewarding loyalty while subtly eliminating rivals. He planted seeds of influence, using his quiet position to shape the empire's future, inching ever closer to his ultimate goal. A goal that now seemed inevitable: the throne itself.

Another opportunity arose when whispers of a growing rebellion in the neighbouring province found their way to him. In Zahir Khan's mind, they were seen as an opportunity—a door ready to be pushed open. As he stood in the emperor's war room, his eyes traced the intricate lines of the map spread across the table. Zahir saw it all with crystal clarity, his mind already calculating the steps needed to turn chaos into control.

"The situation is more delicate than the reports suggest," Zahir said, his voice calm but laced with authority. He tapped his fingers on the map, where lines of communication and trade intersected like veins. "The root of the rebellion is clear—heavy taxes, corrupt local officials, and a growing discontent among the farmers and merchants. The revolt has been brewing for months, unnoticed."

Malik Aslam and the emperor's chief advisor were intrigued by Zahir's composed demeanour. Zahir had always been a man of logistics, meticulous and unassuming. But now, he spoke with the sharpness of a seasoned strategist, his words cutting through the room's tension.

"And what would you suggest we do about it?" Malik asked, his tone cautious but curious.

Zahir leaned forward, his gaze steady, his voice dropping to a low, commanding timbre. "We don't just suppress the rebellion—we suffocate it at the roots. First, we cut their supply lines. The rebels rely heavily on support from the surrounding provinces. Severing those ties will isolate them. Without food, weapons, or reinforcements, they'll be powerless." His finger traced the routes on the map, marking the lifelines he intended to sever. "I'll arrange the logistics to ensure that no supplies make it to their camps."

Malik nodded slowly, but his eyes betrayed a flicker of wariness. "That sounds reasonable, but what of their leaders? We've dealt with uprisings before. There are always those who rally the people."

Zahir's lips curled into a faint, knowing smile. He had anticipated the question. "We eliminate them, quietly. No public executions or bloodshed. We target their key figures— dissolve their command structure. I have operatives who can do this swiftly, without leaving a trace. The rebellion's heart will collapse before it even starts."

The room fell silent, the weight of Zahir's words settling over the advisors like a heavy shroud. Malik exchanged a glance with another advisor, his expression a mix of admiration and apprehension. "But what of the common people?" he asked finally. "Will they not feel betrayed by more punishment? The rebellion's cause is rooted in their suffering. Can we not offer them some reprieve?"

Zahir's smile deepened, though it never reached his eyes. "Of course. We can't just silence them. I propose a temporary tax reduction, combined with the removal of the most corrupt officials. Present it as a gesture of goodwill, a sign that the emperor listens to his people. The tax reduction will soften their hearts, while the removal of the corrupt officials will restore their trust."

Malik leaned back, clearly impressed by the combination of ruthless strategy and political tact. "You've thought this through."

Zahir straightened, his gaze sharp and unyielding. "It's a matter of timing, my lord. Everything will fall into place, and when the rebellion is crushed, it will be swift and without resistance. The empire will remain intact."

Several days later, in the emperor's court, Zahir's plan was set into motion. But what none of the advisors knew was how much Zahir had already influenced the situation behind the scenes. The supply lines were already being severed, and operatives had been positioned to deal with the rebel leaders. The stage had been set long before the emperor's approval.

When the results came in, the rebellion was quelled within weeks. The emperor's name remained untarnished, and the region returned to stability with minimal bloodshed. Zahir's actions were praised, his name whispered with a mix of respect and dread. But his rise was just beginning.

In the aftermath, as the emperor's advisors congratulated him on his success, Zahir stood in the silence, his expression unreadable.

"A brilliant move, Zahir Khan," one advisor said, his voice tinged with admiration. "The rebellion is crushed, and the province is stable again. The emperor will surely reward you."

Zahir smiled, but it was a smile that didn't reach his eyes. "The reward is already mine."

It wasn't just a position of power he sought—it was control. He had moved from being a logistics officer to a trusted advisor, securing his place in the emperor's inner circle. And he had done it all without once drawing a sword.

As the weeks passed, Zahir's name became synonymous with success. His careful manipulation of the court and the rebels had worked perfectly, cementing his reputation as a man of vision, capable of ensuring the empire's survival. But Zahir was no fool. He knew this was only the beginning. The emperor's inner circle grew wary of his rising influence, their whispers laced with suspicion. Yet, Zahir's true power lay not in his current position, but in the carefully laid plans he was yet to put into motion.

Through every step, Zahir masked his ambition behind a veil of humility. He knew when to bow his head in submission and when to press forward. His diligence and loyalty, carefully calculated and strategically placed, earned him the trust of powerful men, positioning him as a figure who was both indispensable and unthreatening. But beneath the surface, Zahir was always calculating his next move, ensuring that no act of kindness or loyalty was given without its price.

It was during these years that Vishakha had entered his life.

***

Zahir sat in the suffocating quiet of his chamber, the scent of jasmine dissipating as the wind shifted. The memories of his past were not just painful—they were his fuel. He had clawed his way up from the dirt, built his power brick by brick, and shed every last remnant of Nasir, the boy who had once dared to dream of love and freedom. But the echoes of that boy, of Afsana's smile and her screams, haunted him still.

The soft knock at his door snapped him back to the present. Zahir straightened, the mask of the cold, calculating officer sliding back into place. "Enter," he commanded.

His lieutenant stepped in, bowing deeply. "My lord, the men are prepared to march at first light. Scouts have been sent ahead to the hills. There are whispers that the villagers of Devran may have sheltered her."

Zahir's lips curved into a faint, humourless smile. "Of course they did. Fear makes fools of even the most cautious.

But they will soon learn that sheltering a fugitive carries a price."

The lieutenant bowed again, stepping back toward the door. "As you wish, my lord. Shall I instruct the men to treat the villagers as hostile?"

Zahir considered the question for a moment, his fingers tapping rhythmically against the hilt of his sword. "No. Not yet. Let them believe they are safe. When we arrive, their trust will be their undoing."

The lieutenant nodded and exited, leaving Zahir alone once more. He stood and walked to the window; his gaze fixed on the distant hills shrouded in darkness. Somewhere out there, Vishakha was running, clinging to whatever fragile hope she believed would save her.

Foolish girl, he thought. She did not realize that there was no escaping him. She carried secrets that could destabilize not just his ambitions, but the delicate balance of power within the entire empire. And she would pay for that knowledge— whether with her life or her loyalty, Zahir had yet to decide.

The stars above the hills twinkled faintly, their light barely reaching the earth. Zahir's grip on the windowsill tightened. Soon, the hills would burn, and with them, the last remnants of defiance against his rise to power. He would see Vishakha's fear, he would hear her confess what she knew, and he would ensure that no one—not even the emperor himself—stood in the way of his destiny.

The past was dead. The future belonged to him. And Zahir Khan would stop at nothing to claim it.

Chapter 5

The village of Devran stirred in the early hours of dawn, a sombre quiet settling over its narrow lanes and clustered huts. The decision to help Vishakha had sparked a flurry of whispered arguments, but now the air was heavy with reluctant acceptance.

Inside the headman's hut, Dharamdas stood with his arms crossed, his stern gaze fixed on Vishakha. Rana leaned against the wall nearby as Dharamdas spoke.

"We've decided to take you away from the village," Dharamdas said, his tone firm. "The Mughals will not stop searching, and keeping you here puts everyone at risk."

Vishakha nodded slowly, her hands tightening around the edge of the blanket draped over her shoulders. "I understand," she said softly. "I never meant to bring danger to your village. I… I'm grateful for your help."

"Grateful or not, you need to tell us more," Dharamdas continued. "Who are you, and why are they after you? The villagers deserve to know what they're risking their lives for."

Rana's sharp gaze shifted to Vishakha. "Start with your name," he said simply.

Vishakha hesitated for a moment before straightening her back. "My name is Vishakha," she said, her voice steady despite the weight of the moment. "I was a servant in the Mughal court. But I… I saw things I wasn't meant to see. Things that Zahir Khan would kill to keep hidden."

Dharamdas exchanged a glance with Rana, his frown deepening. "What kind of things?"

Vishakha's gaze remained unwavering as she met their eyes. "The kind of truth that turns men into corpses," she said, her tone unshaken. "I know enough to be hunted, but not enough to be reckless. If I tell you everything, you'll become loose ends, too. Zahir destroys anyone who knows the full truth, and for your safety, it's better if you stay ignorant."

The room fell into a tense silence, the gravity of her words sinking in. Finally, Rana pushed off the wall and spoke. "You've told us enough for now. Get ready. We leave at first light."

Vishakha nodded, a flicker of relief in her eyes. As she rose to her feet, Dharamdas sighed and rubbed his temples, his expression a mix of frustration and resignation. The weight of the decision hung heavy on them all. Men prepared their weapons—simple spears and makeshift weapons like staff—while women packed bundles of food and water for the group that would escort her to the hills.

Rana stood at the centre of it all, his spear resting against his shoulder as he watched the preparations. His thoughts were divided, split between the task ahead and the ever-present ache of Pari's absence. The image of her red ribbon, clutched in his hand, flashed in his mind. She'd always been fearless, just like the woman now resting in the headman's hut.

Vishakha emerged from the hut, her steps unsteady but determined. Her crimson dupatta was now tied tightly over her head, shielding her face from the curious and wary stares of the villagers. She paused at the threshold, scanning the faces around her, her expression a mixture of gratitude and lingering fear.

"Are you sure about this?" Dharamdas asked, stepping beside Rana. His tone was measured, but there was a flicker of doubt in his eyes. "Taking her out of the village might draw more attention to us. The Mughals…" He let the sentence hang; the unspoken threat heavy in the air.

"Keeping her here is riskier," Rana replied, his voice firm. "The longer she stays, the more danger we invite. We'll lead her away, make sure she's safe, and then return. The village will be fine."

Dharamdas nodded slowly, though his lips pressed into a thin line. "Just remember, Rana, you're not invincible. None of us are. Don't let your pride blind you."

Rana didn't respond, his gaze fixed on Vishakha as she approached them. Her eyes met his briefly, and in that moment, he saw something unspoken pass between them— an acknowledgment of the burden they both carried.

***

The group set out just as the first rays of sunlight kissed the horizon. Rana led the way, his steps purposeful and steady, while Vishakha walked just behind him. Four others accompanied them: Amar, a young blacksmith's apprentice with a quiet resolve; Suresh, a boastful farmer who carried a dagger he barely knew how to use; Chandan, a wiry man with quick eyes who had a reputation for cunning; and Hari, a seasoned tracker who knew the hills better than anyone else, his skills invaluable for the journey.

The forest loomed ahead, its dense canopy swallowing the last traces of daylight. The villagers who had gathered to watch them leave stood in uneasy silence, their expressions a mix of hope and dread.

Pooja, the widow, stepped forward, pressing a bundle of food into Rana's hands. Then, turning to Vishakha, she held out a small cloth bundle.

"These are some of my clothes," she said gently. "You'll need them for the journey."

Vishakha hesitated for a moment before accepting the offering with a grateful nod.

"Take care of her," Pooja said, her gaze shifting back to Rana. "And bring yourself back. The village needs you."

Rana nodded, his grip tightening on the bundle. Without another word, he turned and led the group into the forest.

***

The journey was slow, the cluttered underbrush making progress difficult. The group spoke little, their silence broken only by the occasional snap of a twig or the rustle of leaves. Vishakha kept her eyes on the ground, her mind racing with thoughts of Zahir Khan and the danger she had brought to these people. She felt a pang of guilt as she glanced at Rana, his broad shoulders tense with the weight of responsibility.

Amar, walking beside her, noticed her limp. "You're favouring that leg," he said, his voice light with concern. "Does it hurt too much to keep going?"

"It's fine," she replied quickly, though the strain in her voice betrayed her.

Amar smirked. "'Fine' usually means not fine at all. My sister used to say that right before she fell flat on her face."

Vishakha couldn't help but chuckle softly. "I'll manage. Thank you."

"Well, if you fall flat, I'll make sure to catch you. But just this once," Amar said, his teasing tone drawing a faint smile from her.

Ahead of them, Suresh groaned, throwing his arms up dramatically. "Why are we stopping every five minutes? I thought we were supposed to be escaping danger, not taking a leisurely stroll through the forest."

Chandan snorted. "Says the man who hasn't stopped complaining since we left. Maybe if you carried something heavier than that butter knife you call a dagger, you'd be too tired to whine."

"This 'butter knife' will save your life someday," Suresh shot back. "You'll thank me when it does."

"I'll thank you when you learn to keep quiet," Chandan muttered, his tone dry but not unkind. "Or better yet, when you actually use that thing for something other than peeling fruit."

Amar grinned at Vishakha. "Don't mind them. They're always like this. It's how they show their love."

"Love, huh?" Vishakha raised an eyebrow. "Doesn't sound very affectionate."

"Affectionate is not all that important," Amar replied with a wink. "Practical is better."

Rana's voice cut through their exchange like a whip. "Amar, quit slowing the group down. Unless you're volunteering to carry Suresh next."

Amar fell back a step, but not before murmuring to Vishakha, "Practical and grumpy. That's our fearless leader."

Vishakha glanced at Rana's rigid balance, the tension in his shoulders, and found herself smiling despite the pain in her leg. Amar's light-heartedness was a welcome distraction, but it was Rana's steady presence that gave her a strange sense of security. Even if he did look like he was one wrong word away from snapping someone in half.

Suresh, clearly not done, piped up again. "You know, if we're going to keep stopping, we might as well set up camp. I could use a nap. Or a meal. Or both. Preferably both."

Chandan rolled his eyes. "You're like a child. 'Are we there yet? Can we eat yet? Can I nap yet?'"

"And you're like an old man," Suresh shot back. "'Back in my day, we walked uphill both ways in the snow, and we liked it!'"

"At least I don't carry a dagger that looks like it belongs in a kitchen," Chandan retorted.

"At least I don't carry a stick and call it a weapon," Suresh fired back, gesturing to Chandan's staff.

Rana stopped abruptly, turning to face them with a look that could freeze fire. "If the two of you don't stop bickering, I'll tie you together and leave you for the wolves. Understood?"

The group fell silent, though Amar couldn't resist whispering to Vishakha, "See? Practical and grumpy."

Vishakha stifled a laugh, her hand covering her mouth. For the first time in days, she felt a flicker of something other than fear. It was small, but it was there—a spark of lightness in the heavy air of the forest.

By the time they stopped to rest, the sun was dipping below the treetops, casting the forest in hues of orange and gold. Vishakha sat on a fallen log, her energy drained. Amar offered her a canteen of water, his expression kind but cautious.

"Thank you," she said softly, taking a sip.

He nodded, his gaze lingering on her for a moment before he turned to help Chandan gather firewood. Rana watched the exchange from a distance, his mind working through the challenges ahead. The hills were still a day's journey away, and the forest's silence felt oppressive, as if it were holding its breath.

Hari approached him, his expression laced with concern. "You're putting a lot of faith in this woman," he said quietly.

"And you're putting a lot of doubt in me," Rana replied without looking at him.

Hari's lips tightened, but he said nothing more. Instead, he walked away, his footsteps crunching softly on the forest floor.

***

As night fell, the group huddled around a small fire, its warmth offering a fragile comfort against the biting cold. The flames crackled, sending the scent of burning wood into the crisp night air. Vishakha leaned back against the log, the rough bark pressing into her skin as she shifted, wincing at the ache in her muscles. The distant hoot of an owl broke the silence, mingling with the rustling of leaves as the wind whispered through the trees. Vishakha winced as she shifted her injured leg. Amar settled beside her, handing her a rough piece of cloth.

"For the swelling," he said. "Wrap it tight. It'll help."

"You're too kind," she said softly. "You remind me of my brother."

Amar's grin widened. "I'll take that as a compliment. Unless he was a terrible brother."

"He wasn't," Vishakha said, her voice tinged with sadness. "He was the best."

Rana's gaze flicked toward them, his eyes lingering on Vishakha as she smiled faintly at Amar. Something unspoken stirred within him—an ache he couldn't quite name. He turned away, his hand tightening on the shaft of his spear as he stared into the darkened forest, the flames casting flickering light on his face.

***

The next morning, the forest was shrouded in a dense mist that clung to the trees, muffling the sounds of their movement. Vishakha winced as she tried to stretch her leg before they set off, her body protesting the effort. Amar noticed her hesitation and crouched beside her.

"Let me carry some of your things," he offered, his tone firm when she started to protest. "Don't argue. You need to make it through today in one piece."

"Thank you," she said softly, handing over a small bundle.

Suresh glanced back and smirked. "Careful, Amar. She'll have you carrying her all the way to the hills if you're not careful."

"And I don't remember asking for your valuable advice," Amar shot back, earning a chuckle from Chandan.

Rana, walking ahead, remained silent, his thoughts turning inward. The morning's stillness reminded him of Pari—how she'd loved to run through the dew-soaked fields at dawn, her laughter echoing as she tried to catch butterflies. His hand instinctively brushed against the pocket where her red ribbon was tucked away. A flicker of strain crossed his face, forcing the memories back. He couldn't afford distractions now.

"You okay?" Hari's voice pulled him back to the present. The older man had fallen into step beside him, his sharp eyes scanning the path ahead.

"Fine," Rana said curtly.

"You don't look it," Hari pressed. "Pari is still on your mind, isn't she?"

Rana didn't respond immediately, his gaze fixed on the trail. Finally, he said, "She always is."

Hari nodded, his expression softening. "We'll find her. But first, we get through this."

Behind them, Vishakha's ears caught the exchange, her brow furrowing. She slowed her steps slightly, falling into stride beside Hari as the older man moved forward.

"Who is Pari?" Vishakha asked softly, her voice careful, probing.

Hari glanced at her, his face briefly uncertain, before nodding toward Rana up ahead. "You should ask him," he said simply, then stepped away, leaving her question unanswered.

Vishakha watched Rana in silence, sensing an unspoken weight in the way he moved—measured, almost rigid. There was more to the story, something buried beneath his silence. The name echoed in her mind as she matched his pace, knowing she would have to wait for the right moment to ask him herself.

As they trudged through the mist-laden forest, the silence was only interrupted by the crunch of leaves underfoot and the occasional rustle of unseen creatures. The air was cool, carrying the scent of earth and damp foliage. Vishakha, still limping slightly, walked beside Amar, who was carrying her small bundle. He glanced over at her, a mischievous glint in his eyes.

"You know," Amar began, his voice low but laced with amusement, "when we get out of this alive, I'm opening a shop. 'Amar's Healing Touch.' I'll fix legs just like I'm doing now."

Vishakha shot him a doubtful look. "Oh? And what exactly qualifies you for such an esteemed profession?"

Amar flexed his fingers with exaggerated flair. "These hands. Not just any hands—expert hands. Trained by experience, guided by compassion."

Vishakha let out a soft laugh, shaking her head. "Compassion? I thought they were just good for carrying things."

"Carrying is only the beginning," Amar said, straightening as if his new profession demanded better uprightness. "I can cure headaches too. One press on the forehead, and—gone."

Suresh, who had been walking slightly ahead, glanced over his shoulder with a smirk. "And what next? Free foot massages? Maybe you'll start reviving the dead?"

Amar scoffed. "I'm not a miracle worker, Suresh. Just someone who knows how to keep people moving when they're about to fall apart."

"That's an interesting way of saying you poke at wounds until people stop complaining." Suresh shook his head, grinning. "Maybe next time, try some actual medicine."

Vishakha, still amused, glanced at Amar. "Well, as long as you don't decide your 'healing touch' involves making me walk faster, I'll take whatever cure you're offering."

"Deal." Amar winked. "Slow and steady—I don't want to lose my best patient."

Chandan, who had been quiet until now, finally spoke up. "Since we're all planning our future trades, I might as well share mine."

Amar turned to him with mock suspicion. "Let me guess—you're opening a school for fools?"

Chandan grinned. "Nope. I'm starting an herbal shop. But not just any herbs—special ones. Cures for everything. A broken bone, a fever, even a broken heart."

Vishakha raised an eyebrow. "Special, huh? You mean weeds you plucked off the roadside?"

"Not weeds!" Chandan looked genuinely offended. "Carefully selected, expertly dried, and—most importantly—marketed well."

Suresh eyed Chandan's frayed sandals and muttered, "Maybe then you'll be able to afford shoes that don't fall apart."

Rana, who had been walking ahead, finally spoke, his tone dry. "So, what are we now? Healers, traders, or just fugitives with too much time on our hands?"

Vishakha smirked. "Whatever keeps us from losing our minds."

Amar rubbed his stomach dramatically. "Call me what you want, as long as we have something better than burnt rabbit to eat."

Chandan chuckled. "I burnt the rabbit once, and I'll never hear the end of it, will I?"

Laughter rippled through the group, the weight of exhaustion momentarily lifting. Even Rana, though silent, seemed to relax a fraction.

"Enough talk," he said, cutting through the lingering amusement. "We make it to the hills first. Then you can all debate whether you want to be healers, merchants, or lunatics."

With that, the group fell back into their steady pace, the mist starting to lift as the forest grew lighter. The journey ahead was still fraught with danger, but for a brief moment, the light-hearted conversation provided a rare sense of normalcy.

As the path ahead twisted deeper into the hills, Vishakha's thoughts wandered briefly to Zahir Khan. She shook her head, trying to push him out of her mind. Whatever lay ahead, she couldn't afford to be distracted now.

* * *

Around midday, they reached a small clearing where groups of weary travellers rested, their faces lined with exhaustion. Some huddled together, sharing quiet conversations, while others kept their distance, their eyes watchful. The weight of the journey clung to them all—refugees of war, displaced villagers, people seeking safety where none truly existed.

Rana and his group moved through them, scanning the faces, searching for any sign—any whisper—of Pari.

"Have you seen a little girl?" Rana asked a group of older men sitting beneath a tree. His voice was firm, but there was an urgency beneath it. "She's about this tall, dark eye, always asking too many questions. Her name is Pari."

The men barely glanced at him before shaking their heads.

He moved on. "A girl, maybe taken against her will? Small, thin—"

Another shake of the head. Another door closed.

Amar sighed, rubbing the back of his neck. "We've asked at every stop. If she were nearby, someone would have seen her."

Rana wasn't ready to believe that. He turned to another family—a man, his wife, their daughters huddled close. "Have you heard of a child called Pari?"

The eldest daughter, a girl of about sixteen, looked up sharply. Her lips parted, as if she wanted to speak, but then she hesitated, glancing at her parents.

Rana caught the flicker of recognition in her eyes. "You've heard that name." His voice was steady, but the way he held himself—rigid, expectant—left no room for denial.

The girl swallowed, then took a step forward. "You... you're Rana, aren't you?"

His stomach clenched. "How do you know my name?"

She looked to her father, as if for permission, before answering. "I met a girl. yesterday, near the river. She was with others... but she was different. She kept saying your name."

The world seemed to tilt slightly. "She said my name?"

The girl nodded. "Over and over. 'Rana is coming. He'll find me.' I thought she was just a lost child hoping someone would find her, but she wasn't afraid. Not of being alone. She was afraid of being taken somewhere."

A slow, terrible dread spread through Rana's chest. "Taken where?"

The girl hesitated again, biting her lip. "I don't know. Her gaze dropped, guilt flickering in her eyes. "I asked her where is she from, but before she could say more, some men came. They told her to get up, to move. She didn't want to go, but they made her."

A cold dread settled in Rana's chest. "Who were they?"

The girl shook her head. "I don't know. They weren't dressed like soldiers, but they acted like they had authority. They didn't hurt her, but... they didn't care that she was afraid." She exhaled shakily. "I wanted to help, but what could I do? I was just passing through."

Rana's breath caught. His heart twisted painfully. That was Pari. Trying to be brave. Trying not to be a burden.

"Where was this?" His voice was rough, urgent.

"A village north of here. Not far, maybe a day's walk." She hesitated, then added, "There's a river that cuts through the land. If she's still there... that's where you'll find her."

That was all he needed to hear.

Rana gave her a small, grateful nod before turning to the rest of his group. His face remained tight with restraint; his eyes steely with resolve. "We're changing course. We're heading north. To the hills. Pari is waiting for me, and I'm not letting her down."

Amar, Chandan, and the others exchanged looks, but there was no hesitation in their eyes. They had come this far, and now they had a new mission. No longer was their purpose solely to protect Vishakha—they had to find Pari.

The girl watched them prepare to move, a flicker of something unreadable in her eyes. Before Rana stepped away, she spoke one last time.

"She believed you'd come for her."

Rana exhaled slowly, the weight of those words pressing into him. "She's right."

With that, he turned toward the north, his heart set on the hills. The others followed without a word, each of them knowing that the journey ahead would be fraught with danger. But they had no choice now. They had to find Pari.

Chapter 6

The scent of incense hung in the air, settling into the rich fabrics and wooden carvings of the chamber. Zahir Khan paced, his steps slow but restless, his hands tightening into fists before loosening again.

His lieutenant stood before him, silent, eyes lowered in deference. On the table between them, a map lay sprawled open, a deep red mark slashed across Devran's name—like a wound waiting to be struck deeper.

"You're telling me you know where they're headed?" Zahir's voice was quiet, but the edge of menace in his tone was unmistakable.

The lieutenant nodded cautiously. "A villager spoke. He claimed they're moving north, toward the hills by the river."

Zahir's fingers drummed against the hilt of his sword, the rhythm steady and shrewd. "And this villager?"

"He remains anonymous, my lord," the lieutenant replied. "He refused to give his name but left the information before vanishing into the night."

Zahir's lips curled into a faint sneer. Cowards, he thought. Yet even a coward's words could be valuable if they rang true. He turned to the map, his eyes tracing the paths toward the hills. "Send more men," he commanded. "Double the patrols. Block every route leading to the river. I want them cornered."

The lieutenant hesitated for a moment. "And if they resist?"

Zahir's gaze snapped to him, cold and unyielding. "You know what to do. Bring her to me. Alive. Kill anyone who gets in your way."

The lieutenant bowed deeply, understanding the gravity of his orders. "It will be done, my lord."

As the man left the chamber, Zahir walked to the latticed window, his hands clasped behind his back. The soft murmur of the city's night life drifted up to him, but his mind was far from the bustling streets. Vishakha. Her name echoed in his thoughts, each syllable a reminder of the past they shared. She had once been his ally, his confidant. Now, she was a fugitive, carrying secrets that could dismantle everything he had built.

He closed his eyes, and the memories came rushing back.

***

It had been years ago, in the early days of his ascent, when Zahir was still a low-ranking officer in the Mughal court. He had just earned a position closer to the advisors and governors, a reward for his cunning and ambition. The role placed him within the inner workings of the empire, but it also exposed him to its politics—a web of alliances, betrayals, and power plays.

Vishakha had entered his life during one of the emperor's grand assemblies. She was introduced as the daughter of a fallen noble family, brought into the court to serve as a scribe. Her sharp wit and keen mind set her apart from the other courtiers, and Zahir had noticed her almost immediately. While others underestimated her, dismissing her as just another servant, Zahir saw potential.

Their first interaction had been brief but telling. The governors sat in a semi-circle, their expressions growing uneasy as the discussion of land taxes spiralled into confusion. One of them, a portly man with a heavy gold ring on his finger, declared, "The emperor's decree demands that the tax on grain be increased by five percent across all provinces. It's necessary to account for the shortfall in revenue."

Vishakha, seated in the shadows near the records, looked up sharply. "Forgive me, my lords," she said, her voice calm but cutting through the tension. "The shortfall isn't due to insufficient taxation but mismanagement in the northern provinces. Increasing the tax will only burden the farmers unnecessarily."

The room fell silent, the governors exchanging uneasy glances. The portly man turned to her; his face flushed with irritation. "And what would you, a mere scribe, know of imperial finances?"

Vishakha stood, her movements precise and careful. "I know the numbers, my lord. I've reviewed the accounts myself. The northern provinces have reported consistent discrepancies in their grain production figures. The actual harvests are far greater than the amounts recorded. If we address the corruption in those regions, the shortfall will resolve itself without placing undue pressure on the people."

Her words hung in the air, the governors struggling to refute her logic. Zahir, observing from the edge of the room, leaned forward slightly, intrigued by the composure with which she dismantled the argument. The portly governor's bluster faltered, and he muttered, "Perhaps we should examine these reports more closely."

Zahir's lips curled into a faint smile. While the others saw insubordination, he saw potential. Her intelligence, her calm defiance, and her ability to command the room—these were qualities he could use. And as the discussion resumed, Zahir's mind was already turning, formulating plans to draw her into his fold. The room had fallen silent, the governors exchanging uneasy glances. Zahir, however, had been intrigued.

After the assembly, he approached her. "You're bold for someone in your position," he said, his tone half-amused, half-curious.

She looked up from her parchments, her dark eyes meeting his without hesitation. "I spoke the truth, my lord. Boldness was merely a consequence."

He had smiled then, a rare expression that softened the sharp angles of his face. "Truth has its uses. As does boldness."

From that moment, Zahir began to involve her in his plans. He tasked her with gathering intelligence, decoding messages, and drafting strategies. Vishakha's brilliance complemented his ruthlessness, and together, they became an unstoppable force within the court. She had a way of seeing through the fog of deception, of identifying the weak points in their enemies' armour. Zahir, in turn, used her insights to strike with precision.

But as their partnership flourished, so did Zahir's ambition. He was no longer content with being a pawn in the emperor's game. He wanted control, power, and the respect that came with it. And he was willing to do whatever it took to achieve it.

One of his first major moves had been against Malik Aslam, the senior administrator who had once been his mentor. Malik was a respected figure, known for his integrity and loyalty to the empire. But Zahir saw him as an obstacle—a relic of a bygone era that valued honour over ambition.

Zahir orchestrated Malik's downfall with meticulous care, justifying it to himself as a necessary act of survival and ambition. "The empire needs strength, not outdated ideals," he would mutter in moments of reflection, convincing himself that Malik's integrity was a liability in a world ruled by power.

Zahir crafted an intricate web of deceit to ensure Malik's downfall. He carefully forged letters that mimicked Malik's handwriting, falsified account ledgers to suggest embezzlement, and bribed key officials to corroborate the accusations. Each detail was meticulously planned to withstand scrutiny, creating a tapestry of evidence that was as convincing as it was damning. Each move was calculated— letters forged with painstaking precision, fictitious accounts created to appear seamless, and minor officials bribed to testify against Malik. Zahir silenced the voice in his head that whispered of betrayal, telling himself that sacrifices were inevitable on the path to greatness. Vishakha had her suspicions, but Zahir kept her in the dark, ensuring she played no part in the deception. He couldn't risk her conscience getting in the way.

When the accusations were brought before the court, Malik's protests grew desperate, his voice rising with each denial. "This is preposterous! I have served this empire with unwavering loyalty," he shouted, his hands trembling as he gestured toward the gathered officials. "You all know me! My work, my integrity—it speaks for itself."

The emperor's advisors exchanged sceptical glances, their expressions cold and unreadable. Zahir stood to the side, his face a mask of feigned sorrow, watching as Malik's dignity crumbled under the weight of fabricated evidence.

"My lords," Malik continued, his voice breaking as he turned toward Zahir. "You, of all people, should know the truth! It was I who brought you into the fold, who recognized your potential when others dismissed you. How can you stand there and let this happen?"

Zahir stepped forward, his movements measured, his expression solemn. "Malik," he said softly, his tone laced with regret, "no one here wishes for this outcome. But the evidence... it is overwhelming. We cannot ignore it."

Malik's eyes widened; betrayal etched deeply into his features. "Evidence? Lies, all of it! And you, Zahir... I trusted you. I gave you everything. Without me, you would still be nothing but a scribe!"

A murmur rippled through the chamber as the advisors watched the confrontation unfold. Zahir maintained his composure, his voice steady as he replied, "You are right, Malik. You were my mentor, my guide. And it pains me more than you can imagine to see this day. But loyalty to the empire must come before personal bonds."

Malik shook his head, disbelief mingling with despair. "This is not loyalty. This is ambition. You've orchestrated this, haven't you? You've turned the court against me."

The emperor's chief advisor raised a hand, silencing the room. "Enough," he said firmly. "The accusations have been reviewed, the evidence examined. Malik Aslam, your deeds may have once been honourable, but the corruption uncovered here cannot be overlooked. The empire demands justice."

Malik's shoulders sagged, the weight of his fate pressing down on him. His gaze returned to Zahir, a flicker of defiance still burning in his eyes. "One day, you will answer for this, Zahir. Mark my words."

Zahir's expression remained impassive, but as Malik was escorted from the chamber, his heart remained unmoved. The cries of a fallen mentor were a small price to pay on the path to power. He turned back to the advisors, his voice firm as he addressed them. "The empire must remain strong. Let justice be swift."

The room fell silent, the finality of Zahir's words hanging heavily in the air. And with that, Malik's fate was sealed. The evidence was overwhelming, and the emperor's advisors demanded swift justice. Zahir feigned sorrow as he delivered the final blow, his voice steady as he recommended Malik's execution.

On the day of his execution, the square was packed with onlookers. Soldiers lined the streets, their spears forming an unbroken wall as Malik Aslam was led to the execution platform. The sun was ruthless, casting a pitiless light on the scene. Dust swirled around his bare feet as he took slow, measured steps toward the wooden block.

A hush fell over the crowd. Some whispered in disbelief; others stood frozen, unable to reconcile this fallen man with the commander who had once ruled these very lands with strength and wisdom. Vishakha watched from the balcony of a nearby haveli, her hands gripping the stone railing. She had not spoken a word since the verdict was delivered, but her silence was heavy with suspicion. She wasn't certain, but something in her gut told her it was Zahir's doing.

Malik knelt before the executioner; his hands bound behind his back. His face, though lined with exhaustion, bore no fear. His gaze swept over the crowd before finally settling on Zahir, who stood near the imperial guards, his arms crossed over his chest. Their eyes met, and for the first time, Zahir saw something he had never seen in his former mentor—pity.

Malik exhaled slowly, shaking his head. "I was wrong about you, Zahir," he said, his voice calm, almost resigned. "I thought I had forged a warrior. Instead, I created a man who would sell his soul for power."

Zahir drew in a slow, controlled breath but he said nothing.

Malik's lips curled into a weary smile. "Remember this moment. When your time comes—and it will come—you will stand in my place. And when that day arrives, your end will come at the hands of one you trust. One who knows your secrets. One you never see coming."

A murmur rippled through the crowd. Zahir's face remained impassive, but a flicker of something unreadable passed through his eyes.

Malik let out a dry chuckle. "Mark my words, Zahir. The blade meant for you has already been forged. And when it finds your back, remember this day."

The executioner raised his blade. The crowd held its breath. With one swift motion, it was over.

The body crumpled, the head rolling onto the platform with a dull thud. The silence was shattered by the wail of a woman in the distance, followed by murmurs of disbelief. Blood seeped into the wood, a deep crimson stain that the sun would dry, but never erase.

Vishakha turned away, her nails pressing into her palms. She had suspected, but now the feeling gnawed at her—this had Zahir's stench all over it. The signs were there, too many to ignore. And yet, she held her silence. Some truths were better left untouched, some suspicions too dangerous to confirm, some battles not worth waging.

The day Malik was beheaded; Zahir took his place as the senior administrator. It was a position of immense power, one that allowed him to control the empire's resources and influence its policies. But it came at a cost. Vishakha, though unaware of the full extent of his betrayal, sensed a change in him. She grew quieter, more reserved, as if questioning the path they were on. Yet she stayed by his side, driven by her own desire for survival and advancement.

Zahir Khan's rise to power was a tale of ruthless ambition and calculated brutality. No longer content with the confines of his lowly beginnings, he now held the position of the empire's senior administrator, and his ambitions stretched far beyond mere administration. The empire was his to command, and he intended to shape it in his image.

With Vishakha by his side, Zahir's ascent was not only swift but unstoppable.

In the early days of their alliance, Zahir and Vishakha had been a formidable team, each complementing the other's strengths. Vishakha's intellect and sharp perception made her invaluable to Zahir, while his ruthless ambition pushed her to see beyond the surface of court politics and think strategically. Together, they quickly grew in influence within the Mughal court.

One such instance of their cunning partnership came when Zahir was aiming to secure favour with the emperor, Qasim Khan, whose trust and resources were the final piece of the puzzle in Zahir's rise to power. The emperor, however, was a man of many advisors, and Zahir knew he would need to approach the matter with precision and subtlety. It was here that Vishakha's mind, ever sharp and analytical, came into play.

They devised a plan to infiltrate the emperor's court during a grand assembly meant to discuss matters of taxation and military strategy. Qasim had been growing increasingly frustrated with the inefficiency and corruption in his empire, and Zahir saw an opportunity to position himself as the solution to the emperor's growing concerns. However, to earn the emperor's trust, Zahir needed to appear both capable and indispensable—someone who could not only manage the empire's vast resources but also see through the veils of deceit that clouded the court.

Vishakha, ever astute, realized that the emperor's insecurities about his court were the key to manipulating the situation. "The emperor values loyalty above all," she had said to Zahir one evening, her fingers lightly tracing the edges of a scroll they had been reviewing. "But he's surrounded by men who only flatter him to climb higher. He's not interested in yes-men—he needs someone who speaks truth, even if it stings."

Zahir had nodded, a plan already forming in his mind. "Then we must be the ones to show him the truth."

Together, they crafted a scheme that would place Zahir at the forefront of the emperor's thoughts. Vishakha would use her position as a scribe in the emperor's inner circle to glean sensitive information from the royal records. She carefully studied Qasim's handwritten notes and court documents, spotting discrepancies and signs of corruption that the emperor himself was too close to notice. Armed with this knowledge, she passed it to Zahir, who, under the guise of a loyal officer, would present his findings at the next assembly.

The day of the grand assembly arrived, and the emperor's court was filled with nervous anticipation. The room was a labyrinth of political rivalries, whispers, and shifting alliances. Zahir, dressed in his finest robes, stood at the periphery, waiting for his moment. Vishakha, seated among the scribes, carefully observed the proceedings. As the conversation turned toward the empire's financial woes, Zahir rose to speak, his voice calm yet commanding.

"The issue here is not merely a lack of funds, my lords," Zahir said, addressing the gathered nobles. "It is a failure of trust. The reports submitted by your governors and administrators are riddled with inconsistencies, as are the tax records. If the emperor wishes to restore the empire's prosperity, he must first restore the trust between his people and his officials."

The assembly fell silent. The emperor's advisors exchanged nervous glances. Vishakha's heart pounded in her chest as she watched the scene unfold. She knew that Zahir's words had hit their mark—they were precisely what the emperor needed to hear. Qasim's brow furrowed, but there was a flicker of recognition in his eyes as he glanced at Zahir.

"You claim there is corruption in my court?" Qasim asked, his voice both curious and cautious.

"I do not claim, my lord," Zahir replied, his voice steady. "I have evidence. If you trust me to speak further, I will show you the truth that lies hidden beneath the surface."

With Vishakha's intelligence guiding him, Zahir revealed the discrepancies in the empire's financial records, pointing out the false reports and embezzled funds that had been funnelled into the pockets of corrupt officials. He spoke with such conviction that the emperor could not ignore him, nor the implications of what he was saying. The emperor, though initially defensive, was soon captivated by Zahir's honesty and insight.

As the assembly concluded and the courtiers filed out of the room, a heavy silence settled over the grand hall. Zahir stood firm, his poise unyielding as the emperor, Qasim Khan, motioned for him to follow. The grandeur of the palace seemed to recede, leaving the two men alone in the shadow of imperial power. The emperor's gaze bore into Zahir, the candlelight wavering as its warmth failed to soften the cold bite of the stone walls.

The emperor, his regal presence commanding yet burdened, walked slowly toward the window, his back to Zahir. The vast city of Dilli sprawled beneath them, the palace towers rising like sentinels against the darkening sky.

For a long moment, Qasim Khan did not speak. He stood there, looking out into the distance, as if searching for the answers he had been too reluctant to face. Zahir, standing quietly behind him, let the silence stretch, allowing the tension to mount.

Finally, Qasim Khan spoke, his voice low but laden with a kind of weariness Zahir had never heard before.

"You have shown me a truth I did not want to see, Zahir Khan," he said, turning to face him, his expression thoughtful but not yet trusting. "But perhaps it is a truth necessary for the future of my empire."

Zahir stood tall, the weight of the emperor's scrutiny upon him. He had always been prepared for these moments—when men of power would resist change and challenge the truths that might unsettle them. Yet, despite his calm demeanour, a flicker of anticipation moved through him. This was the moment that would solidify his place at Qasim Khan's side.

"I do not say these things lightly, my lord," Zahir replied evenly, his gaze never wavering from the emperor. "I have no loyalty to those who wear false masks of power and glory. I am loyal to the empire, to the strength it can have, if only it is built on truth."

Qasim Khan studied him for a long moment, his piercing eyes assessing the man before him. "And you think you are the one to give me that truth, Zahir Khan?" There was a slight edge to his voice, but it was not dismissive—it was the curiosity of a ruler who had seen betrayal too many times to accept trust easily.

"I have nothing to gain by hiding the truth from you, my lord," Zahir said, stepping forward, his tone sincere but unwavering. "Your empire is crumbling under the weight of deception. The truth must be exposed, even if it risks shaking the very foundations of power. Only by confronting it can we rebuild."

Qasim Khan's eyes narrowed slightly. "You would dare to speak of rebuilding to me, Zahir Khan? You who has manipulated the court, outmanoeuvred my own advisors?" His voice was colder now, but there was no venom in it— only the sharp edge of a man confronted by a truth he had long denied.

"I've only acted in the service of the empire, my lord," Zahir responded, his voice steady but laced with the quiet authority of someone who had already seen beyond the game of politics. "This empire was built on strength, yes. But it will only endure if that strength is aligned with the truth. The corruption is not in the people—it is in the men who betray their emperor's trust, in those who would mislead you for their own gain."

Qasim Khan's gaze softened as he absorbed Zahir's words, his expression momentarily distant. The candlelight trembled, highlighting the deep lines of weariness etched into his face—the weight of rulership pressing heavy upon him.

"I have trusted many men before," the emperor murmured, almost to himself. "And each of them has betrayed me, Zahir. How can I trust you not to follow the same path? How can I believe you when I've seen nothing but treachery in this court?"

Zahir took another step forward, his voice more earnest, more personal. "I do not seek to betray you, my lord. I seek to serve you, to strengthen the empire—not by manipulation, but by revealing the truths that others fear to speak." He paused, letting his words sink in. "Trust, my lord, must be earned. I understand that. But I ask you to trust me—not as a mere officer, but as someone who sees beyond the politics. I want to see this empire flourish as you do. Not as a vessel of power, but as a beacon of strength and justice."

Qasim Khan's lips tightened as if he were wrestling with the weight of a decision. The room was filled with the tension of unspoken words, the weight of history pressing down on both men.

"You would have me believe that your loyalty lies with me and not with your own ambitions?" the emperor asked, his voice a little more vulnerable than before.

Zahir's gaze never wavered. "Yes, my lord. My ambition lies with this empire. With you."

There was a long silence. Then, at last, Qasim Khan stepped away from the window, his eyes never leaving Zahir's. Slowly, almost imperceptibly, he nodded.

"You are not wrong," the emperor said, his voice steadying. "The empire is failing because the truth has been hidden from us. I have surrounded myself with sycophants who praise me to my face, but no one tells me what I need to hear. They tell me what I want to hear, and in doing so, they have led me astray."

Zahir inclined his head slightly, acknowledging the emperor's words. "You have my word, my lord. I will not do the same. I will speak the truth, even when it is difficult."

Qasim Khan studied him for a moment longer, then spoke again, this time with a tone of finality. "I will trust you, Zahir Khan. You have shown me what the others could not, and for that, you have earned my trust."

Zahir's expression remained unchanged, but his heart quickened. He had done it. He had earned the emperor's trust.

"You will have my counsel, and you will have my ear," the emperor continued, his voice now authoritative. "From now on, Zahir Khan, I will look to you for advice. Not just on matters of finance and strategy, but on the very future of this empire."

A flicker of something—something that bordered on satisfaction—flashed in Zahir's eyes, but he did not show it. Instead, he bowed low, his voice steady but filled with respect. "Thank you, my lord. I will not fail you."

As the conversation drew to a close, Qasim Khan's words echoed in Zahir's mind. The emperor had placed his trust in him, and Zahir would not squander it. This was the beginning of something far greater than mere loyalty—it was a partnership born out of necessity, and one that would shape the future of the empire.

For the first time, Zahir felt the weight of power settle firmly on his shoulders. He had crossed a threshold, and there was no turning back. With the emperor's trust, the path ahead was clearer than ever.

In that moment, Zahir had secured his position as one of the emperor's most trusted advisors, and Vishakha had been the mastermind behind the scheme. Together, they had outmanoeuvred the court's political players, proving themselves indispensable. Their partnership, built on shared ambition and mutual respect, had brought them to the pinnacle of power.

But as time passed, Vishakha began to feel the weight of their success. The cost of Zahir's ambition had become clearer with each passing day—the bloodshed, the manipulation, and the cold ruthlessness that had come to define their rise. She had helped him climb to the emperor's side, but now she found herself questioning the price of their power.

And so, the woman who had once trusted him would soon find herself at odds with the very man she had helped become the most dangerous figure in the empire.

Zahir had always been a man of precision, and now that he had the power, he wielded it without hesitation. When Malik Aslam, his former mentor, had fallen, it was just the beginning. Zahir began to systematically dismantle anyone who stood in his way, not through brute force alone, but with a cold, calculating strategy that left nothing to chance.

Under the emperor's command, Zahir's ruthless reputation spread like wildfire across the empire. His reputation as a man of unwavering loyalty and brutal efficiency became a tool for the emperor's will—one he wielded with cold precision. When Emperor Qasim Khan ordered the capture of a rebellious province, it was not a matter of strategy alone; it was an opportunity for Zahir to solidify his dominance, showing the empire the cost of defiance.

Zahir's methods were as merciless as they were calculated. When a region dared to rebel, he did not simply seek to subdue the rebels—he sought to eradicate the very notion of resistance. His first act was always to send his men to deal with the soldiers who had laid down their arms. Those who surrendered were given no mercy, not even the dignity of death on a battlefield. Instead, Zahir ordered the captives to be lined up in rows, their heads bowed in submission.

"No mercy for the unfaithful," Zahir would say, his voice unwavering and devoid of any emotion as he gave the command. "Those who do not submit to Islam will die as traitors; their blood will cleanse the land."

His soldiers would carry out the order swiftly, slaying those who refused conversion to Islam with brutal efficiency, their swords raised high as they cleaved through necks and limbs, ending lives with casual indifference. Zahir watched, impassive, as the men who had once been soldiers for a cause were reduced to mere corpses, left to rot under the sun, a grim reminder of the consequences of defying the emperor's rule. The cries of those who were forced to convert echoed in the air, their voices torn between fear and anger.

Once the captives were dealt with, Zahir's soldiers turned their attention to the homes of the fallen. The houses of the surrendered soldiers, once symbols of their defiance, were burned to the ground. The flames would rise high into the sky, a towering inferno that consumed the hopes and lives of entire families. The smell of burning wood and flesh filled the air as the village was reduced to ashes.

"The cost of disloyalty," Zahir would say, his gaze fixed on the horizon, watching as the smoke from the burning homes billowed into the sky. "Loyalty is not a privilege—it is a necessity."

And yet, the carnage did not end with the burning of homes. Zahir's men, driven by the desire for blood and riches, were given free rein over the villages they had captured. The women, once the wives and daughters of the villagers, were taken as spoils of war. Zahir turned a blind eye to their fates as his soldiers violated them, their screams lost in the chaos of the burning villages. The men, no longer able to protect their families, watched helplessly as their lives and dignity were stripped away.

Vishakha had been by Zahir's side through every campaign, studying the enemy, analysing weaknesses, and crafting strategies that led to his victories. But as the carnage unfolded before her, something inside her fractured. She had always known Zahir was ruthless, but the depths of his cruelty, the sheer precision with which he commanded slaughter, made her stomach twist with turmoil.

She saw a woman—no older than herself—dragged into a soldier's tent, her terrified pleas swallowed by the night. Vishakha clenched her fists, bile rising in her throat. She had stood by Zahir, played her role in his ascension, and yet, when faced with the horrors of conquest, she could no longer ignore what they had become.

Later, as they stood atop a hill overlooking the smouldering remains of the village, Zahir spoke, his voice unnervingly calm. "It's always the families that pay the price," he mused. "But it's necessary. The children will grow up fearing rebellion. The land will be cleansed."

Vishakha's hands trembled, but she willed herself to remain composed. She looked at him then—not as the man she had once admired, but as something else entirely. The moment the last scream had faded, the weight of his actions settled over her like a shroud. She had thought herself strong enough to ignore the bloodshed, but she had been wrong.

That night, as the embers of the ruined village flickered in the dark, sleep eluded her. The cries of the fallen echoed in her mind, their suffering an accusation she could no longer silence. Power, she had always believed, came at a cost. But this? This was something else.

At dawn, as Zahir prepared to march to his next conquest, she made a decision. She had followed him for power, had helped shape his rise, but she could not walk the path he had chosen.

That evening, in the stillness of their chambers, Vishakha sat beside the oil lamp, its unsteady glow illuminating the room with a fragile warmth. Her heart bore the weight of everything she had witnessed—everything she had chosen to overlook.

"Vishakha," Zahir's voice broke through her thoughts. He stood in the doorway, his silhouette dark against the moonlight streaming through the window. "We've secured another victory. The empire is ours to shape."

Vishakha didn't respond at first. She simply stared at the flame, the heat from it only serving to deepen the coldness that had settled in her chest. Finally, she spoke, her voice quiet but firm.

"At what cost, Zahir?" she asked. "How many lives must be sacrificed for this 'empire' you speak of? How many villages must burn before you're satisfied?"

Zahir's gaze hardened, and he stepped closer to her, his expression darkening. "You knew what you were getting into," he said, his tone laced with warning. "Power is not given, Vishakha. It is taken. The weak are crushed, and the strong rise. That is the way of the world."

Her heart sank as she realized that the man she had once believed in had become something else entirely—a man who would stop at nothing to attain his goals, even if it meant destroying everything in his path. She had helped him rise, but she could not continue to support him as he became a monster.

"I can't do this anymore," she whispered, her voice trembling. "I won't be part of this... this destruction."

Zahir's eyes flashed with anger. "You think you can walk away from this? You think you can turn your back on the power we've built? You have no choice, Vishakha. You are as much a part of this as I am."

But Vishakha knew that she could no longer be complicit in his rise. She had seen enough bloodshed to last a lifetime, and she could no longer stomach the man Zahir had become. She had dreams of her own—dreams of power, yes, but not at the expense of innocent lives.

Without another word, she gathered her things and left. It was a decision that would cost her dearly, but it was one she had to make.

With heavy steps, she left him, her heart filled with both fear and relief. The empire Zahir sought to build would be one built on the bones of the innocent, and she no longer wanted to be a part of it.

As she disappeared into the distance, she whispered to herself, "I've made my choice. I will not follow him down this path any longer."

Zahir, meanwhile, stood at the head of his army, oblivious to her departure, his thoughts fixed on his next conquest. His vision of power was unstoppable, and in his eyes, the cost of loyalty was one that others would pay—but not him.

***

But as the image of the battlefield faded, a soft voice interrupted his thoughts.

"Zahir?"

He blinked, coming back to the present with a sharp inhale. The noise of the army, the weight of the ambitions that had carried him so far—all of it faded into the background as his gaze fell upon the woman standing in the doorway of the room. She had entered unnoticed, her presence quiet but commanding.

Her voice had brought him back, but her gaze, laced with subtle concern, caused a brief flicker of something in him. Zahir, who had trained himself to focus solely on power, found himself unexpectedly caught in the quiet moment between them.

"Is something troubling you?" Her voice was soft, but it held the authority of one who had long known him, one who could sense the shifts in his demeanour.

Zahir stood motionless for a long moment, the weight of his inner thoughts pulling at him. His focus shifted from the plans in his mind to the woman before him. His thoughts remained sharp, as always, but he couldn't ignore the way she looked at him—like someone who had always been by his side, watching, waiting, understanding.

"No," he replied, his voice steady, but his words lacked the sharpness they usually held. "There's just much to be done. Few things have to be taken care of."

She studied him, her eyes searching his face for a moment longer, as if she could peel away the layers of ambition that cloaked him. But she said nothing more. Instead, her expression softened, and she nodded, her gaze lingering for a brief moment before she turned.

"I'll be in the study, Zahir. Should you need anything."

Her presence lingered in the room as she left, the door clicking softly behind her. Zahir exhaled slowly, returning his focus to the task ahead. Yet, for a moment, a slight shift in his thoughts lingered. The sharp edge of his ambition hadn't dulled, but the quiet exchange had unsettled him.

He quickly pushed those thoughts away. There was no time for distractions. The throne awaited, and everything was moving according to plan. He would have it all, but at what cost?

Chapter 7

The air was damp with the scent of earth and dew as Rana's group pushed into the dense forest. Moist leaves brushed against their arms, their surfaces slick with the remnants of dawn's mist. The ground, uneven and softened by the night's moisture, gave slightly beneath their steps. Distant birdcalls echoed through the canopy, punctuated by the occasional crack of a branch as unseen creatures moved through the undergrowth. Each breath carried the crispness of morning, yet beneath it all, a tension coiled in the air—silent, unspoken. Rana felt it pressing against his ribs, but deeper still, something hotter stirred within him, a force that would not let him stop.

The mention of Pari's name by the girl had been enough to ignite a fire within him. She was alive. The thought of her being somewhere out there, waiting for him, kept him moving through the wilderness, each step forward filled with the hope that he would find her before it was too late.

The group walked in silence, their faces grim, their minds occupied with the mission ahead. Vishakha, though still weak from her injuries, trudged along beside Rana, her thoughts distant. The weight of their journey—the uncertainty of the path they were on—was a burden she couldn't ignore. But there was something in Rana's steady stride, the way he never wavered, that gave her a sense of strength. She had seen that same strength in him when he had decided to protect Pari, and though she had her own doubts about the future, she couldn't help but admire his unwavering resolve.

Amar and Chandan were walking ahead of the group, their voices low but full of humour, trying to cut through the pressing silence that had settled over the others. Amar had always been the one to bring some levity to their travels, and even Chandan, usually the more reserved of the two, couldn't resist joining in.

"You know," Amar said, his voice teasing as he glanced at Chandan, "I have another idea for a business."

Chandan raised an eyebrow, glancing sideways. "Another? What's that now?"

"Yeah!" Amar's grin was wide. "I'll sell 'Amar's Guide to Survival'—it'll be a bestseller. You know, tricks for traveling through forests, how to survive danger, and of course, how to stay alive while carrying all these weapons."

Chandan chuckled, shaking his head. "And I suppose you'll be the star of your own guide?"

"Of course!" Amar replied with a mock bow. "How else would it work? You'll get your copy at a discount for being my favourite traveling companion."

Chandan rolled his eyes. "I don't need any tips from you on how to survive, Amar. I've been doing just fine."

Amar's eyes twinkled as he nudged him. "Are you sure about that? You've got a way of getting into trouble, you know."

"Trouble? Me?" Chandan said with mock outrage. "No more than you! If it weren't for my quick thinking, I'm sure you would've gotten us all caught by now."

Vishakha, who had been walking quietly beside Rana, caught their exchange. She couldn't help but smile at the lightness between the two men. Despite the heavy journey ahead, it was moments like these that made the hardships bearable.

But as she glanced over at Rana, she saw the quiet, distant look in his eyes. She turned her attention back to the path, her leg throbbing with every step, but her thoughts remained on him.

In a world of hardship and survival, men like Rana stood apart—driven, relentless, their minds consumed by the battles ahead. He was the kind who saw only the path before him, unyielding in his focus. But a world filled with men like Rana would be a grim, merciless place. There was strength in resolve, but survival demanded more than just determination. It needed those who could cut through the weight of fear and uncertainty with laughter, who could find light even in the darkest moments.

To the outside world, men like Amar and Chandan might seem like fools, their easy words and quick wit mistaken for carelessness. But in truth, they were just as essential as the warriors and strategists. The weight of uncertainty, the exhaustion of the journey, the fear of what lay ahead—it pressed down on all of them. The road they travelled was harsh, their mission uncertain, and without the lightness that Amar's sharp tongue and Chandan's endless banters, the tension might have consumed them. In moments of silence, when doubt threatened to take hold, it was their laughter that reminded the group to keep moving forward.

At the back of the group, Suresh's voice cut through the light banter, harsh and frustrated.

"This is ridiculous," he muttered, scowling as he looked at the pace they were setting.

The others fell silent, the shift in mood palpable. Suresh didn't hold back. "We're moving too slowly. You're letting her injuries hold us back. You're all focused on helping her, but we've got a bigger problem—Pari's out there. What's more important? Finding her, or helping some stranger we barely know?"

The group's mood shifted as Rana, walking ahead, stopped and turned toward Suresh, his face stern.

"No one wants to find Pari more than I do," Rana's voice was calm but unwavering. "But we can't trade one life for another."

Suresh's frustration boiled over. "That's not what I'm saying. We're wasting time. Every minute counts, and we're moving at a crawl because we're babysitting her."

Amar's light-heartedness faltered as he stepped closer to Suresh. "She's not a 'babysitting' case, Suresh. You think we're not all worried about Pari? But we can't just abandon people because they're injured. That's not who we are."

Suresh's eyes narrowed. "I know we set out to protect Vishakha, but things have changed. Now that we know about Pari, shouldn't our priority shift?"

Rana, his gaze sharp and unwavering, took a step toward Suresh, his voice low. "You think I don't know that?" He paused, his eyes hardening. "But if we start making decisions like that—sacrificing one life for another—where does it end? No one gets left behind, Suresh. Not now. Not ever. Not on my watch."

The weight of Rana's words hung in the air, and the tension was palpable. Suresh, momentarily taken aback by Rana's response, didn't say anything more. He was silent for a long moment before he muttered, "Fine."

The truth was, Suresh didn't care much about Pari—he just didn't like Vishakha. Some people simply rub you the wrong way, and she was one of them. He didn't like her and couldn't even explain why. He hadn't wanted to come on this mission in the first place, but Dharamdas had forced his hand. Now, stuck in this endless march through the wilderness for someone he had no interest in saving, he couldn't help but voice his frustration whenever the opportunity arose.

The air grew dense, the banter fading into silence. The group, now fully grasping the gravity of their situation, pressed on with a sombre, more reflective mood. Vishakha, still limping from her injury, felt the weight of the moment tighten around her chest. They were bound to this mission, tied by the promise to find Pari, but with each step, the true cost of loyalty—of carrying one another through hardship—became more evident.

Rana's words rang in her mind as she watched him lead the way, resolute as ever. No one would be left behind. And somehow, no matter how difficult the journey, she believed him.

***

As the group continued their journey through the hills, the sounds of the forest grew more ominous with each step. The mist had gathered as the day wore on, making the narrow path ahead more difficult to navigate. The air was cool, and the occasional rustling in the underbrush sent an eerie chill down their spines.

Rana, his mind occupied with thoughts of Pari and the distant memory of the ribbon he had found, led the group with unwavering determination. The trek had taken longer than expected, but they were finally nearing the river—the place where the girl had told him Pari had been last seen.

As the sun dipped lower in the sky, they arrived at a clearing near the riverbank. The peaceful sound of rushing water filled the air, but there was a heaviness that lingered around them. The once gentle breeze had turned cold, as if the land itself had grown wary of the travellers.

Several other figures had gathered around a small campfire in the clearing. They were a mixed group, weary travellers and families, some sitting quietly, others murmuring among themselves. Rana approached them, his eyes scanning the crowd for anyone who might know about a missing child.

"Has anyone seen a young girl, around ten or eleven?" Rana asked, his voice firm yet tinged with urgency.

The group fell silent. One man, an older farmer with a weathered face, shook his head. "I haven't seen anyone like that. There are many of us searching, but it's all the same. Children go missing, and we find nothing."

Rana's heart sank. He looked at the group, noting the same haunted look in their eyes that he had felt in his own. A woman spoke next, her voice barely a whisper. "Many children are being taken by the forest. No one knows why. They vanish, and all that's left are these symbols, these circles of stones."

Rana's mind raced. The mysterious circles, the glowing symbols, the vanishing children—it all pointed to something more than mere superstition.

"We've seen the same thing," the farmer continued, his voice quivering. "A circle of stones, always in the same pattern. In the centre, a piece of clothing or some other memento. The last we saw... a boy from our village. We found his hat, but not him."

Rana's breath caught. The memory of the red ribbon returned to him with sharp clarity. The circle of stones, the symbols, the eerie glow in the twilight—it was the same thing he had seen in the forest when he had been searching for Pari. This was no coincidence.

"Where exactly did you find the circle?" Rana asked, his voice low, barely above a whisper.

The farmer pointed toward the deeper reaches of the forest. "It's not far from here. Just past the river, where the trees get dense. We thought it was just a superstition at first, but then... so many children have gone missing. It's a place cursed by the forest, no doubt."

Rana's grip tightened on his spear as he exchanged a quick glance with Hari and Suresh. There was no mystery here, no unknown force at work. Someone—something—was taking the children, and it was no superstition. The forest had become a hunting ground, and Rana knew that he couldn't leave it like that. He had to find out who was behind this.

As the group began to settle down for the night, Rana stood at the edge of the river, his mind racing. The others were talking in low voices, discussing the missing children and the mysterious signs, but Rana could barely hear them. His focus was entirely on the task ahead.

"We need to go to the river's edge," he said abruptly, his tone resolute. "Now."

Hari, who had been sitting by the fire, looked up in confusion. "What do you mean?"

Rana turned to him; his gaze intense. "If we're going to find Pari, we need to understand what's going on. The circle, the missing children, they're connected. We need to see this for ourselves."

Suresh, still uneasy, spoke up. "Are you sure? This doesn't feel right, Rana. I don't trust those woods. No one does."

Rana's expression hardened. "We can't leave this unsolved. Not when it could be the key to finding Pari."

With that, they made their way toward the riverbank, the last streaks of sunlight barely clinging to the sky. A cold breeze slithered through the trees, carrying the damp scent of the river and the distant rustling of unseen creatures. The deeper they went into the forest, the denser the silence became— smothering, watchful, as if the very trees were holding their breath. Every snapped twig underfoot sent a jolt through their nerves, the weight of the unknown pressing down on them. Ahead lay the place where the strange circle had been found, and though none spoke of it, a quiet discomfort curled in their chests, settling in the pit of their stomachs like a warning left unspoken.

As they reached the clearing, the trees parted to reveal the familiar stone circle, eerily glowing in the last light of the day. The stones were arranged with unnerving precision, just as the farmer had described. Each symbol carved into them glowed faintly in the twilight, casting strange shadows on the forest floor.

In the centre of the circle, a single piece of clothing—a small torn scarf—lay discarded. The same haunting feeling Rana had experienced in the forest returned to him, stronger now. He could feel the weight of the forest, as though it was watching them, waiting.

"See," Hari muttered under his breath, his voice tinged with fear. "It's just like they said. The forest... it's taking them."

Suresh stood frozen, his eyes wide with terror. "This is not just superstition. There's something out there, and it's taking our children."

Rana stepped forward, kneeling beside the torn scarf, his fingers brushing lightly over the fabric. His face remained impassive, but his mind raced. This wasn't some curse, nor was it the forest acting on its own. Someone was behind this—someone who knew the land well enough to lure children into the woods, to make them disappear without a trace.

Slowly, he reached into his tunic and pulled out the ribbon he had taken from Pari's circle. He held it between his fingers, his grip tightening for a moment as he stared at it. The edges were frayed, worn from being carried so long, yet it was the only tangible piece of her he had. He exhaled sharply before tucking it back into his tunic, as if sealing away both the ribbon and the emotions it stirred. Then, his gaze hardened, and he rose to his feet. Whoever was behind this had made a mistake. And Rana intended to find them.

"There's someone behind this," Rana said quietly, his voice grim. "And I will find them."

The forest, once a place of refuge and solace for Rana, now felt like a sinister labyrinth. He would not rest until he uncovered who was taking the children—no matter the cost.

As Rana and his group made their way back to the clearing near the riverbank, an uneasy stillness settled over them. The discoveries they had just made left an unspoken tension hanging in the air. The circle of stones and the piece of clothing weren't just remnants of superstition—they pointed to something stern, something resolute. This wasn't just fear of the unknown. Someone had shaped it, controlled it. And that realization was far more unsettling than any legend.

The travellers they had spoken to earlier were still sitting by the fire, their faces weary and their voices hushed, as though the forest itself had already begun to creep into their thoughts. They looked up as the group approached, their gazes filled with uncertainty and distrust.

Rana, his mind restless with the thought of Pari and the children taken by the forest, strode up to the group without hesitation.

"Where can we go?" he asked bluntly. "We need to find out where the children are being taken. We can't just sit here."

The travellers exchanged nervous glances, their faces contorting with doubt and fear. The man who had first spoken to Rana—the farmer—shook his head, his voice trembling.

"The forest is cursed, I tell you. No good comes from venturing into it at night. I lost my own daughter to it, and there was nothing but silence when we looked for her."

Another man, his face pale, nodded. "We don't enter the forest after dark. It's the way of the land. We've learned to leave well enough alone."

Rana's gaze hardened, frustration growing with each passing second. "Do you think hiding from the truth will protect you? You don't even know who's behind this!"

His words were met with silence, the group's expressions a mix of fear and defiance. The fire crackled, filling the quiet moments between them with an eerie rhythm, as if the forest itself were listening.

"We know the stories," the woman spoke, her voice low. "The forest is cursed, and no one who's ventured in after dark has ever returned the same, or at all."

"And you think that's what's happening to the children?" Rana pressed, his anger rising. "That the forest is some kind of curse?"

Before anyone could respond, a figure emerged from the shadows, moving with a structured and quiet grace. A man, dressed in dark, tattered clothing, appeared by the edge of the firelight. His face was obscured by the shadows, but his presence seemed to fill the space. His eyes, however, gleamed with an unsettling knowledge.

The man glanced at the gathering, eyes dark with something between frustration and pity, before turning to Rana and his group. "You're wasting your time debating with them," he said, his voice low but firm. "They've already given up. And to hide the guilt of their own choices, they cling to superstitions. It's always easier to believe that some unseen force stole their loved ones than to admit they could have done more to save them. Demons and cursed forests make for convenient excuses—they help them sleep at night, free of blame."

The gatherings grew still at his arrival, recognizing something in his demeanour that made them wary, but he spoke calmly, his voice barely more than a whisper carried on the wind.

Without waiting for a response, he gestured for them to follow. Leading them away from the gathering, he walked with purpose, his steps sure despite the uneven ground. Only when they were deep enough into the trees, where the flickering village torches were nothing but distant specks, did he finally stop.

His jaw was set, eyes sharp as he finally spoke "The forest is no curse," the man said cryptically, his eyes briefly meeting Rana's. "It's a tool—used by those who know how to wield it. The real power is not in the trees, but in the men who make the forest seem like a mystery."

Rana's eyes narrowed, his heart racing. "Who are you?"

The man's lips curled into a small, knowing smile, though his expression remained controlled. "A man who has seen too much and spoken too little. The children... they are being taken to a place. Not a forest. Not a curse. A market. Where the highest bidders come to claim them."

Rana's pulse quickened as he stepped closer, his voice demanding answers. "A market? A market where children are sold?"

The man's eyes darkened, and he glanced around, lowering his voice even further, as though speaking too loudly might give away something vital. "Buyers come from Kabul. They trade in people—women, children. Slaves for the west. Those who don't get sold... they vanish. Used by the men who take them, kept for their own purposes. They make it look like the forest is cursed, to keep the villagers too scared to pursue. It's been happening for years."

Rana felt a cold rage settle in his chest as he absorbed the weight of the man's words. He had suspected something dark, but hearing it spoken aloud made it real. This was no superstition. This was human trafficking, hidden under the guise of fear.

"That's why the forest is cursed in the stories," the man continued, his voice growing more urgent. "It's easier to make people believe in ghosts and spirits than it is to make them believe that their neighbours—men they've known all their lives—are selling their children into slavery."

Rana's hands clenched into fists. The realization hit him like a physical blow. The missing children, the symbols, the eerie circles—none of it had anything to do with magic or curses. It was men. And they were hiding in plain sight, preying on the very people who were too scared to even question the reality of what was happening.

Chandan, who had been silent until now, spoke with a tremor in his voice. "And you think we can just march into the heart of that? No, Rana. This is madness. We're not warriors. We're just a group of villagers. There's no way we can go after them."

But Rana, his mind burning with the need for justice, stepped closer to the man. "How do we find them?"

The man gave him a look, his eyes narrowing with an almost imperceptible hint of warning. "Follow the path that the children leave behind. It's not hard to see when you know what to look for. But do it before they cover their tracks, before they disappear into the darkness."

Rana looked back at the group, his gaze hard. The others were still processing the new information, their faces drawn with the weight of it all. But the path ahead was clear to him. He couldn't wait for the safety of daylight.

"I'll go tonight," Rana said, his voice resolute. "I'll find out where they've taken the children. If it's a market, I'll ruin it. I don't care how dangerous it is. No one should have to live in fear like this."

"Rana, wait!" Suresh's voice broke through his resolve. "This is madness! We're not prepared for this! The forest is dangerous enough during the day. At night—"

"No," Rana interrupted, his tone unwavering. "I will not wait. If they've taken Pari, I will not sit idly by while others suffer."

Vishakha, who had been quiet until now, looked at Rana, her gaze filled with quiet concern. "Rana, please... We don't know what's out there. The others are right. We should wait until dawn."

Rana shook his head. "We don't have time to wait. Every moment counts. But if you all wish to rest, I will go alone. But I'll find her. I'll find Pari."

There was a heavy silence among the group. After a moment, Hari spoke, his voice low. "We can't just send you off alone, Rana. We need to stick together."

But Suresh, his face still filled with apprehension, put in his final word. "We rest. We move at first light. The forest isn't safe at night."

Reluctantly, Rana nodded, his jaw locked with unspoken frustration. He knew they were right. As much as he wanted to push on, the others were right to be cautious. The forest was no place for recklessness, not when they didn't know what else might be waiting in the shadows.

***

The fire had long since died down, its last embers casting faint glows against the darkness. The night was still, the only sound the soft rustle of leaves and the occasional murmur of the river flowing beside the camp. Most of the group had fallen into an uneasy sleep, but not Rana. He sat at the edge of the riverbank, his eyes fixed on the dark waters that reflected the pale light of the moon.

Vishakha, her mind restless from the day's revelations, noticed him there, sitting alone, a figure of quiet strength and unspoken grief. She moved quietly toward him, her steps muffled by the soft earth, careful not to disturb the others. When she reached him, she stood there for a moment, watching him, unsure of how to break the silence.

Rana's posture was tense, his gaze distant, lost in thought. He didn't turn when she approached, but after a moment, his voice broke the stillness.

"You should be resting," he said quietly, his tone flat but with an undercurrent of concern.

Vishakha hesitated before sitting beside him, keeping a respectful distance. The cool night air brushed against her face, but it did little to calm the turmoil inside her. She folded her arms, staring out at the river.

"I couldn't sleep," she admitted, her voice soft. After a long pause, she spoke again. "I... I wanted to thank you."

Rana didn't respond at first, but the tension in his bearing seemed to ease slightly.

"You took a risk when you brought me with you," she continued, her voice sincere. "You didn't have to. Everyone else was ready to abandon me, and you stood by me. Even when Suresh wanted to leave me behind, you didn't. You could've saved yourself so much trouble, but you chose to help me instead. I won't forget that."

Rana finally turned his head toward her, his eyes reflecting the soft moonlight. He said nothing, but his silence was enough to show that he understood the weight of her gratitude.

"I'm not doing this just for you," he replied quietly. "I'm doing this for Pari. But..." His voice faltered for a moment, and he paused, as if uncertain whether to share more. "If there's anything you know that could help, now's the time."

Vishakha's gaze drifted to the river again. She was silent for a while, as though deciding how much to reveal. Her fingers traced the edges of the blanket around her shoulders, the weight of the past pressing down on her.

"I might know where they've taken the children," she said finally, her voice low but steady. "There's a market in Agra. I've heard whispers about it, and I've seen things... things I wish I could forget."

Rana turned toward her fully now, his expression sharp with curiosity and concern. "A market? What do you mean? What kind of market?"

Vishakha exhaled slowly, gathering her thoughts before speaking. "A market where women and children are bought and sold. It's not a place for trade in goods—it's a place for people. Buyers come from all over, including Kabul. They take the children, the women—anyone they can use for whatever purpose they want. Some are sold; some are kept for other reasons. The ones who aren't bought... they disappear. Left behind. Used for other dark purposes."

Rana inhaled sharply. He could hardly fathom what he was hearing, but the anger inside him burned brighter than ever.

"But how do you know about this?" he asked, his voice rough, filled with suspicion and disbelief. "How could you have possibly known about something like this?"

"I worked in the Mughal court," she began. "Not as a mere servant, but in the inner circles—where whispers shaped destinies, where a single word in the wrong ear could change the course of a kingdom."

"I wasn't born into that world. I was placed there," she said, her voice carrying the weight of the past. "I was born into a family of scholars. My father was a man of great learning, respected by many. He believed in the power of knowledge, that wisdom could shape the world into something better." Vishakha's lips curved into a soft smile, the kind that comes from memories too precious to forget. "My mother... she was the heart of our home. She had a laugh that could fill every corner of the house, a kindness that made everyone feel like they belonged."

She let out a small, breathy chuckle, her fingers brushing away a tear that had slipped down her cheek. "And my brothers... they were my protectors, my partners in mischief. No matter how much trouble I got into, they were always there, shielding me, teasing me, making me feel invincible." She paused, her smile lingering, but the glisten in her eyes betrayed the ache beneath it. Another tear followed the first, and she let it fall, unbothered by the contradiction of joy and grief entwining in her expression. "We were happy. We were whole."

For a fleeting second, it was as if she had stepped back into that life—before it was taken from her. But the present pulled her back, and her smile, though still there, carried the sadness of something lost forever.

She swallowed hard, her fingers tightening around the edge of her blanket. "But the world doesn't care about happiness. It doesn't care about families or dreams or the lives people build. It only cares about power. And when power shifts, it destroys everything in its path."

Her voice broke, and she took a moment to steady herself. "There was a rebellion. A faction rose against the empire, and my family... we were caught in the middle. My father refused to take sides. He believed in peace, in dialogue. But neutrality is a luxury the powerful cannot afford."

Her fingers curled into fists in her lap. "I was barely more than a child when it happened. One day, we were a family. The next... they were gone. Our home was burned, our lands seized. My father, my brothers, slaughtered like they were nothing. My mother..." Vishakha's voice wavered, and she looked away, forcing herself to steady her breath before she continued. "She didn't survive the grief. I suppose she did, for a while, but she wasn't really there. She stopped speaking. Stopped eating. I remember holding her hand, feeling how cold it had become. She was still breathing, but she had already left me. And then, one morning, she was gone too."

She swallowed hard, her throat burning. "I was alone. A girl, barely old enough to understand why my world had crumbled overnight. And I had nothing. No home, no family, no one to turn to." She let out a bitter laugh, shaking her head. "And do you know what the world does to girls like that, Rana? It doesn't give them a chance to grieve. It doesn't let them bury their dead with dignity. It eats them alive."

Vishakha exhaled softly, her gaze lost in the fire. "I wouldn't have survived in this world if it weren't for Bairam Chacha," she said, her voice quieter now, as if speaking his name after all these years carried a weight she wasn't sure she could bear. "He was an officer in the Mughal court… a friend of my father's. When my family was gone, I had nothing—no home, no protection, and no one to claim me." A faint, wistful smile crossed her lips before vanishing just as quickly. "It was Bairam Chacha who took me in, who gave me a place to stay, who kept me safe from the men who—" She swallowed hard, shaking her head. "From the men who saw nothing but an unclaimed girl. Without him, I would have been swallowed whole by that world.

She paused, wrapping her arms around herself as if bracing against a cold only she could feel. "Maybe he pitied me at first. Maybe he just wanted to do right by my father. But over time, it felt like something more. He never said it, but I think he saw in me the daughter he never had. And I... I suppose he was the closest thing to family I had left."

Her fingers tightened around the fabric of her clothes, as if grounding herself in the present. "But he taught me how to survive. He made sure I wasn't seen as weak. He introduced me to the court, told me who to trust, who to fear. He gave me a name, a place… and in return, I learned how to navigate that world. How to be more than just a girl they could use and throw away."

Her hands trembled, but she clenched them into fists. "I learned quickly. If I wanted to survive, I had to be useful. So, I did what I had to. I learned how to listen, how to blend into the background, how to speak when it mattered and stay silent when it didn't. I became a shadow in the court—watching, observing, gathering the secrets of men who would never think twice about crushing people like me beneath their boots."

She exhaled shakily; her eyes distant. "For years, I told myself I was doing what was necessary. That I had no choice. But the more I saw, the more I understood—there was no justice in that world. There was no fairness, no mercy. Power wasn't earned through honour or loyalty. It was stolen through betrayal, through cruelty."

Her voice dropped to a whisper. "I lived in a golden cage, surrounded by silk and jewels, but it was still a cage. I wasn't free. And one day, I realized… if I stayed, I would become just like them. And I would rather have died than let that happen."

She finally turned to face Rana, her eyes shining with unshed tears. "So, I ran. I left everything behind—everything I had clawed and bled for, every ounce of security I had built. I walked away from the only life I knew, because I couldn't live with myself if I stayed. And I have been running ever since."

For a long moment, there was silence. The fire crackled softly between them, the only sound in the heavy night air.

Rana's heart ached as he saw the raw pain in her eyes. He had never imagined that someone like her, so composed and calculated, had endured such devastation. He could feel the weight of her grief; the depth of the loneliness she had carried with her for so long.

"I'm sorry," Rana murmured after a long silence, his voice softening. "I had no idea. I didn't know what you went through."

Vishakha's eyes briefly met his, and for the first time, there was something vulnerable in them. "It's not something I talk about," she said softly. "But you asked, and I think you deserve to know."

There was a long pause. The moonlight reflected off the river, casting its faint glow on the water as the weight of her confession settled between them. The sound of the river was soothing, but it didn't erase the heaviness in the air.

Rana cleared his throat, his voice rough with unspoken emotion. "I'm sorry you had to endure that. You didn't deserve it. If I could change your past, I would, but I can't. I know what it means to lose someone you love, how it shatters you in ways no one else can truly understand. People try to imagine the pain, but unless they've felt it, they never really know. And I wouldn't wish that kind of loss on anyone."

His words carried an honesty that made Vishakha's chest feel heavy. She wasn't used to hearing such raw vulnerability and compassion from anyone, least of all a man like Rana, whose stoic demeanour had kept him distant from everyone around him.

But now, as she looked at him, she saw something more than just the protector. She saw a man who, like her, had suffered. A man who had known loss.

Vishakha hesitated, choosing her words carefully. She had asked about Pari before, but Rana had never answered. And so, she had waited—waited for a moment when the weight of it all would sit heavily enough on his shoulders that he might finally share it. Now, as she watched him, saw the way his fingers tightened around his spear, the way his gaze flickered with something unspoken, she knew this was the time.

"Rana," she said gently, her voice steady but laced with quiet insistence. "I've heard her name from you many times. Pari." She searched his face, watching the way a muscle tick his jaw at the mention. "She's not just a child you're trying to save. She means something more to you, doesn't she? Who is she to you?"

Rana let out a quiet breath, a sad smile tugging at the corner of his lips. His fingers traced absent patterns on the shaft of his spear as he spoke, his voice softer than usual.

"Sometimes, it doesn't make sense how someone unknown suddenly becomes important to you. How, out of nowhere, the universe places a person in your life—someone different from the rest. For me, that was Pari." His gaze drifted toward the river, the moonlight catching in his eyes, making the emotion there almost unreadable.

"She didn't have anyone else. No parents. Her mother... her mother was taken by the forest," Rana said, his voice barely above a whisper. He looked down, his fingers tracing the worn edges of his spear. "It was the forest that took her. That's what people said, anyway. The villagers believed it was cursed. But I knew better. Her mother had gone into the woods one day, and she never returned. The forest... it had taken her. Left her child behind."

His voice caught in his throat, and the pain of the past, of things he couldn't undo, seemed to settle in the spaces between his words.

"Her father, he wasn't much better off. He turned to drinking to forget, to numb the pain of losing his wife. But in the end, it destroyed him. He died in his sleep, alone and forgotten. And there was little Pari, alone in the world. She didn't even have a home to return to. She became a beggar, living at the temple, surviving on scraps and whatever people would give her. It was where I first met her."

Rana's eyes darkened as he recalled the first time, he had seen Pari. A small, thin child sitting alone by the steps of the temple, her eyes wide with fear and loneliness. It had broken something in him.

"I couldn't let her stay like that. I couldn't just walk by and pretend I didn't see her. So, I started giving her food—little bits here and there, whatever I could spare. But it wasn't just the food... I would check on her, make sure she was safe. It became routine, something I couldn't ignore. And slowly, she started following me around. Wherever I went, there she was. She always found a way to me."

"I have stayed alone for most of my life," he continued, his voice steady but heavy with something unspoken. "I kept my distance from the villagers. I knew who they were, and they knew me, but it never got personal. I taught myself that getting close to someone only meant one thing—that when they were taken from you, it would hurt. And I didn't want to feel that pain. So, I built walls. High, unshakable walls. To make sure I never cared too much."

His grip on the spear tightened. "But then... she came along. This girl. Pari." A faint chuckle escaped him, tinged with sorrow. "I don't know why, but when she was around, I felt different. Lighter. Happier. I tried to keep her away, to make sure she wouldn't matter to me. But she never listened. She always clung to me, followed me around like a shadow. And the strangest thing was... when she wasn't there, I found myself searching for her."

His smile faded, replaced by something rawer, something filled with quiet regret. "She doesn't know this, but I loved spending time with her. More than I ever admitted, even to myself. I wish I had told her that."

He paused, the memories flooding his mind like a storm breaking loose. A lump started to form in his throat, and for the first time in a long while, his usually stoic expression softened with the weight of those memories.

Rana's eyes darkened, the weight of regret pressing heavily on his chest. His fists clenched as the ache of loss threatened to consume him.

"I know what it is like to lose family," he said, his voice low, raw. "When I saw Pari, I saw myself in her. I didn't want her to go through the same pain I did, didn't want her to feel that same hollow emptiness. Maybe that's why I felt so connected to her. Maybe that's why, now that she's gone, it feels like I failed her."

His breath hitched slightly; his gaze fixed on the ground as if searching for answers that would never come. "Why didn't I keep her with me? Why did I keep her at a distance? Maybe if I had held on tighter, if I hadn't pushed her away, no one could have taken her." He exhaled sharply, a bitter edge creeping into his tone. "She believed in me. She trusted me. And I—" He broke off, shaking his head, his chin dipped slightly. "I kept pushing her away, scared of getting too attached. Scared of losing her. And now..." His voice dropped to a whisper, quivering with grief. "Now, when she's gone, all I have left is regret. The same pain of losing. The same pain of not doing enough."

Vishakha was silent for a long moment, her gaze softening as she watched Rana, her heart aching for the depth of his grief. The raw vulnerability in his words, so rarely revealed, stirred something in her. She had seen him as a protector, someone who stood strong and unwavering, but now she saw the man behind the armour—the one who had been shaped by loss and hardened by a life without family.

"I'm sorry," she said quietly, her voice gentle.

For a moment, she wanted to reach out—to place a reassuring hand on his arm, to offer him something tangible, something real to hold onto. Maybe even an embrace, something to ease the weight of his pain. But she hesitated. The walls he had built around himself were strong, and she wasn't sure if he would let her in. So instead, she remained still, letting her words be the only comfort she could offer.

Rana shook his head, a bitter smile tugging at his lips. "I made a promise to her, and I'll keep it. No matter what happens. She's out there, and I'll find her. I won't fail her again."

For a moment, the two of them sat in silence, the weight of their shared words lingering in the air, so close yet so distant. Two souls with a painful past. Universe has been hard on both of them. The river beside them continued its steady flow, unchanging and indifferent to the turmoil within the hearts of the travellers.

Vishakha finally spoke, her voice quiet but resolute. "You're not alone in this, Rana. You have me, and you have all of us. We'll help you find her. Together."

Rana looked at her then, his expression softening just a fraction. For the first time in a long while, he allowed himself to believe in the possibility that maybe, just maybe, he wouldn't have to carry this burden alone.

Chapter 8

Zahir Khan sat in the quiet study, his fingers lightly tracing the edges of a map that lay before him, though his mind was far from the parchment. The room was dimly lit by the soft glow of oil lamps. His gaze was fixed on the woman seated across from him—his wife, her presence a quiet reminder of the price he had paid to reach his current position.

Her features were soft and composed, her eyes focused on a book in her hands, though Zahir knew her mind was elsewhere, just as his often wandered. It was a rare moment of peace in the ever-turbulent court, a time when Zahir allowed himself to briefly let down his guard.

His thoughts lingered on her, on how she had been the key to his ascent—an unassuming pawn in the game of power, one he had turned into his greatest asset. When he first married her, she had been just another connection, another step toward his grand ambition. But now, as he watched her, he couldn't deny that her influence had become more than he ever expected. She had helped him in ways even he hadn't anticipated.

A flicker of a smile tugged at the corner of his mouth, but it quickly vanished as his mind shifted back to the journey that had brought him to this moment. The years of scheming, the alliances forged in shadow, the careful manipulation of every step. It all led him here—into the heart of power, where he had managed to carve his name among the elite.

It was then, as he observed his wife, that his mind slipped back in time, remembering how it all started—how he had maneuverer his way to a throne not through brute force, but through careful planning, through patience, and through her.

***

Back in the time when Zahir was senior administrator, Emperor Qasim Khan had lived a long life, filled with the triumphs and burdens of ruling one of the largest empires in the world. But now, as the years weighed heavily upon him, the task of maintaining control seemed more daunting with every passing day. He had six sons, each born to different queens, and three daughters—each of them his flesh and blood. The empire was vast, but it was also fragile. With every new victory, his sons grew more ambitious, each carving out their own place in the world, but none of them fully trusted one another. They each ruled over a different province, each carrying the weight of his imperial name, yet each seemed to be looking for a way to surpass the others.

Shahid Khan had been the first-born, the eldest son, and as such, had been entrusted with the North West Frontier—the most critical and dangerous region in the empire. This stretch of land was constantly under threat from foreign invaders, tribal factions, and rebellious kingdoms that sought to escape Mughal rule. Shahid's rule over the frontier was firm, his strength and ruthlessness well known across the empire. He was the emperor's first line of defence, but it was also clear that his ambitions stretched far beyond the borders of his assigned region. His successes on the battlefield made him a hero in the eyes of the people, but also a potential threat in the eyes of his brothers.

Farhan Khan, the second son, had been given Gujarat—a province that was rich with wealth and opportunity. Gujarat was the heart of the empire's trade routes, its ports the gateways to foreign lands. The province was crucial not only for its resources but for the revenue it brought in from merchants, traders, and foreign dignitaries. Farhan, unlike Shahid, was not a man of war. He was a man of commerce, diplomacy, and subtlety. He governed Gujarat with a deft hand, maintaining peace with the local rulers and ensuring the continuous flow of trade. He was respected by the merchants and feared by those who sought to disrupt the flow of wealth, but his gentleness was often seen as weakness by his more ambitious brothers.

Zain Khan, the third son, ruled Bengal—another region rich in resources and crucial to the empire's economy. The province was known for its fertile land, teeming with crops like rice and jute, and its rivers that brought goods from all corners of the empire. The province was also important for the trades with the eastern world through seas. Zain was pragmatic, an astute administrator who understood the importance of agriculture and trade in maintaining the empire's prosperity. He was well-liked by the people, but his tendency to avoid conflict left him vulnerable to the growing ambitions of his siblings. While Zain worked tirelessly to protect the interests of Bengal, his indecisiveness when faced with rebellion or external threats made him seem weak in the eyes of his more aggressive brothers.

Raza Khan, the fourth son, was placed in Deccan, a sprawling region filled with mineral wealth and a history of resistance against Mughal rule. Raza's role was to collect taxes from the southern kings, many of whom had long resisted the empire's influence. Raza was known for his ability to extract tribute from even the most rebellious rulers, using force, when necessary, but always with an eye on the long-term stability of the region. His ruthlessness in dealing with the southern kingdoms made him a feared figure. But his iron grip on Deccan came at a price—many whispered that his methods were too harsh, that his desire for power was becoming more apparent with each passing year.

Imran Khan, the fifth son, ruled Allahabad, a crucial city situated at the crossroads of the empire's central trade routes. Allahabad controlled the passage between the north and the south, and its location made it a vital hub for the flow of resources even from east to west. Imran was a strategist, quietly overseeing the trade routes and ensuring that the wealth from all corners of the empire passed through his hands. He was not as vocal as his brothers, nor as flamboyant, but his influence in the empire grew with each caravan that passed through Allahabad. Some saw him as a quiet king, while others feared his growing control over the heart of the empire's economy.

Suleiman Khan, the youngest son, had yet to be entrusted with a province of his own. Still a boy in many respects, he was learning under his father's watchful eye. Qasim Khan had high hopes for Suleiman, believing him to be the one son who might one day bring the family together, restoring unity where there had been division. For now, Suleiman served as his father's advisor, shadowing him at court and learning the complexities of ruling a vast empire. He had much to prove, but his father saw potential in him—potential that could one day surpass his brothers' ambitious hearts.

Despite the relative success of each of his sons in their appointed regions, Qasim Khan could not escape the gnawing feeling that his empire was becoming more divided with each passing year. The provinces, once held together under his rule, were beginning to splinter under the weight of his sons' ambitions. His empire was vast, stretching across land and sea, from the fertile plains of Bengal to the rocky highlands of the North West Frontier. But it was fragile— held together not just by his power, but by the delicate relationships between his sons. His legacy would not be determined by his battles or his conquests, but by how well he could hold together the empire that was slowly beginning to unravel before his eyes

Qasim Khan had granted each of his sons immense power, believing that this would unite them under the banner of the Mughal Empire. But in truth, it only created a volatile mix of rivalry, distrust, and competition. Each son was loyal to the empire, but each son was also loyal to his own ambitions. And the emperor, though wise and powerful, found himself caught between them.

He had entrusted his sons with the empire's future, but now, as he sat alone in his chambers, he wondered if he had made the right choice. Would his legacy survive the ambitions of his own flesh and blood, or would the empire crumble under the weight of their rivalries? Only time would tell, but one thing was certain—Qasim Khan could feel the shifting winds of change, and they were blowing with the force of inevitability.

Emperor Qasim Khan had always taken pride in his family, but the political alliances forged through his children's marriages were both a blessing and a curse. His three daughters—each as distinct as the provinces they represented—were not just heirs in their own right; they were pieces in a larger game of power and influence that transcended familial bonds.

Amina Khan was the eldest daughter, a woman of grace and intelligence. Her marriage to the Nizam of Hyderabad, a powerful and wealthy ruler in the Deccan, had been an alliance forged to secure the southern borders of the empire. Amina was the embodiment of diplomacy, carrying the weight of her father's legacy with quiet dignity. Her marriage to the Nizam had been one of political necessity, but it had allowed Qasim Khan to solidify his control over the southern kingdoms, making her one of the most influential women in the empire.

Leela Khan, the second daughter, had been married off to a Rajput king in an attempt to forge an alliance with the northern Rajput clans, whose loyalty to the emperor had always been tenuous. Leela, fierce and determined, had inherited much of her father's strategic mind, and her marriage had not been without friction. Though the Rajputs had initially resisted the marriage, Leela had managed to win them over with her wisdom and keen insight into their ways. However, her role in the court was largely one of secondary importance, as the Rajputs were reluctant to place their trust fully in the Mughal court, despite their bond through her.

Then there was Saira Khan, the youngest of the three daughters. She had beauty that captured the attention of all who met her. She had yet to be married, and with her father aging, her marriage had become the next strategic move. But unlike her elder sisters, Saira's future was clouded with uncertainty. The emperor had yet to find a suitor worthy of her, and many saw her as a symbol of both hope and vulnerability—an unclaimed piece of the royal bloodline.

Saira had always been sheltered, kept in the palace away from the machinations of court politics. Her father, though benevolent, was distant, and the power struggles among his sons were things she rarely heard about. She was content with her books and dreams of a future she could barely understand, but that all changed when Zahir Khan began to seek her out.

Zahir had, for years, maintained his position as the emperor's most trusted advisor, but in his heart, his ambitions stretched far beyond that role. He had come to realize that to rise to true power, he needed to secure a place within the royal bloodline itself. The most direct path to that was through Saira Khan. The youngest daughter, though her family ruled vast swathes of land, was still somewhat naïve about the complexities of the court and the manipulations that surrounded her every move. Zahir saw an opportunity—a chance to ingratiate himself into the royal family's inner circle by seducing Saira and eventually marrying her, positioning himself as the future ruler of the Mughal Empire.

He was careful with his approach, always appearing as a protector and confidant. He listened to her frustrations about the court, about her father's health, and about the marriage prospects that seemed to weigh heavily on her heart. Zahir's words, laced with sympathy and understanding, became a lifeline to Saira, who felt increasingly isolated in her position.

One night, as they strolled through the palace gardens, the moonlight casting a soft glow on the paths, Zahir spoke, his voice low and soothing.

"Saira, you are not just a pawn in the court's games," he said, his tone gentle, "You are the daughter of an emperor, and your future holds far more than just marriage to a foreign prince or king. You deserve someone who sees you—not just as an asset to an empire—but as a woman who can rule alongside him."

Saira's heart skipped at his words. The notion that she could rule, that her life could be more than an arranged marriage, stirred something deep inside her. She had always felt somewhat powerless in the shadow of her brothers' ambition and her father's legacy. Now, Zahir was offering her a vision of herself that she had never dared imagine.

"But what if I do not know how to take such a future into my hands?" she asked, her voice filled with uncertainty.

Zahir smiled, a hint of sadness in his eyes. "That's why I am here. To help you understand that your path is yours to decide. The emperor may be old, and your brothers may be driven by their own ambitions, but you—Saira—are capable of shaping your own destiny. I would stand by you, protect you, and guide you."

Her gaze met his, searching for any hint of deceit. But there was none. To her innocent eyes, Zahir's sincerity appeared genuine, his words a balm to her uncertainties.

"You would protect me?" she asked softly, her voice trembling with the emotion of the moment.

"I would do more than protect you," Zahir replied, stepping closer, his gaze intense. "I would make sure your dreams are realized. I would make sure no one dares take advantage of your kindness. You deserve more than what has been promised to you."

Saira's pulse quickened as he spoke, the warmth of his words making her feel seen in a way she had never felt before. She had always been the youngest, the one whose voice was often ignored. But now, here was a man—powerful, respected, and strategic—who was offering her everything.

"You truly think I could rule alongside you?" Saira whispered, unsure of the enormity of the dream he was planting in her heart.

Zahir's smile widened, and his voice dropped to a whisper. "I don't just think it, Saira. I know it. Together, we could achieve greatness. You, me, and the empire."

She believed him. Her heart, full of longing for a purpose, didn't question his sincerity. It was the first time she had felt like she mattered in the grand design of the empire. She smiled, her eyes shining with newfound hope. "Then let's start, Zahir. Let's shape the future together."

As Zahir continued to manipulate Saira, his plans grew bolder. He knew that Saira Khan, once married to him, would cement his position as a future king—one who would rule not only the empire but the royal bloodline itself.

Her naïveté had made her the perfect pawn, and she would never see the depth of his ambitions. But for Zahir, this was no longer about love. It was about power. The throne awaited, and he would stop at nothing to claim it.

And as the days passed, Zahir knew that the final move was approaching—one that would lead him to the throne, to a future where he was no longer just an advisor, but an emperor in his own right.

Saira, caught in his web, could not see the danger that lay ahead. She thought Zahir loved her, and in that belief, she would play her part. But love, for Zahir, had long since been a casualty of ambition.

***

As the weight of his past and unspoken desires settled between them, Zahir was suddenly pulled back to the present. The dim light of dawn crept into the study, softening the harsh lines of his face. He had spent the entire night lost in thought, reflecting on the choices that had led him to this point.

The quiet morning was broken by the sound of footsteps approaching. A soldier entered; his face grim. "My lord," the soldier said, bowing respectfully, "our spies have confirmed it. Vishakha and her group were spotted near the river. They spent the night there, but only left moments before we arrived. They're on the move, and our men are already in pursuit."

Zahir's eyes narrowed, his mind already calculating their next move. He rose from his chair, his hands clasped behind his back. "They won't get far," he muttered, his voice low and determined. "We will catch them soon. Send the men in every direction from that point."

As the soldier nodded and left to carry out his orders, Zahir stood at the window, watching the first light of dawn break over the horizon. His thoughts shifted toward the chase ahead, the pursuit of a woman who carried secrets—secrets that should never come out in the open.

Chapter 9

The moonlight shimmered on the surface of the river as Rana and Vishakha sat in the quiet stillness of the night. The group had fallen asleep hours ago, their exhaustion finally catching up to them after days of relentless travel. But Rana couldn't sleep—not with thoughts of Pari consuming him, and not with the strange pull he felt toward Vishakha, a woman whose past seemed to echo his own pain.

The quiet night was interrupted by hurried footsteps and urgent whispers. Hari emerged from the dark, his face pale and tense.

"Rana," Hari said, his voice low but edged with urgency. "We have a problem."

Rana stood immediately, his hand instinctively reaching for his spear. "What is it?"

"The Mughal army," Hari said, glancing over his shoulder as though expecting to see soldiers materialize from the darkness. "They've been spotted near the river. One of the travellers coming from that side told that they are searching everywhere for a group of fugitives escaping with a girl. They're close."

Vishakha stiffened, her hands tightening around the edge of her blanket. "How close?"

"Too close," Hari replied grimly.

Vishakha pulled Rana towards the side of the camp where other travellers were sleeping while Hari moved swiftly through the camp, his voice a harsh whisper as he shook Amar by the shoulder. "Get up!"

Amar groaned, rolling onto his side. "Five more minutes," he mumbled.

Hari scowled and moved on to Chandan, nudging him none too gently. "Chandan, wake up! If you don't, I swear I'll—"

Chandan cracked one eye open and grinned. "Why can't I just sleep for one night!"

Hari smacked the back of his head. "Mughals are close."

That got Chandan up. He bolted upright, glancing around. "Wait—what?"

Suresh, still half-asleep, grumbled as Hari shook him next. "If this is another one of your pranks, Hari, I swear—"

"Mughals," Hari hissed.

That woke Suresh up faster than a bucket of cold water. He shot up, eyes wide. "Why didn't you start with that?"

The group packed their things in a flurry, the weight of exhaustion momentarily replaced by urgency. As they slung their belongings over their shoulders, Suresh muttered, "This is madness. Running blindly into the night? We'll be caught before sunrise."

Just then, Rana emerged from the shadows, leading six horses by the reins.

Amar's mouth fell open. "We have horses now?" He shot a look at Chandan. "Did I wake up in the wrong camp?"

Chandan shook his head. "No, no, I see them too. Either we're hallucinating, or Rana's got some explaining to do."

Rana tossed the reins to them, with urgency. "No time for all that now. Mount up. We'll talk once we've put enough distance between us and the soldiers."

The decision to move under cover of darkness was not up for debate. They had packed quickly, their meagre supplies slung over the saddles of their newfound horses.

***

By dawn, the group had put enough distance between themselves and the river to feel a brief sense of relief. The first light of the sun stretched across the horizon, painting the sky in delicate hues of pink and orange, while the cool morning air carried the faint scent of damp earth and wild foliage. The rhythmic clatter of hooves slowed as they reached a bend in the forest where the river curved once again, its waters murmuring softly over smooth stones. They stopped beneath the shade of a cluster of trees, the air filled with the steady exhale of their horses, nostrils flaring as they snorted and pawed at the ground. The scent of sweat and leather mixed with the damp musk of the animals as they shook their manes, tails swishing lazily. Nearby, the horses tugged at tufts of grass, their teeth tearing through the blades with quiet, repetitive crunches, a stark contrast to the tense silence that had followed them through the night.

Amar stretched his arms above his head, yawning dramatically. "I have to admit," he said, his voice low but cheerful, "these horses make running from certain death so much more comfortable. It's like a traveling luxury I never knew I needed."

Chandan smirked, leaning back against the tree trunk. "Luxury? I wouldn't go that far. But I will admit, not having to use my legs for hours on end is a welcome change. My feet might actually survive this journey."

Amar gave him a mock glare. "You'll change your tune when I establish my empire of horse-drawn travel. I'll call it Amar's Express. Quick, efficient, and far more comfortable than walking through forests of death."

Chandan snorted. "I'll invest. But only if you promise to keep those royal ideas of yours to yourself while we ride."

The group chuckled softly, their voices breaking the heavy quiet of the forest. Even Suresh, who had remained silent for most of the night, allowed himself a small smile.

"You can thank Rana for the horses," Chandan added with a grin, gesturing toward the leader of their group.

Rana, seated on a rock and scanning the treeline, shook his head. "It wasn't me," he said simply, his tone calm but amused.

Amar paused mid-stretch, his brow furrowing. "Wait... what? Then who...?"

Rana inclined his head toward Vishakha, who was seated cross-legged under a nearby tree, a faint smile played on her lips.

All eyes turned to her, and she looked up with a small sigh, clearly anticipating the flood of questions.

"You got us the horses?" Amar asked, his tone incredulous.

Vishakha gave a small nod.

Chandan whistled softly, leaning forward. "Now that's impressive. I don't even want to know how you pulled that off."

"You're right," Vishakha replied smoothly, a faint smirk tugging at her lips. "You don't want to know."

Amar, of course, was undeterred. "Oh, but we do want to know. What did you do? Charm someone? Steal them? Bribe someone?"

"Maybe all three," Chandan chimed in with a grin.

Vishakha chuckled softly but didn't answer, instead taking a sip of water from her flask. "I think it's more fun to leave you guessing," she said, expertly changing the subject. "Shouldn't we be talking about which way we're headed next?"

Amar groaned, throwing up his hands in mock frustration. "She's not going to tell us. Fine. But I'll figure it out eventually."

Rana watched the exchange with quiet amusement before standing and approaching Hari, who was seated nearby sharpening his knife. "What's the plan ahead?" Rana asked in a low voice.

Hari glanced up; his expression serious. "If the man we spoke to was telling the truth, the market is less than a day's ride from here. But we'll need to stay off the main paths.

The Mughal army is close, and they'll be hunting for us now that they know we're in the area."

Rana nodded, his gaze drifting toward the forest ahead. "We have to reach that market before it's too late."

Hari's voice was firm. "We will. But we need to be careful. This isn't just about speed—it's about staying alive."

As the group finished their meal and prepared to set off again, Rana walked over to Vishakha, who was checking the saddle on her horse. He stopped beside her, his tone quiet but curious. "So, are you finally going to tell me how you managed to get the horses?"

Vishakha glanced at him, her brows knitting together briefly before softening into something thoughtful. Then she sighed softly. "It's not much of a story," she said. "Years of working with the Mughals taught me one thing—you can't survive without resources. I made sure to save some gold for myself over the years. I used a little of it to buy these horses. It's the least I could do, considering everything your group is doing for me."

Rana studied her, surprised by the admission. "You spent your gold... for us?"

"For all of us," she corrected, her gaze meeting his. "Including myself. Let's not pretend I'm not benefiting from this. My injured legs can definitely use the rest."

Rana's sharp eyes softened as he watched her. He could see the strength in her, the resilience of someone who had endured far more than she let on. "So that's what you've been hiding in that satchel of yours?" he said quietly, with a playful smile on his face.

Vishakha shrugged, a faint smile playing on her lips. "It came handy, didn't it?"

A quiet pause settled between them, filled with words neither of them spoke. The way she looked at him—wary yet open, strong yet vulnerable—made something shift in him.

And in the way he looked back, there was an unspoken recognition, as if, for the first time, he was truly seeing her.

The moment passed as quickly as it had come, and Vishakha turned her attention back to her horse. "We should get moving," she said lightly, pulling herself into the saddle. "The market won't wait for us."

Rana nodded, mounting his own horse. "You're right. Let's go."

As the group resumed their journey, the bond between Rana and Vishakha deepened, unspoken but undeniable. The spark of something more lingered between them, quietly growing as they pressed on toward the unknown.

***

The late morning sun dappled through the trees as the group rode steadily onward. The tension of the past few nights had begun to ease, and for the first time in days, there was a sense of camaraderie among them. Amar, as usual, was the one to break the silence.

"You know," he said, glancing at Vishakha with a mischievous grin, "you might just be the most mysterious woman I've ever met. First, you get us horses. Now, you have us riding straight into Agra like it's a Sunday stroll. What's next? Will you pull a palace out of your pocket at the next bend?"

Vishakha laughed softly, shaking her head. "If I could conjure palaces, I wouldn't have been sharing a campfire with you lot, eating stale bread and pretending it was a feast."

Amar gasped, clutching his chest as if wounded. "Stale bread? That was *artisanal* stale bread, thank you very much. Aged to perfection, like a fine wine."

Chandan snorted, leaning slightly from his saddle. "Amar, the only thing aged to perfection about that bread was the Mold growing on it. I'm pretty sure even the horse will refuse to eat it."

Vishakha smirked. "Well, you're not wrong. But don't worry, I'll make sure we get something edible soon. Can't have you two collapsing from hunger and blaming me for it."

Amar placed a hand dramatically over his chest. "Well, that would be great, Didi!"

"Didi, huh?" Vishakha raised an eyebrow, amused.

"Of course," Amar said with a grin. "You definitely are like an elder sister to us. You got us horses, now you're talking about getting us food!"

"That's true," Chandan added, winking. "We'll officially declare you the sensible one in the group. Just don't expect too much from us. Amar, in particular, is a lost cause."

Vishakha chuckled, her laughter lightening the air. "I'll take that as a compliment, though I'm not sure if it says more about you or me."

The group continued their journey, the horses' steady hooves crunching against the dirt road. The mood had grown lighter, a stark contrast to the tension of the previous night. Amar, of course, started the conversation again.

"You know," Amar began, glancing around dramatically, "these horses are a blessing. If we'd kept walking, I'd have needed a new pair of feet by now."

Chandan snorted. "A new pair of feet? I'd say you'd need a whole new body. The way you complain, Amar, you'd make a 92-year-old grandpa sound healthier."

Amar grinned. "Laugh all you want, but admit it, Chandan. You're grateful for the horses too. Just think how much farther we'd be if we had them from the start."

"Grateful doesn't begin to cover it," Chandan replied, patting his horse's neck. "This fine beast is the best thing that's happened to me in weeks. Better company than you, at least."

Amar feigned a wounded expression, clutching his chest. "You wound me, Chandan. After all we've been through together, I thought we had something special."

"Special, sure," Chandan quipped. "Specially annoying."

The group chuckled at their exchange, even Suresh cracking a rare smile. Vishakha, who had been riding quietly, finally joined in, her voice light. "If you two are done bickering like an old married couple, maybe we can focus on reaching Agra without driving each other mad."

Amar turned to her with a mock bow. "As you command, Didi. But you have to admit, these horses are a miracle. How did you even manage to get them?"

Suresh, who had been unusually silent, glanced at her with hesitant curiosity. "He's right," he muttered. "You never told how you did it."

Vishakha smirked, waving a hand dismissively. "Oh, it's nothing. Just a bit of luck and a few kind words."

"Luck, huh?" Chandan said with a sly grin. "Somehow, I doubt that. Spill it, Vishakha. What's the real story?"

She shook her head, her smile widening. "I don't know if I should tell you. It might ruin the mystery."

"Come on, tell us!" Amar pleaded, leaning forward dramatically in his saddle. "We're all dying to know."

"You'll survive," Vishakha replied, her tone teasing. "Besides, a woman needs to keep some secrets."

The group laughed, and even Rana, who had been riding slightly ahead, allowed himself a small smile. "Let her keep her secrets," he said, glancing over his shoulder. "Some mysteries are better left unsolved."

Hari chuckled softly, shaking his head. "A wise man once said, 'If you dig too deep, you might not like what you find.'"

Amar sighed, throwing his hands up in mock defeat. "Fine, fine. Keep your secrets. But one day, we'll figure you out, Vishakha."

"Good luck with that," she replied, her eyes sparkling with amusement.

Suresh, who had been quietly observing the exchange, finally spoke up again, his voice softer this time. "For what it's worth... I appreciate what you did. Getting the horses, I mean. It's made things easier."

Vishakha turned to him, her expression warm but playful. "Is that your way of apologizing, Suresh? Because if it is, you're terrible at it."

The group erupted into laughter, and even Suresh couldn't help but smile. "All right, all right," he muttered. "I'm sorry. Happy now?"

"Very," Vishakha said with a wink.

Amar and Chandan chimed in simultaneously, their voices overlapping. "And just like that, the impossible happened— Suresh apologized!"

"Mark this day," Amar added with mock solemnity. "The heavens must be rejoicing."

"Enough, all of you," Suresh grumbled, though his tone lacked any real irritation.

Rana shook his head, a rare flicker of amusement crossing his face. "If you all put half as much effort into planning as you do into talking, we'd be at Agra by now."

"And if you smiled more often, Rana," Amar shot back, "the rest of us might not feel like we're traveling with a grumpy old man."

Chandan clapped him on the back. "See? That's progress. We're becoming a real team now!"

Hari, who had been riding near the back with Rana, smirked. "It's a miracle you all haven't driven each other mad yet."

"Give it time," Rana replied dryly, though there was a hint of amusement in his tone.

The group laughed again, and even Rana let out a soft chuckle, his usual stoicism momentarily broken. For a brief moment, it felt as though the weight of their journey had lifted, replaced by a fleeting sense of normalcy.

The laughter was still echoing in the air, Amar and Chandan trading barbs while Vishakha shook her head, trying to suppress a smile. Even Rana had softened, allowing himself to enjoy the rare moment of levity. The warm sun filtered through the trees, and for the first time in days, the group felt almost at ease.

But the mood shattered in an instant.

From around the bend in the road, the unmistakable sound of hooves broke through the peace, sharp and unnerving. Three Mughal guards appeared, their crimson-and-gold uniforms catching the sunlight as they rode into view. The clinking of their weapons, the disciplined stature on their horses—there was no mistaking who they were.

Rana's hand shot up, signalling the group to stop. The humour vanished from his face, replaced by a deadly seriousness. The others followed his lead, their horses coming to a halt with a nervous shuffle. The tension was immediate, crackling like a thunderstorm on the verge of breaking.

"Stay calm," Rana said, his voice low and firm, though his grip on the reins hinted at his readiness for anything. "Let me do the talking.

Amar's usual grin disappeared, his knuckles whitening as he tightened his hold on the saddle. Chandan swallowed hard, his earlier jokes now a distant memory. Even Suresh looked stricken, his lips pressed into a thin line.

The guards hadn't spotted them yet, their focus elsewhere as they spoke among themselves. But as the group tried to remain still, the sound of their horses shifting broke the fragile silence. One of the guards turned his head sharply, his eyes narrowing as he caught sight of the small group.

"There," he said, his voice cutting through the air like a blade. The guards turned their horses toward them, approaching with reflective speed.

Rana straightened in his saddle; his expression unreadable as the guards neared. The rest of the group tensed; their earlier camaraderie replaced by a silent fear. Vishakha's hand drifted to her dupatta, instinctively pulling it tighter over her head, masking her face.

The guards stopped a few paces away, their eyes scanning the group. The leader, a tall man with a scar running down his cheek, looked them over with suspicion.

"Travelers," the scarred guard said, his tone clipped. "What brings you this close to Agra?"

Rana's voice was calm, steady. "We're on our way to the city, sir. Just villagers heading to the market."

The guard's eyes narrowed, moving from Rana to the rest of the group. His gaze lingered on Vishakha, and she stiffened under the weight of his scrutiny. Beside her, Amar shifted uncomfortably, and Chandan's hand twitched toward his belt, though he thought better of it.

"And what are you trading?" the guard asked, his tone carrying a faint edge of suspicion.

"Livestock," Rana lied smoothly, gesturing vaguely behind them. "We sold what we had in the last village and are headed to the market to see if there's anything worth buying."

The guard's eyes flicked back to Rana, studying him for a long moment. "Odd time to travel," he said, his tone sharp. "With the forest so dangerous. Bandits. Wild animals. I'm sure you've heard the rumours."

Rana nodded, his expression calm but firm. "We've been careful. Just trying to make an honest living."

The scarred guard seemed to consider this, his gaze darting once more to Vishakha. Her head was bowed, her face partially obscured by her dupatta, but the tension in her demeanour was impossible to miss.

"What about her?" the guard asked suddenly, his voice cutting through the air. "She doesn't look like a farmer."

Rana's hand tightened slightly on the reins, but his voice remained steady. "My cousin's wife," he said without missing a beat. "Her husband was taken by the forest. We're looking after her."

The guard's gaze didn't waver, his eyes narrowing further. The air felt heavy, every second stretching into eternity. Then, finally, he grunted, turning to his men.

"Keep moving," he said, waving them off. "They're no threat."

The tension began to ease as the guards nudged their horses forward, moving past the group. But just as the group exhaled, a voice called out from behind them.

"Wait."

The fourth guard emerged from the treeline, his sharp eyes scanning the group with suspicion. Though younger than the others, he carried himself with the same air of authority. His hand rested on the hilt of his sword as he stepped forward, his tone clipped and commanding.

"Get off your horses. All of you," he ordered.

Rana's group tensed, their hands instinctively shifting toward their weapons. Amar shot a glance at Rana, his breath hitched for a moment, while Chandan muttered under his breath. Suresh looked ready to protest, but Rana gave a subtle nod, his voice calm but firm.

"Do as he say."

Reluctantly, they dismounted, their boots hitting the ground in near unison. The soldiers did the same, the air crackled with dismay, every movement measured and cautious.

As the group stood facing their captors, the young Mughal guard's gaze landed on Vishakha. His expression shifted, a flicker of recognition flashing across his face.

"You," he said, pointing directly at her. "I know you."

The group froze as the young Mughal guard stepped closer; his sharp eyes fixed on Vishakha. His earlier certainty now turned to rude insistence as he gestured toward her. "You," he said, his voice laced with arrogance. "Remove the dupatta from your face. Let me see who you are."

Vishakha casts a nervous glance toward Rana. Before she could say anything, Rana stepped forward, placing himself slightly in front of her, his expression calm but his voice carrying an unmistakable edge.

"She is my cousin's wife," Rana said, his tone firm but diplomatic. "There's no need for her to remove her veil."

The young guard smirked, crossing his arms. "Your cousin's wife, you say? Convenient story. But I don't take the word of strangers, especially ones traveling near Agra under such... suspicious circumstances."

"She has no need to prove anything to you," Rana replied, his voice steady, though his fingers twitched near his belt. "We're just travellers. Leave us be."

But the guard wasn't deterred. His smirk widened into something more sinister as he leaned closer, his eyes gleaming with cruelty. "You think you can give me orders, farmer? I'll decide who can pass here and who cannot. Now, woman," he snapped, pointing at Vishakha, "remove your veil."

Vishakha's shoulders stiffened, but she stayed silent, her defiance evident even through her trembling hands. The guard's patience seemed to wane, and he reached forward, his fingers aiming for her dupatta.

Rana's voice was sharp as a blade. "Don't touch her."

The guard froze for a moment, his head snapping toward Rana. But the moment passed as quickly as it had come. With a sneer, the guard reached for Vishakha's face.

That was when Rana moved.

In a flash, faster than anyone could react, Rana's spear was in his hands, and with one swift motion, he drove it through the guard's neck. Blood sprayed as the young soldier gurgled a strangled cry, his hands clawing at the wooden shaft lodged in his throat before collapsing to the ground, lifeless. Rana pulls the spear back from the corpse.

The air seemed to freeze. The remaining three guards stared in stunned disbelief for a heartbeat before roaring in anger. Their hands went to their weapons, and chaos erupted.

Rana faced the largest of the guards, a towering figure with arms as sturdy as tree trunks and a presence that seemed to dwarf everyone around him. The soldier's blade, almost as massive as the man himself, gleamed ominously in the sunlight, each swing a promise of death. But Rana stood his ground, his eyes locked on the opponent with an intensity that unnerved even the hulking brute before him.

The first swing came with brutal force, the sheer weight of it slicing the air with a menacing whistle. Rana sidestepped just in time, the blade missing him by inches. He countered with a quick jab of his spear, the sharp steel head grazing the soldier's forearm. Blood beaded where the weapon struck, but the guard barely flinched, a low growl rumbling from his chest.

The soldier swung again; a wide arc aimed to cleave Rana in two. But Rana moved with precision, ducking under the blow and spinning to strike the man's side with the blunt end of his spear. The guard stumbled slightly, more out of surprise than pain, and glared at Rana with a renewed fury.

"You're quick," the soldier spat, his voice a deep, guttural snarl. "But speed won't save you."

Rana didn't respond. His grip on the spear tightened, and his movements became sharper, more calculated. He knew brute strength would never win this fight—this was a battle of endurance, of precision, and of patience.

As the soldier lunged again, Rana twisted his body with lightning speed, slashing at the man's thigh with the steel-tipped spearhead. The guard roared in pain, the cut shallow but enough to slow him.

"You'll need more than that," the guard sneered, charging at Rana like a bull.

The guard charged with fury, his sword coming down in a reckless arc. Rana raised his spear, blocking the strike, but the force of it splintered the shaft in two. Now armed with the steel-tipped head in one hand and the wooden shaft in the other, Rana shifted his stance, his movements fluid and quick.

The guard's swings became increasingly desperate as Rana darted in and out of reach, landing shallow cuts with each pass. The man's breathing grew laboured, his strength waning as frustration mounted. Rana, in contrast, moved like a predator—calm, focused, and relentless.

Seizing an opening, Rana hurled the wooden shaft at the guard, forcing him to deflect. In that brief moment, Rana darted toward the fallen soldier from earlier, grabbing the sword from his lifeless grasp. Armed now with a blade and the sharp spearhead, Rana advanced, his strikes faster and more precise.

The guard roared in defiance, but Rana was unyielding. His blade sliced across the man's side, and the spearhead landed a deep cut on his thigh. Each attack drained the towering guard of strength until he staggered, his knees buckling under the weight of exhaustion.

Chandan and Suresh found themselves locked in a desperate fight against the second soldier, who towered over them with his gleaming sword. They had no weapons—only two solid wooden logs they'd found near the trees. Their breaths came in ragged gasps as they darted around the trunk of a massive tree, using it as their only shield against the soldier's relentless swings.

"You cowards!" the soldier roared, his voice echoing through the forest. He lunged, his blade slashing dangerously close to Chandan's shoulder as he ducked just in time. "Stop hiding and fight me like men!"

"We're not hiding," Chandan shot back, his voice trembling as he gripped the log tightly. "We're employing advanced tactics... very advanced tactics.

Suresh barked a nervous laugh as he narrowly dodged another swing. "Great tactic, Chandan. Let's see how long this brilliant plan keeps us alive!"

The soldier, already furious, snarled as his swings became wilder, his frustration mounting with each missed attack. He lunged again, but this time his foot slipped on the uneven ground, and his balance wavered. Seizing the moment, Chandan and Suresh charged simultaneously, swinging their wooden logs with all their strength.

The first blow struck the soldier's shoulder, and the second landed squarely on his back. He staggered forward, letting out a grunt of pain, but quickly turned, his sword flashing in the sunlight. With a powerful slash, he caught Suresh on the leg, the blade cutting deep into his calf. Suresh cried out and collapsed to the ground, clutching his bleeding leg.

Chandan hesitated, his eyes darting between Suresh and the soldier, who now turned his attention to him. "Oh no," Chandan muttered, backing away as the guard advanced with murderous intent.

The soldier swung his blade in a brutal downward arc. Chandan barely managed to lift his log in time to block the blow. The sword pierced into the wood with a sickening crack, embedding itself deep and got stuck in the log. The soldier growled, yanking at the blade, but Chandan held onto the log with desperate strength, his knuckles white as he wrestled against the guard's pull.

The soldier's patience snapped. With a vicious kick, he struck Chandan square in the stomach, sending him sprawling onto the ground. The log slipped from his grasp, and the soldier freed his sword, raising it high for the final strike.

Chandan stared up at the blade, his heart pounding in his chest. He scrambled backward, trying to put distance between himself and the descending blade. Just as the soldier prepared to bring the sword down, a shadow lunged at him from behind.

Suresh, blood dripping from his injured leg, had forced himself to his feet. With a feral cry, he jumped onto the soldier's back, his small dagger—his infamous "butter knife"—gripped tightly in his hand. The soldier staggered under the sudden weight, his sword swing faltering as Suresh drove the dagger into the side of his neck.

The soldier let out a strangled roar, trying to throw Suresh off, but Suresh held on with everything he had. He stabbed again, and again, each thrust more determined than the last. Blood sprayed onto the forest floor as the soldier's struggles grew weaker. Finally, with a gurgled breath, the guard collapsed to his knees and fell face-first into the dirt, his body motionless.

Panting heavily, Suresh rolled off the lifeless guard and lay on his back beside Chandan, clutching his injured leg. His chest heaved as he struggled to catch his breath. Chandan, still shaken, stared at him in stunned silence before breaking into a shaky grin.

Suresh tilted his head toward Chandan, a weak smile tugging at his lips. "Told you... this butter knife... would save you one day."

Chandan let out a breathless laugh, shaking his head. "You're unbelievable."

The two of them lay there for a moment, the adrenaline still coursing through their veins, the sounds of the forest slowly returning around them. The fight was over—but the cost was heavy, and the day was far from won.

The third soldier, surrounded by Amar, Vishakha, and Hari, circled them with a predator's intensity, his sword gleaming under the faint light filtering through the trees. His sharp eyes flicked between his opponents, assessing the weakest link.

Suddenly, Hari bolted, his footsteps echoing through the forest. "Hari!" Amar shouted after him, stunned. But the older man didn't stop, disappearing into the underbrush.

The soldier smirked, his gaze locking onto Amar and Vishakha. "Cowards," he sneered, stepping closer, his sword raised.

"Run!" Amar shouted at Vishakha, his voice trembling. But she didn't move. Her lips twitched before setting firm, her gaze steady.

"No," she said firmly. Her eyes darted to the ground, spotting a patch of loose dirt. In one swift motion, she scooped up a handful and hurled it into the soldier's face.

The man stumbled back, cursing as he tried to rub the dirt from his stinging eyes. "Run!" Vishakha yelled, grabbing Amar's arm and pulling him. They both started to move, but her injured leg gave out, sending her tumbling to the ground with a cry of pain.

"Go!" she urged, pushing at Amar. "Save yourself!"

Amar turned to her, his face set with determination. "Not a chance, Didi," he said, gripping his wooden log like a weapon. His gaze burned with a protective fury.

The soldier, his vision clearing, let out a furious growl. He charged toward them, his sword cutting through the air. Amar met him head-on, shouting as he swung his log with all his strength. The impact struck the soldier's side, but it wasn't enough. The soldier retaliated with a vicious punch to Amar's chest, sending him sprawling to the ground, gasping for air.

The soldier turned his attention to Vishakha, who was trying to crawl backward, her injured leg dragging uselessly. He towered over her, his sword gleaming as he raised it high for the killing blow.

"Didi!" Amar gasped, trying to rise, but he was too dazed. It seemed like there was no hope.

And then, out of nowhere, Rana appeared. He moved with lightning speed, his hand snapping out to grip the soldier's wrist mid-swing. The soldier's blade froze inches from Vishakha's neck.

With his other hand, Rana drove the sharp head of his spear into the soldier's side, right into the liver. The soldier's breath hitched, his body going rigid as his strength drained away. He gasped, his grip on the sword weakening before he crumpled to the ground, lifeless.

But Rana wasn't done. His sharp gaze flicked to the towering soldier he had been fighting earlier, who was staggering to his feet in the distance, bloodied but still dangerous. Without hesitation, Rana yanked the spearhead free from the corpse at his feet, his movements fluid and precise.

In one smooth motion, he hurled the spearhead through the air with the force of a tempest. The sharp steel sang as it flew, striking the towering soldier directly in the heart. The giant's eyes widened in shock, his hands clawing at the weapon lodged in his chest as he collapsed with a thunderous crash, lifeless.

The forest fell silent, the sounds of the battle replaced by the heavy breathing of the survivors. Vishakha, still on the ground, stared at Rana with wide, stunned eyes. Amar, clutching his chest, managed a weak grin despite the pain.

Rana stumbled amidst the carnage, his chest heaving and his hands stained with blood. He looked down at Vishakha, his eyes softening. "Are you all right?" he asked, his voice low but steady.

Before she could answer, Amar's voice cut through the silence, hoarse but laced with humour. "You know, Rana," he said between gasps, "next time you could try being a little faster."

A stunned silence lingered before Chandan and Suresh's laughter broke the tension, and even Vishakha let out a breathy laugh. The group burst into laughter; their relief palpable.

But their laughter faded when they noticed Rana falling on the ground, his body slumped against a tree, motionless.

"Rana!" Vishakha cried, scrambling toward him.

Amar leaned over him, panic in his voice. "He's unconscious!"

The group gathered around their fallen leader; the weight of their victory now overshadowed by the fear that Rana might not wake.

Chapter 10

The room was bathed in a soft, flickering glow, as lanterns cast shifting shadows across the walls. Zahir Khan sat at the head of a carved wooden table; his piercing gaze fixed on the men before him. Behind his every calculated move, every shadowy plot, stood his three most trusted aides—men who had pledged their lives to his cause and whose loyalty was as unwavering as his ambition. After Vishakha left him on the battlefield, Zahir knew he needed someone—or rather, several someone's—to fill the void she had left. Her sharp mind, resourcefulness, and knowledge of his ambitions had been unmatched, but her departure taught him a valuable lesson: no single person could ever hold such power over his plans again.

He found his solution not in one, but in three men, each selected with painstaking precision. Together, they were more than just a replacement for Vishakha—they were the perfect tools to execute his vision. Each brought a unique skill set to the table, and each served with an unyielding loyalty that Zahir ensured through fear, respect, and reward. Where Vishakha had been a singular pillar, these three would form the foundation of his empire.

Imran, the strategist, had known Zahir since the earliest days of his rise. A seasoned warrior with a sharp mind for military tactics, Imran was Zahir's right-hand man when it came to securing regions and eliminating enemies. His knowledge of the empire's military and its weaknesses made him indispensable to Zahir's conquest of power. Imran made sure that anyone who came in the way of Zahir was eliminated with precision.

Danish, the spy, was Zahir's eyes and ears within the empire. A master of subterfuge, he gathered information from the most unlikely sources. His network of informants extended far beyond the palace walls, and he knew every secret, every whisper that passed through the court. Danish was the one who had kept Zahir informed about Saira's growing frustrations with her position, her hesitations about marriage, and her increasing vulnerability. It was Danish who had helped arrange Zahir's first secret meeting with Saira, laying the groundwork for the affair that would eventually give Zahir the leverage he needed.

Ayaan, the diplomat, was the smooth-talker who knew how to navigate the complex politics of the Mughal court. He had been instrumental in ensuring Zahir's rise within the emperor's inner circle, helping him gain the trust of Qasim Khan and his sons. Ayaan was the one who smoothed over tensions between Zahir and the emperor's sons, ensuring that no one suspected Zahir's true intentions.

Imran leaned forward with a map spread across the table, his calloused finger tracing routes and locations. "Vishakha has slipped through our grasp again," he said, his voice edged with frustration. "Every time we close in, she evades us. It's as if she knows our every move."

"She doesn't know our moves," Danish interjected with a sly smile, "but she knows you, Zahir. She's predicting your strategies because she's seen them before. She's clever. And dangerous."

Ayaan sat back in his chair, stroking his neatly trimmed beard. "This is becoming a problem," he said. "If she's allowed to continue running free, she could expose everything. The emperor's trust in you is absolute, but even he can't ignore whispers forever."

Zahir's stiffened as he gripped the armrest of his chair. The mention of Vishakha's name was like a thorn lodged deep in his side, a constant reminder of the loose end he couldn't afford to leave untied.

"She must be eliminated," Zahir said coldly, his voice like a blade slicing through the air. "I don't care how long it takes or how far you have to go. She is the only thread that could unravel everything we've built. She cannot be allowed to live."

Imran nodded. "Our men are closing in. She was spotted near the river with a group. If they continue toward Agra, they'll be within our reach soon."

Zahir's lips curved into a thin, humourless smile. "Good," he said. "I want updates hourly. Leave no path unchecked. Danish, ensure our spies in Agra are watching every gate. If she dares to enter the city, I want her captured."

Danish inclined his head. "It will be done, my lord."

Imran added, "What about you, Zahir? Should we delay our journey to Agra until she is dealt with?"

Zahir waved a dismissive hand. "No. Agra is the only place that calms my mind. We'll travel as planned, but I expect constant reports. If your men fail me again, it will not be them I hold accountable—it will be you."

The three aides exchanged quick glances but nodded in unison. They had seen Zahir's wrath before and knew better than to test his patience.

***

As the carriage rolled steadily toward Agra, Zahir reclined against the plush interior. The rhythmic clatter of wheels on stone was soothing, yet his mind was far from calm. He had bid farewell to his wife at the palace gates, her quiet gaze following him as his entourage disappeared down the road.

He gazed out of the window at the landscape passing by, but his mind slipped into the past, to the events that had cemented his position in Qasim Khan's family.

***

The room was filled with tension as Qasim Khan paced the polished marble floor of his private chamber. The faint scent of burning incense lingered in the air, but it did little to soothe the emperor's mounting frustration. He clutched a letter in his hand—the one delivered from Hyderabad earlier that day. Behind him, Ayaan and Danish stood in silence, their expressions carefully neutral as they awaited his next outburst. Zahir Khan, standing at the edge of the room, leaned against a pillar, his sharp eyes observing every flicker of emotion on Qasim's face.

The hunting accident had been a tragedy. The Nizam of Hyderabad, one of the empire's most powerful allies, had died suddenly, leaving the throne to his young and ambitious son. As the newly crowned Nizam, the son had wasted no time in making his intentions clear—he wanted to marry Saira, Qasim Khan's youngest daughter.

"This is absurd!" Qasim barked suddenly, shaking the letter as though it were a physical embodiment of his frustrations. "Amina is already in Hyderabad, married to the late Nizam! And now his son—his son—wants to marry Saira?" He turned sharply to face his aides, his dark eyes blazing with indignation. "What will Saira call Amina? Mother? Sister? How is this not disgraceful?"

"My emperor," Ayaan said cautiously, his tone soothing, "perhaps we can delay the decision. The new Nizam is young. If we stall, his interest may fade, and the request may quietly disappear."

"Delay?" Qasim growled, his pacing resuming. "Delay will only create suspicion. Hyderabad is too important an ally to offend with games. If we reject his proposal outright, it's an insult. But if we agree..." He trailed off, pressing a hand to his temple as if the thought alone gave him a headache. "Amina's life will be ruined. She'll be humiliated. Forever in the shadow of her own sister. This is unbearable."

Danish exchanged a quick glance with Ayaan, but said nothing. Zahir, however, straightened abruptly, a sudden, sinister thought flashing across his mind. A plan, dangerous yet full of promise, began to take shape. He had to present it carefully, though—this was an unexpected opportunity, one that could finally fulfil his long-held ambitions. With calculated calm, he stepped forward, his mind already working through the next move.

"My emperor," Zahir began, his voice low and thoughtful, "perhaps there is... another way."

Qasim turned to him sharply, his brows furrowing. "Another way? Speak clearly, Zahir. What do you suggest?"

Zahir bowed slightly; his expression composed yet grave. "Bring Amina and her children back to Dilli."

The words hung in the air for a moment, and then Qasim's face darkened further. "Bring them back? For what purpose? If Saira marries the Nizam, Amina will have no role there. But bringing her back here? Who will care for her? She's nearly forty! No king will marry her. And her daughter—"

"She has served her purpose in Hyderabad," Zahir interjected gently. "The alliance was secured when she married the late Nizam. Now, Saira's marriage will strengthen it further. Amina need not remain in Hyderabad, where her presence may become... complicated."

Qasim stopped pacing, his gaze narrowing as he considered Zahir's words. "And if we bring her back? Then what? What becomes of her, Zahir? She's not young anymore. Who will want her now? She has a daughter, and kings marry to produce sons, not take on burdens."

He turned away; his shoulders heavy with the weight of the decision. "And what about me? I am no longer the man I once was. My sons are too preoccupied with their own ambitions, and my daughters have their own lives to lead.

When I am gone, Amina will have no one to care for her. No protector, no companion. She'll be left alone, forgotten."

Qasim's voice dropped, a rare tremor of vulnerability seeping into his words. "She's given everything to this family, and now I can't even guarantee her a dignified life. What kind of father am I?"

Zahir hesitated, as if carefully choosing his next words. He lowered his voice, his tone almost hesitant. "If it pleases you, my emperor... I will."

The room fell silent.

Qasim froze, staring at Zahir as though he had misheard. His eyebrows knitted together, and his voice trembled slightly, disbelief and confusion lacing his words. "You? You would marry Amina? At this age of her, you would take her as your wife?"

Zahir stood still, his gaze steady, but his heart raced as he carefully considered his next words. He had walked this tightrope before—cunning and diplomacy often were his closest companions—but today, the stakes were different.

Zahir remained calm, his demeanour steady and composed. He lowered his head slightly in a respectful bow, maintaining an air of humility. "Yes, my emperor. I would marry Amina."

Qasim narrowed his eyes, scanning Zahir's face with suspicion. "And why now, Zahir? Why this sudden offer? You, a man of your stature, with all your ambition—why marry a woman nearing forty with a daughter?"

Zahir hesitated for a moment, his gaze steady but his voice carrying a rare softness, as though he were revealing something deeply personal. He took a step closer to Qasim, his tone measured and sincere. "My emperor, if I may speak freely... I understand your hesitation. You have been betrayed before, and trust does not come easily to you. But I hope you will hear me out, not as your advisor, but as a man who has long admired Amina from afar."

Qasim's eyes narrowed slightly, but he did not interrupt, allowing Zahir to continue.

"Amina," Zahir began, his voice warm with genuine affection, "is a woman unlike any other. Her beauty, her strength, her grace, her unwavering loyalty—these are qualities I have admired for years. But she was married, and I would never have overstepped that boundary. I respected her too much to even let my feelings be known. Now, with her husband gone, I see an opportunity to offer her the life she deserves. Not out of pity, my emperor, but out of deep respect and admiration."

Qasim looked at him, his gaze unyielding. "You claim to admire her... but why, Zahir? You have power, wealth, and influence. You can marry any girl you want. A girl who could give you sons."

Zahir took a slow, planned step forward, lowering his voice slightly. "Amina has always commanded my respect, but only recently have I allowed myself to see her with new eyes. She is not just another noblewoman—she is a woman of great strength, intelligence, and wisdom. Her years have added to her beauty, not detracted from it."

Zahir paused, letting his words sink in before continuing, the sincerity in his voice unmistakable. "As for her age, I see it as an asset, not a hindrance. A woman with such experience, such character—she holds more value than any young, fleeting beauty."

Qasim's expression remained guarded, but there was a flicker of curiosity in his eyes. "You speak of admiration, Zahir, but what of practicality? I still don't understand. What do you gain from this union?"

Zahir's gaze softened, and he took a moment before responding. "What do I gain? The companionship of a woman who has endured more than most could bear and still carries herself with dignity. A woman who has raised a daughter as strong and intelligent as Sahiba. I gain a family, my emperor. Something I have long desired but never pursued, for my duties to the empire always came first. But now, I see a chance to build something meaningful—not just for myself, but for Amina and Sahiba as well."

Qasim swallowed thickly, tension radiating around him. He looked away for a moment, his thoughts clearly troubled. Zahir pressed on, his tone earnest. "There is also the matter of politics, my emperor. If Amina remains unmarried, she will be forced to stay there while Saira is married to young Nizam. That is not a comfortable situation for either of them. Amina would be isolated, and Saira would have to be Queen while her elder sister plays role of her step mother. It would be a difficult existence for them both. But if I marry Amina, I can take them under my care, away from the complexities of the court. They would have a home, a future, and the respect they deserve."

Qasim turned back to Zahir, his eyes searching for any hint of deception. "And what of your ambitions, Zahir? You are a man of power and influence. Marrying Amina would tie you to her family, to her past. Are you prepared for that?"

Zahir met his gaze without flinching. "My ambitions have always been in service to the empire, my emperor. Marrying Amina would not change that. If anything, it would strengthen my ties to you and to the empire. Amina is a woman of great wisdom and insight. She would be an asset, not a burden. And Sahiba... she is young, but she is bright. With the right guidance, she could grow into a woman of great influence herself. Together, we could build a legacy that benefits us all."

Qasim studied Zahir closely, his mind unravelling the layers of the proposal. His frown deepened, but his posture softened, as though the weight of Zahir's words had started to take root. As a father, Qasim knew well the complexities of family—how delicate alliances and relationships could be, especially when it involved his daughter.

He thought of Saira, who was soon to be married to late Nizam's son. The idea of her elder sister, Amina, living in the same house, not as a mere relative but as a stepmother, would create an uncomfortable situation. The very thought of it stirred a protective instinct in Qasim. He had seen the challenges of raising daughters in a world where power, marriage, and duty were inextricably linked, and he understood how delicate it was to balance family dynamics without causing friction.

Zahir's words had struck a chord with him, and for a brief moment, Qasim saw beyond the political manoeuvring. He saw Zahir's offer as an opportunity to ease the situation, to provide Saira and Amina with a sense of stability that he could not secure on his own. Amina deserved better than to be left in the shadows and Zahir might be able to provide her the future that she deserves, and Saira needed the protection of a strong, secure position before she entered a marriage.

As the silence stretched, Qasim's expression softened, his gaze fixed on Zahir. The emperor was still wary, but the emotional weight of fatherhood, the need to ensure his daughters' futures, had guided him toward understanding Zahir's proposal not just as a political strategy, but as a genuine, personal offer. "You may be right," he murmured, his voice softer than before. "For the sake of my daughters, perhaps this is what is needed."

Qasim studied him for a moment longer, then nodded slowly. "Very well. If Amina agrees to this union, I will not stand in your way. But remember, Zahir—this is not just a marriage. It is a promise. A promise to protect, to provide, and to honour. Do not make me regret trusting you."

Zahir placed a hand over his heart, his expression solemn. "You have my word, my emperor. I will honour Amina and

Sahiba as they deserve. This is not just a political alliance or a duty—it is a choice I make with my whole heart."

Qasim took a deep breath. The tension in his shoulders eased, and he relaxed slightly. "You truly surprise me, Zahir. I have trusted you with the empire, but I never thought you would offer such a thing... not out of obligation, but out of genuine care."

Zahir bowed his head, his expression humble. "It is a privilege, emperor. And I give you my word that I will take care of Amina and her daughter as my own."

Qasim stepped forward, his hand resting briefly on Zahir's shoulder. "You have my blessing. I know you will make her happy."

Zahir's eyes gleamed with satisfaction, and he bowed deeply. "Thank you, my emperor. I will not let you down."

As Qasim turned to make arrangements, Zahir allowed himself a moment to savour the success of his manipulation. His plan had worked far better than expected. Marrying Amina was far simpler and more advantageous than marrying Saira. The emperor trusted him, and now he would be firmly entrenched within the imperial family.

But there was still one hurdle left—Saira. Convincing her would be a delicate task. But Zahir, ever the master of persuasion, was confident that he would succeed. And in the end, it would all fall into place.

***

Saira's anguished cry echoed through the chamber, a raw, unfiltered sound of betrayal. Her hands clutched at her chest, her eyes wide with disbelief as tears streamed down her face. "You were supposed to protect me!" she cried, her voice cracking under the weight of her heartbreak. "I trusted you, Zahir. I thought you loved me. I gave you everything, and this is how you repay me?"

Zahir stood in front of her, his expression carefully composed, his insides twisting in a knot of satisfaction and guilt. He knew the pain he was causing her, and yet, it was necessary. He had to do this. He had to push her away for his own ambition. "I did love you, Saira," he said softly, his voice low, as though he was feeling the sting of his own words. He took a step forward, reaching out to her, but she pulled away, her anger flaring anew.

"I did," he repeated, his voice laced with feigned regret, his eyes clouded with false sorrow. "But how could I say no to your father? To the emperor's will?" His gaze shifted momentarily to the floor, as if to imply that his duty had been too great to defy. "The emperor's will is absolute, Saira. If I defied him, it would only bring disgrace upon us both. Do you understand? This is not something I could change. Not without losing everything. The new Nizam has asked for your hand, why would your father deny his will to fulfil mine? I'm nobody."

Saira's breath hitched, her fists clenched at her sides as she tried to make sense of his words, her heart racing with disbelief. The realization settled on her like a cold stone, and her tears flowed even faster. "So, that's it?" Her voice cracked with the weight of her disappointment. "I'm just... a pawn in some alliance? A means to an end?"

Zahir flinched slightly at her words, but his expression remained steady. He took a deep breath, trying to calm the turmoil rising within him. He stepped closer, reaching for her hands, his fingers gently brushing against hers, a touch meant to soothe. "No, Saira," he said, his voice quieter now, almost tender. "You are so much more than that. You've always been more than that to me."

His words were carefully chosen, each one designed to lure her into believing him once again. "This alliance—it's important, yes. For the empire, for your father. But it's also for your own protection. The Nizam... he will treat you well. I'll ensure it, Saira. You will have everything you need. And no matter where you are, no matter what happens, I will always be here for you. Always."

He saw the conflict flicker in her eyes—her hope, so fragile and fleeting, wavering like a candle flame in the wind. But it wasn't enough. It wouldn't be enough. Saira's heart was breaking, and no matter how much he lied, no matter how many comforting words he spoke, he could see the fire in her spirit slowly dimming.

Her sobs quieted, but her face was hollow, drained of the joy that had once been there. "I hate this," she whispered, her voice small and broken. "I hate myself for believing in you. For thinking you cared... for thinking you would protect me. I thought you would choose me over everything else." Her voice faltered as she turned away from him, unable to meet his eyes any longer.

Zahir's hand hovered in the air for a moment before he lowered it. The sight of her pain twisted something inside him—something he quickly pushed away. He couldn't afford to feel. Not now. Not when everything was falling into place.

"I'm sorry, Saira," he murmured, his voice soft, as if the words held the weight of a love he no longer felt. He placed his hand on her shoulder, turning her gently to face him once more. "I wish things were different. Believe me, I do. But this is for the best. For both of us."

Saira's eyes were wet, her heart shattered, but there was a resigned quiet in her now. She took a step back, her lips trembling as she fought to keep her composure. The fire in her eyes—the fire he had once seen as love—was gone, replaced by emptiness. "I'll go," she said quietly, her voice barely a whisper as she backed away. "But I'll never forgive you for this. I'll never forgive myself for believing that you were different."

As she turned and walked toward the door, her shoulders sagged under the weight of the emotional burden, the last shred of hope she had left slipping away with every step she took. Zahir watched her leave, his face impassive, but inside, he felt something stir—something sharp and cold, but also victorious.

He allowed himself a faint smile as the door closed behind her. Another step closer to his ultimate goal. Another obstacle cleared.

As he walked back toward his desk, Zahir's thoughts drifted to the future. His plan was falling into place, and soon, everything he had worked for would be his. He had used Saira, yes. But in the end, it was all for the greater good. He would have the empire. He would have the power.

But Saira? Saira would be just another casualty of his rise. She would fade into the background, her love for him no longer a burden. And that, to Zahir, was all that mattered.

***

The carriage jolted, bringing Zahir back to the present. Agra's walls were visible in the distance, their grandeur silhouetted against the rising sun. He leaned back, his fingers drumming against the armrest.

He had come too far, gained too much. He couldn't let Vishakha unravel it all. She had to be stopped. At any cost.

Chapter 11

The warmth of the fire crackled in the small, humble home, filling the room with light smoke. Rana, only 6-7 years old, sat on a low stool, his small feet dangling off the edge, his face bright with joy. His mother, with a gentle smile, hummed as she stirred a pot of food on the stove. The aroma of the stew filled the air, making Rana's stomach growl in excitement.

"Is it ready yet, Amma?" he asked eagerly, his eyes wide and full of anticipation.

His mother laughed softly, brushing a strand of hair from her face as she glanced over at him. "Just a little longer, my darling. You're too excited tonight."

Just then, the door creaked open, and his father entered. He was a tall, broad man, his face weathered from the long hours of work, but his eyes were warm as he greeted his son. Rana jumped up excitedly, running to his father and wrapping his arms around his legs.

"Bapu!" Rana's voice was full of energy. "Amma's making the best food tonight! You're going to love it!"

His father laughed, ruffling his son's hair. "I'm sure she is, little one. I can smell it from here." He bent down to kiss Rana on the cheek, his hands still rough from his day's labour.

The family exchanged a quiet, loving moment, their hearts at ease, as they sat down to share their meal. The room was filled with laughter, simple but deep, a warmth that no one can get enough of...

But that peace was short-lived.

A distant shout pierced the air, followed by a cacophony of screams and the sound of hurried footsteps. The joy in the room instantly vanished, replaced by an overwhelming tension. Rana's father's face went pale, and his mother's smile faltered as she stood, her instincts already on alert.

Rana's father immediately rushed to the door, peeking out to see what was happening. His eyes widened in horror as he saw the Mughal army advancing on the village. The flames of burning houses flickered in the distance, casting an eerie light on the chaos that had erupted outside.

"They're here," his father muttered, his voice trembling for the first time in years. "They're attacking us."

His mother gasped, fear flooding her eyes. "No... no, not us. Not our village..."

"Hide, Rana. Hide," his father said, his voice trembling as he grabbed the boy and pushed him toward the corner of the room. He pointed at the stack of wooden logs by the wall. "Behind those logs, Rana. Stay still. Don't make a sound. You hear me?"

Rana's small face was filled with confusion, his innocent eyes wide with fear. "Bapu, what's happening?"

"Just listen to me," his father said, crouching down to kiss his son on the forehead. His lips trembled, and his eyes glistened with tears. "If you don't make a sound, they won't find you. You must be brave, little one. You must be very brave."

His mother, with tears in her eyes, reached out for her son. "We love you, Rana. Don't be scared. Just stay still. Don't make a sound."

Rana nodded, his heart pounding in his chest as his father kissed him again. His father stood, his back stiff with resolve. "I'll go out the back. Don't move, Rana. And don't listen to anyone, even if I shout for you to run. Stay here."

With one last look at his wife and son, his father opened the back door, his face grim. But just as he stepped outside, the front door was kicked open with a loud crash, and the soldiers stormed in.

His father spun around to face his family, his eyes full of love and pain. "Run Rana! Run, my son!"

But Rana remembered his father's words. He stayed still, hidden behind the logs, holding his breath. His heart pounded in his chest as he watched his father's desperate face. His mother screamed, "Run Rana! Run!" But Rana stayed silent, frozen in place.

With a single, swift motion, one of the soldiers swung his blade through the air, and his father fell to the floor, lifeless. His mother screamed, but the soldiers ignored her, pulling her roughly from the ground. "Take her!" one of the men shouted. "We'll deal with her after we finish with the boy!"

The soldier who had been sent to find Rana looked around and then ran out the back door. "He's gone! He's running!" he shouted.

But Rana, hiding in the corner, remained motionless, the words echoing in his mind: "Stay still. Don't make a sound."

As his mother's cries echoed in his ears— "Run Rana, run!"—the soldiers dragged her away. But her words, "Run Rana, run!" haunted him. The words changed in his mind. The call of his mother turned into his own name— "Rana... Rana..." And with that, he jolted awake, gasping for breath, his heart racing.

The voice was no longer his mother's. It was Vishakha's. He looked around, dazed, realizing he was no longer in that dark place but lying on the ground in the midst of the forest. Vishakha's voice had pulled him back from the nightmare that had plagued him for years.

He breathed heavily, his body still trembling. But the pain of the past didn't go away. It never would.

The soft trickle of water splashed against Rana's lips, and he blinked rapidly, shaking the fog from his mind. As the cool liquid flowed down his throat, he slowly regained full consciousness, his vision clearing.

Vishakha, kneeling beside him, helped him sit up. Her eyes were filled with concern. "Rana... what happened? You were unconscious for so long."

Rana let out a slow breath, his head throbbing as he blinked against the dim light. His body felt heavy, every muscle aching from the fight. He ran a hand over the sore spot on his temple, his fingers brushing against the dried blood.

"The big guard," he murmured, his voice hoarse. "He got me good." He paused; his thoughts sluggish as he tried to piece everything together.

Vishakha's brow furrowed, her worry deepening. "You scared us. You've been out for so long. How do you feel?"

Rana took a deep breath, his hand dropping to his side as he tried to sit up straighter. "Like I've been trampled by a herd of elephants," he said with a weak chuckle, though it was clear he was still in pain. He glanced around, his eyes finally focusing on the others who had gathered nearby.

His stomach growled in protest, and he exhaled a weary chuckle. "Guess I'm hungrier than I thought. Fighting really works up an appetite."

Amar chuckled, handing him a piece of bread. "I'm sure you'll feel better once you get some food in you. You've been pushing yourself too hard."

Chandan, still keeping a close eye on the surroundings, added, "You looked pretty unstoppable out there, Rana. Three soldiers, all by yourself. That was just awesome."

Suresh raised an eyebrow, then smirked. "Guess we should all start taking lessons from you." His voice was light, but there was respect in it.

Rana smiled wryly, feeling the warmth of their camaraderie, but he didn't let on how deeply the battle had shaken him. "Maybe another time," he said, brushing off the compliment.

But Vishakha wasn't convinced. Her gaze lingered on him, trying to read his expression. "I see," she said slowly, then changed the subject. "Well, we've got a little victory to celebrate. We've got five extra horses now. And we should make the most of them."

Before Rana could respond, Amar let out a frustrated scoff. "A little victory?" he muttered, shaking his head. "That coward Hari ran the moment the fight started. He left us there to fend for ourselves." His nostrils flared; the anger still fresh in his voice.

Rana sighed, rubbing his forehead before looking at Amar. "Hari isn't a fighter, Amar. He's an old man with a family to think about. What else was he supposed to do?"

"He could have stayed," Amar shot back, his voice quieter but no less bitter. "He could have tried."

Rana met Amar's glare with a calm, steady look. "And gotten himself killed? Tell me, what good would that have done? Some men survive by fighting, others survive by running. Hari did what he had to."

Amar exhaled sharply and looked away; his hands clenched into fists. He didn't argue further, but the resentment in his silence made it clear he didn't agree.

Rana let the matter drop, knowing there was no point in pushing. Instead, he shifted his focus back to their next move. "Yes, we'll take these horses and head to the Agra market. We'll pretend to be horse sellers—shouldn't raise any suspicion that way. What do you think?"

Chandan slapped his hands together. "Brilliant idea! They won't expect us at all."

Amar nodded. "We're resourceful, I'll give you that."

Suresh, though still a bit hesitant about the whole idea, shrugged. "We're already in deep, might as well keep going. I trust you, Rana."

With everyone in agreement, they began preparing to move. As they mounted their horses and set off down the road, the silence between them was filled with the occasional sound of hooves and the distant call of birds.

Vishakha, riding next to Rana, glanced at him again, her curiosity piqued, "I'll say... you killed three trained soldiers by yourself. Where did you learn how to fight like that?"

Rana leaned back slightly, trying to avoid the question. "Ah, we can talk about that another time," he said, his tone light and casual.

Vishakha, watching him closely, raised an eyebrow, "But I'm wondering... when you woke up, there were tears in your eyes. What happened?"

Rana stiffened for a moment, caught off guard by the question. He quickly diverted his gaze, pretending to adjust his saddle. "Oh, probably something got in my eyes while fighting" he said dismissively, trying to mask the discomfort in his voice.

Vishakha didn't believe him for a second. She could tell there was more to it. But she didn't press him further, letting the question linger unanswered. "I see," she said softly, though the question remained in her mind.

They rode in silence for a few moments, but Vishakha couldn't shake the feeling that there was something deeper in Rana's past, something that made him vulnerable in ways he hadn't revealed yet.

But she also couldn't ignore the strange pull she felt towards him, the way he seemed to always be there when she needed him most. He had saved her life again, and somehow, that made her heart ache. She hasn't felt like that for a man before in her life.

As they continued their journey, a quiet thought settled in Vishakha's mind: She was falling for him. But even if she didn't fully know why, she could sense the growing connection between them. She just hoped that, someday, he'd let her in—let her understand the person he truly was.

***

The streets of Agra were alive with noise, the hum of conversation and clatter of hooves echoing through the narrow lanes. Lanterns swung in the evening breeze, casting flickering shadows across the cobbled streets. The group of five moved cautiously, their horses' steps muffled by the dampness of the ground. Conversations had grown heavy as their nerves stretched taut with every passing moment. Each one of them knew what they were looking for, but no one dared to say it out loud.

Rana led the group, his eyes scanning every face in the crowd with a sharpness that betrayed his tension. Vishakha rode close to him, her face partially obscured by the veil of her scarf. She was visibly uneasy. Her hands clenched the reins tightly, and her gaze flitted nervously from one person to another, her fear of recognition palpable.

"Rana," she whispered softly, her voice barely audible above the chatter of the market. "Someone might recognize me here. I... I don't know if this is a good idea."

Rana glanced at her, his expression softening for a moment. "I know," he said quietly. "But we'll be careful. Stay close to me. If anything feels off, we leave—Pari or no Pari." His voice was firm, but the weight in his eyes betrayed his inner conflict. He couldn't afford to lose Vishakha, not after everything they'd been through. But the thought of Pari— alone, scared, and suffering—was a wound that wouldn't heal. He clenched his jaw and forced himself to focus.

They moved through the crowd, speaking in hushed tones to locals, asking coded questions about where they could sell their "horses" to "wealthy foreigners." The responses were mostly blank stares and confused head shakes.

"Foreigners don't buy horses here," one man scoffed before walking away.

At another stall, a merchant laughed nervously. "Horses? For foreigners? You must be lost. Try the outskirts."

Their attempts felt futile, and the weight of their mission pressed heavier with each failed conversation. But they couldn't afford to give up. Time was slipping through their fingers like sand.

Finally, as they lingered near a quieter stretch of the marketplace, a man emerged from the crowd. He was tall and lean, his face partially hidden beneath a hood. His piercing eyes darted to each of them before settling on Vishakha, lingering a little too long. She instinctively pulled her scarf tighter around her face, shifting uncomfortably under his scrutiny.

"You're looking for something," the man said, his voice low and deep. It wasn't a question—it was a statement.

Rana stepped forward, his hand resting subtly on the hilt of his sword. "We're just travellers," he said casually, though his tone carried an edge. "Looking for a place where we can trade horses. We heard foreigners pay well."

The man smirked, his gaze flicking to the horses and back to Rana. "Foreigners, huh? That's an interesting way to put it."

The tension between them was palpable. The man's eyes narrowed slightly as he studied Rana, as if trying to read the intent behind his words. "You don't look like regular horse traders," he said after a moment. "And you..."—his gaze shifted to Vishakha again— "don't look like you belong in the market at all."

Rana's grip tightened on his half-spear, but he forced a calm smile. "She's with me. That's all you need to know."

The man's gaze flicked over the group, lingering on Vishakha for a moment too long. Rana stepped slightly in front of her, his expression hardening.

"I might know a place," the man said, his voice slow and firm, "but these are dangerous streets for strangers. What business do you really have here?"

Rana didn't falter. "Our business is just what we said—selling horses. Nothing more."

The man smirked, clearly unconvinced. "Foreign buyers don't come to Agra for horses. They come for... other things. What are you really after?"

Amar, standing nearby, shifted uncomfortably. Rana shot him a warning glance before turning back to the man. "If you know someone who can take us to the right market, we're willing to pay for the help."

The man considered this, his eyes once again flicking toward Vishakha. "I might know someone. But it'll cost you."

Rana nodded. "We'll pay. Take us to him."

The man hesitated for a moment, then gestured for them to follow. He led them through a series of winding alleys before stopping abruptly at the edge of the Yamuna River. The moon hung high in the sky, casting a silver glow over the water. They were near a patch of forest that ran along the riverbank, secluded and eerily quiet.

"You'll wait here," the man said, pointing to a spot near the water. "I'll bring someone who can help you."

Rana didn't like the situation. He exchanged a quick glance with Vishakha, who was tense but said nothing. They had no choice but to wait.

As the man disappeared into the dark, Amar, Chandan, and Suresh tried to lighten the mood with nervous humour.

"What if this is a trap?" Chandan muttered, trying to suppress a laugh. "We might end up getting sold instead of these horses."

Amar chuckled uneasily. "If that happens, I'll make sure to get a good price for you, Chandan. You're worth at least two camels."

Suresh joined in, shaking his head. "Forget the camels. He's worth maybe a goat, if we're lucky."

Despite the humour, the tension in the group was palpable. The moonlight bathed the Yamuna's waters, casting a faint silver glow on the group as they waited, nerves stretched taut. Rana sat slightly apart, his half-spear resting at his side, his hand tracing the carved wood as if drawing strength from it. His expression was blank, but the tension in his stance betrayed his restlessness.

Would they find Pari? What would they do if they did? And if this was a trap, how would he protect everyone? His thoughts were interrupted by Vishakha.

Vishakha, who had been pacing quietly, finally approached him. She sat beside him, her movements careful, almost hesitant. For a moment, neither of them spoke. The soft rustle of the riverbank and the distant hum of the city were the only sounds that filled the air.

"You don't talk much about yourself," she said softly, breaking the silence.

Rana glanced at her, his lips pressing into a thin line. "Not much to tell," he replied.

She gave him a look—a gentle, probing gaze that told him she didn't believe a word of it. "You didn't learn to fight like that by accident. You killed those soldiers like you'd been doing it your whole life. Where did you learn to fight like that?"

Rana let out a breath, his shoulders sagging slightly. He turned to the river, his eyes fixed on the shimmering surface as memories began to surface. "It wasn't by choice," he began, his voice low, almost a whisper.

Vishakha said nothing, waiting for him to continue.

"I was seven," Rana said, his words heavy with the weight of years gone by. "A happy boy. Carefree. I had Amma... and Bapu. They were my world." He paused, pressing his tongue against his teeth as if forcing the words out. "Bapu worked long days, but he always came home with a smile. And Amma... she'd be cooking by the fire, humming her favourite songs. I used to sit by her, asking a hundred questions about everything—why the stars shine, why the moon changes shape. She always had an answer."

Vishakha smiled faintly at the image, but her heart clenched at the sorrow in his tone.

"That night," Rana continued, his voice faltering, "Bapu came home late. I was so happy to see him—I ran to him, hugged him. Amma laughed, telling me to let him wash up. She was making our favourite dish. It felt like... any other night." His voice cracked slightly, and he paused to steady himself.

"Then we heard it," he said, his tone dropping, his eyes darkening. "Shouts. Screams. Flames."

Vishakha's breath hitched, but she didn't interrupt.

"Bapu told us to stay inside. He went to see what was happening." Rana swallowed hard, his fists clenching. "When he came back, his face... I'll never forget that look. Fear. Real fear. He pulled me to the corner of the room, behind a pile of wooden logs. 'Stay here,' he said. 'No matter what you hear, no matter what happens, stay quiet. Don't make a sound.'"

Rana's voice shook as he spoke. "I didn't understand. I asked him why. He just kissed my forehead and said, 'Amma and I love you more than anything. Don't be scared, my boy.'"

Vishakha reached out instinctively, her hand brushing his arm.

"I stayed there," Rana continued, his eyes glistening with unshed tears. "Frozen. Helpless. I saw them come in. Four soldiers in Mughal uniforms. Bapu tried to fight them. He picked up a stick—just a stick—and they... they killed him with one swing of a sword."

Vishakha gasped softly, her hand flying to her mouth.

"Amma screamed. She fought, too—threw a pot at one of them. But they overpowered her. Dragged her out. I... I just sat there. I didn't move. I didn't breathe. I heard her screams outside. I heard them laughing, and then... silence."

Tears spilled down Rana's cheeks now, but he didn't wipe them away. "I don't know how long I stayed there. Hours, maybe. When it was quiet, I came out. They were gone. The house was... in ruins. Amma and Bapu were gone. I found them outside, their bodies..." He broke off, his voice choked with emotion.

Vishakha's own eyes were brimming with tears. "Rana..." she whispered, her voice trembling.

"I sat there, beside them," he said hoarsely. "I cried until I couldn't anymore. I howled. I begged them to wake up. But they didn't."

He drew a shaky breath. "I was alone after that. An orphan. No home. No family. I wandered until I found Devran village. Dharamdas, the village head, found me. He took me in. The people there accepted me, gave me a place to belong. I started sleeping in the village temple. But the dreams... the nightmares never stopped. I saw Bapu's face every time I closed my eyes. I heard Amma's screams. I swore to myself that I'd never be that helpless again."

Rana straightened slightly; his body language rigid as he wiped the lingering tears from his face. When he spoke again, his voice was steadier, but there was a hard edge to it, like a blade sharpened by pain.

"When Dharamdas took me in, I was grateful, but I knew that kindness wouldn't protect me if the same thing happened again. So, I started training—every single day. At first, I didn't have anything but sticks. So, I fought with them—against trees, against rocks, against the boys in the village. I didn't care if I came back with bruises or cuts. I had to be better, faster, stronger."

Rana's eyes darkened, his gaze fixed on the distance, as if he were seeing those long, gruelling days play out again in his mind. "I wrestled with the older boys in the village, boys twice my size. They laughed at me at first, called me a scrawny orphan who didn't stand a chance. But I didn't care. I kept coming back, every day, until they weren't laughing anymore. Until I could take them down. One by one, I became the strongest among them."

Vishakha listened in silence, her heart aching for the boy he had been and the man he had become.

"I learned to hunt," Rana continued, his voice quieter now, but no less intense. "Not just to survive, but to become deadly. I spent hours in the forests, tracking animals, moving silently, waiting for the perfect moment to strike. I learned patience. Precision. How to read my prey, how to anticipate its movements.

He looked down at his hands, calloused and rough, and let out a bitter chuckle. "I didn't have a real sword, so I practiced with sticks until my arms felt like they would fall off. I studied the way the village warriors moved when they trained— watched how they held their blades, how they fought. When I finally got my hands on a real sword, it felt like an extension of myself. And the spear..." He patted the half-spear at his side, a faint smile tugging at his lips. "It became my second weapon. A weapon that gave me reach, that allowed me to take down an enemy before they could even touch me."

Rana's eyes met Vishakha's, and she saw a storm of emotions there—anger, sorrow, determination. "Every bruise, every scar, every drop of sweat and blood... it was all for one purpose. To make sure that no one—no man, no soldier, no army—would ever take away what was mine again. If anyone tried, they'd have to go through me first. And I'd make sure they'd regret it."

His voice softened, but it carried an unshakable resolve. "I made a small hut for myself. I became the best hunter, the strongest fighter, because I refused to be that helpless boy again. I refused to sit in silence while the people I love are ripped away from me. Not anymore."

Vishakha felt her throat tighten, but she said nothing. Words felt inadequate, too small to hold the weight of what he had just shared. The silence between them stretched, weighted with emotion, yet she didn't break it. She simply reached out, her fingers trembling slightly, and took his hand in hers.

Rana stiffened for the briefest moment, unaccustomed to such quiet tenderness. But then, something in him eased. The tension in his shoulders, the tightness in his features— slowly, they unravelled. He let out a breath he hadn't realized he was holding, as if something inside him was finally exhaling after years of suffocating in grief.

The warmth of her hand grounded him, pulled him from the depths of painful memories and brought him to the present. He turned his palm slightly, his calloused fingers wrapping around hers. It was a small gesture, but it felt monumental. A lifetime of battles, loss, and loneliness had made him forget what it meant to simply be held—to be understood without the need for explanations or reassurances.

She didn't offer him sympathy or empty words. She didn't tell him she was sorry or that things would be alright. Instead, she shifted closer, and with a quiet sigh, she rested her head on his shoulder.

Rana froze. Not out of discomfort, but out of sheer disbelief. It had been so long since someone had leaned on him—not for strength, not for protection, but simply to share in the silence. To be with him, not as a warrior, not as a leader, but as the man who had lost everything and rebuilt himself from the ashes.

A lump formed in his throat, and for once, he didn't fight it. He let himself feel. The grief, the longing, the unbearable weight of loneliness that had been his constant companion—it all came rushing to the surface, raw and unfiltered. His grip on her hand tightened, not in desperation, but in quiet gratitude.

The world outside faded. The past, the battles, the scars—they all blurred into insignificance. Here, in this moment, there was only her warmth against him, only the quiet rise and fall of her breath, only the steady beat of two wounded hearts finding solace in each other.

His eyes burned, and for once, he didn't blink away the tears. He let them fall, silent and unseen, soaking into the dust and sweat of his skin. And Vishakha, without a word, squeezed his hand as if she had felt them, as if she knew.

They sat like that for what felt like an eternity, neither of them moving, neither of them speaking. They didn't need to. Their grief, their pain, their unspoken understanding—weighed heavier than any words ever could.

For the first time in years, Rana felt something shift deep within him. A barrier, a wall he had built around himself, cracked ever so slightly. And through that crack, something unfamiliar seeped in—something soft, something warm.

Something that felt a lot like home.

"You didn't possibly think you could go through the streets of Agra without getting caught, did you?"

The spell broke instantly, and they pulled apart, their heads snapping toward the source of the voice. A man in a Mughal uniform stepped out of the shadows, his structure confident, his gaze sharp and calculating. Behind him stood the mysterious man who had led them there, a sly smile tugging at his lips.

The tension in the air shifted instantly, turning electric. Rana's hand instinctively went to his sword, his other gripping the half-spear beside him. Behind him, Amar, Chandan, and Suresh tensed, their hands inching toward the weapons they had taken from the fallen soldiers from their fight.

The Mughal officer's gaze lingered on each of them before settling on Vishakha. His eyes narrowed, a cunning smile spreading across his face.

Rana's grip on his weapons tightened, his body coiled like a spring, ready to strike. The moment of intimacy had passed, replaced by the cold, sharp reality of danger.

The air was filled with tension as Rana and his companions instinctively gripped their weapons, their muscles tensed for a fight. But before the moment could spiral into violence, Vishakha took a step forward, her expression shifting from wariness to something softer.

A small, knowing smile curved her lips. "Akram," she greeted warmly, her voice filled with familiarity.

The man in front of them—a tall, sharp-eyed figure with a neatly trimmed beard and the dignified form of someone used to power—tilted his head slightly, his lips curling into a smile of his own. "Vishakha," he said, his tone carrying both relief and amusement. "You haven't changed."

Rana, his grip still firm on his half-spear, narrowed his eyes. Amar, Chandan, and Suresh exchanged bewildered glances, silently demanding an explanation. But Vishakha remained composed, stepping closer to Akram as though greeting an old friend.

"I'm happy to see you," she said sincerely.

Akram's expression softened. "And I, you. I never thought I'd find you here, of all places." He exhaled sharply before his face turned more serious. "Vishakha, do you realize that half the city is searching for you? Everyone on Zahir's payroll is hunting for a woman matching your description. You're lucky that Aasif—" he gestured to the man standing beside him, the one who had led them here, "—found you before Zahir's spies did."

Rana's shoulders eased slightly, but his stance remained guarded. He trusted Vishakha, but he didn't trust Akram—not yet. Meanwhile, Amar, Chandan, and Suresh were still visibly confused.

Vishakha turned toward them, sensing their unspoken questions. "This is Akram," she explained. "He was a close aide during my time in the Mughal court. He is fiercely loyal to Emperor Qasim and his family. He's not our enemy."

Akram gave them a brief nod.

Chandan, ever the blunt one, furrowed his brows. "Your time in the Mughal court?" he echoed, exchanging a quick look with Amar and Suresh. "There's a whole past of yours we don't know, isn't there?"

Vishakha hesitated but nodded. "There is," she admitted. "But we don't have time for those stories now."

Akram studied her for a long moment before asking, "What brings you to Agra?"

Vishakha took a deep breath. "I was running from Zahir's men. I took a fall from a hill while running and that's how I ended up in Devran." She cast a glance toward Rana, as if drawing strength from his presence before continuing. "The people of Devran gave me shelter, and they have been helping me stay hidden. But there's something more pressing that brought us here."

Akram frowned. "What is it?"

"A girl—Pari. She's from Devran. She was taken." Vishakha's voice wavered slightly, but she steadied herself. "At first, we thought the forest had swallowed her. But we found out that she might have been taken by men and sold. There's a chance she's here in Agra."

A flicker of something passed through Akram's eyes. He shifted uncomfortably, his gaze momentarily dropping to the ground.

Vishakha noticed immediately. Her breath hitched. "You know something."

Akram's chin lifted. "Vishakha—"

"You know something," she pressed, stepping forward. "Where is she?"

Akram hesitated. His gaze flickered toward Aasif, as if weighing his options. Finally, he exhaled sharply. "I don't want to be involved in this."

Rana's fingers twitched around his weapon, his patience thinning. "You don't want to be involved?" he said, his voice dangerously low. "A child was stolen from her home."

Akram turned his gaze to Rana. "You don't understand," he said quietly. "The Mughals aren't involved in this trade. But we receive rewards for keeping our eyes closed."

Vishakha's stomach twisted. "So, you've known all along?"

Akram's face betrayed a flicker of shame. "I have known that girls disappear. But I never asked questions. That's how you survive in this city." He hesitated, then sighed. "If Pari hasn't already been sold, I can point you toward where she might be held."

A rush of hope surged through the group. Rana straightened, his grip tightening with renewed determination.

"Aasif will take you there," Akram continued. "But whatever you do, you must do on your own. I can't interfere."

"I understand," Vishakha said, her voice firm. "And I'm grateful for your help."

Akram's expression softened again. "If you're going to act, do it before dawn," he warned. "That's when security is at its weakest."

Vishakha turned to Rana. "We need to leave. Now."

But before Rana could respond, Akram raised a hand. "I think you misunderstood," he said carefully.

Vishakha frowned. "What do you mean?"

Akram's gaze was steady. "The group can go after Pari," he said. "Aasif will guide them." His eyes flickered toward Vishakha. "But you must come with me."

A tense silence fell over the group.

Rana's pose stiffened immediately. "She's not going anywhere without us."

Akram met his gaze evenly. "There's someone who wants to meet her."

Vishakha's brow furrowed. "Who?"

Akram didn't answer immediately, and that only made Rana more suspicious.

"We don't have time for this," Rana snapped. "We either leave together or not at all."

Akram sighed. "I understand your hesitation. But think. You have only a few hours before dawn. If you waste time, Pari could be lost forever."

A muscle in Rana's jaw twitched. He knew Akram was right. But the thought of letting Vishakha out of his sight—

Vishakha turned to him, her voice softer now. "Rana, I'll be fine."

His fingers twitched at his sides. "You don't know that."

She gave him a small smile, one that was meant to reassure but only made his stomach knot further. "I trust Akram."

A heavy pause settled between them. Rana looked at her for a long time, his chest rising and falling with barely restrained frustration. But then, reluctantly, he exhaled.

A muscle twitched in his cheek. "If anything happens to her—"

Akram raised a hand. "She'll be safe."

There was still hesitation, but eventually, Rana nodded.

The weight of parting settled heavily over the group. The urgency of their mission loomed in the air, yet none of them moved. Vishakha stood before them, her eyes glistening in the dim moonlight, her heart torn between duty and attachment.

She turned to Amar first, her lips curving into a bittersweet smile. "You know, Amar," she said, her voice trembling slightly, "the next time I see you, you better have that one of your many businesses up and running."

Amar blinked back his tears and scoffed lightly. "Of course." He smirked. "Chandan will be my business partner, obviously."

Chandan, despite the tears pooling in his eyes, puffed out his chest. "Obviously! Someone has to make sure you don't go bankrupt on the first day."

Vishakha laughed, a sound filled with both warmth and sadness. "Yes, and I'm sure the business will double as a storytelling hub with all your endless chatter." She sniffled; her voice choked with emotion. "I'll miss you both."

Amar's playful mask cracked, and he pulled her into a tight embrace. "We'll miss you too, Didi. Stay safe, okay?"

When he let go, Chandan immediately wrapped his arms around her. "If you don't come back," he muttered, voice shaking, "I swear I'll find you and drag you back myself."

She let out a shaky breath, fighting back her tears. "I'll come back. I promise."

As she stepped back, her gaze landed on Suresh. The man who once barely tolerated her, who had been quick to mistrust, now stood before her, his eyes lowered, his fingers clenching and unclenching at his sides.

"I never thought I'd say this," he muttered, rubbing the back of his neck, "but… I was wrong about you." His voice faltered, then steadied. "You're one of us now."

A lump formed in Vishakha's throat. She stepped closer, placing a hand on his arm. "And you? You're not as much of an unbearable brute as I thought you were."

Suresh let out a short laugh, shaking his head. "Don't make me regret this."

She smiled through the tears threatening to spill over. "Take care, Suresh."

And then, her eyes met Rana's.

The world around them blurred. The others faded into the background.

Rana stood there, silent, his hands clenched into fists at his sides. His face was stiff, his expressions were blank, but his eyes—they betrayed everything.

"You don't have to do this," he said, his voice quiet but firm.

She stepped closer, close enough to see the conflict raging within him. "I do," she whispered.

Rana shook his head, his frustration barely concealed. "This isn't a good idea, Vishakha. You don't know what you're walking into."

She reached up, her fingertips grazing his arm in the gentlest of touches. "You've done enough for me, Rana. More than I could have ever asked for."

His breath hitched, but he said nothing.

She forced a smile, though her heart was breaking. "Now it's time to stop worrying about me. Pari needs you. Go get her."

He exhaled sharply, his hands twitching as if he wanted to reach for her, to pull her back, to stop this. But he didn't.

"I'll be fine," she reassured him, her voice softer now. "I'm in good hands."

Rana's eyes darkened with doubt.

She took a step back, but not before murmuring, "When this is over, I'll come to Devran. I want to see Pari." She swallowed hard. "And I know you'll bring her home."

Rana's throat bobbed as he struggled to say something, anything, but words failed him.

Instead, he simply nodded. There was nothing left to say.

With a final glance at each of them, Vishakha turned and walked toward Akram. The group watched in heavy silence as she moved further away.

And then, just as she was about to disappear into the shadows, she turned.

Rana turned at the same moment.

Their eyes met one last time.

A teary smile.

A silent goodbye.

Then, the darkness swallowed them both.

Chapter 12

The palace rose ahead, its towering walls stark against the pale moonlight. The closer they got, the heavier Vishakha's chest felt. She sat rigid on the horse beside Akram, her fingers gripping the reins tighter than necessary.

The entrance was grand—arched domes, towering gates, and guards stationed at every corner. The moment they crossed the first gate, a strange fear settled in Vishakha's chest. Something about this place felt different. Mughal banners hung from the high walls, their emerald and gold fabric shimmering under the flickering torchlight. Every glance exchanged between the soldiers, every whispered conversation in the dim corridors, sent a shiver through her. She had trusted Akram, forced herself to believe in him, but doubt began to gnaw at her mind. What if she had been wrong? What if this was a trap? What if she had walked straight into Zahir's hands?

One gate closed behind them, then another. The heavy thud of wood and iron felt final, each barrier shutting her deeper inside. The air felt colder, heavier, as though the palace itself was swallowing her whole. Her fingers twitched at her sides, and she had to force herself to steady her breathing. Why so many guards? Why so many gates? The deeper they went, the more her instincts screamed at her to turn back.

By the time they reached the final corridor, her pulse was hammering in her ears. Akram stopped and turned to her with a strange smile on his face. "The king is waiting for you inside," he said.

The words sent a cold shiver down her spine. Her throat went dry. The king?

Something was wrong. Panic clawed at her insides. She took a step back instinctively, her body tensing, her mind racing. Was this Zahir? Had Akram betrayed her? She searched his face for answers, but his expression remained calm, controlled—too controlled. The silence stretched between them.

"Go," he said.

She hesitated, but there was no other choice. Forcing herself to move forward, she stepped toward the massive doors as they creaked open.

The courtroom was vast, its towering walls adorned with intricate gold inlay. Chandeliers cast a dim, golden glow over the chamber, and the scent of burning sandalwood lingered in the air. The weight of the room pressed down on her, its grandeur doing nothing to ease the suffocating tension that curled around her chest.

Then, a voice—smooth, assured.

"We've been waiting for you for a long time, Vishakha."

Her heart stilled.

A man sat at the centre of the room, his stance regal, his dark gaze sharp and assessing. He wasn't Zahir. He wasn't anyone she had expected. Recognition hit her like a blow. Raza Khan. The fourth son of Qasim Khan, the Mughal ruler of the Deccan.

Her mind reeled. Raza Khan? Not Zahir? This was something else entirely. But before she could fully grasp the implications, her eyes fell on another figure seated beside him.

Saira.

Vishakha froze.

The breath left her lungs, her confusion turning to alarm.

"What is this?" she whispered, barely able to push the words out.

Saira looked at her, but there was no relief in her gaze, no explanation, only something unreadable—something that deepened Vishakha's distress.

Nothing made sense. Why was Raza Khan waiting for her? Why was Saira here? What had she just walked into?

Vishakha's pulse thundered in her ears as she stood in the grand courtroom, facing Raza Khan and Saira. The weight of their gazes pressed against her like an invisible force, demanding answers.

Raza leaned back in his cushioned seat, his fingers idly tracing the rim of his cup. His voice was smooth, unhurried. "Saira and I are in Agra to see the grand monument my father is building," he said. "It is magnificent. Once complete, it will be unlike anything the world has ever seen." He smiled faintly. "And yet, I find my curiosity drawn elsewhere."

His curious eyes met Vishakha's. "My spies tell me you are here as well. And I hear that Zahir has been looking for you." He tilted his head slightly. "You have something that he wants." His smile didn't reach his eyes. "I would like to know what that is."

Vishakha stiffened, her mind racing.

She had spent so long running, hiding, keeping her secret buried in the depths of her soul. But now, she was cornered. Raza's presence here… was it coincidence? Or something else?

She forced herself to stay composed. "And why would that interest you, Raza Khan?" she asked cautiously.

Raza chuckled, swirling the dark liquid in his cup. "Let's call it divine intervention," he said. "It's as if the gods themselves wanted us to meet."

Vishakha narrowed her eyes. "Or perhaps Zahir's enemies are simply too eager to see him fall."

Raza's expression darkened slightly. "That is true," he admitted. He leaned forward, resting his forearms on his knees. "And I suspect you are one of them."

Vishakha inhaled sharply, trying to read his face. Could she trust him? Was this a trap?

Raza seemed to sense her hesitation. He exhaled, then said, "I don't blame you for being wary, Vishakha. You have every reason to be. But you are out of options." His gaze sharpened. "You can either tell me what you know, or you can keep running for the rest of your life. Zahir will never stop looking for you. You know that, don't you?"

Vishakha swallowed. He was right.

Saira shifted in her seat; her voice softer but filled with steel. "I told my brother everything, Vishakha," she said. "About what Zahir did to me. How he used me." Her fingers trembled as they clutched the folds of her silk dupatta. "He made me believe I was important to him. And when he had no use for me, he discarded me like I was nothing."

Raza's gaze darkened. "I don't trust Zahir," he said bluntly. "I never have." His voice lowered. "His rise to power was too easy. Too convenient. My father may not see it, but I do." He met her gaze. "It is not a coincidence that two of my brothers died within a year of his marriage to Amina."

Vishakha's breath caught.

She had suspected it. But hearing it from Raza himself…

Raza exhaled; his voice quiet yet firm. "I know something doesn't add up. But my father is blind to it. And my sister…" His lips pressed together. "Amina is under his charm. She won't hear a word against him."

Vishakha's hands clenched at her sides. She had spent so long guarding her secret, not knowing who to trust. But now, here was a man whose hatred for Zahir ran just as deep as hers. Maybe she couldn't trust Raza as a man, but she could trust his hatred—hatred for the man who had hurt his sister.

Her heart pounded as she made her decision. Her voice was barely above a whisper.

"I know something that can destroy him."

The room seemed to tighten around her.

Raza leaned in; his eyes gleaming with interest. "Then now is the time, Vishakha," he said softly. "Tell me."

The room was brimming with tension, the flickering torches casting dancing shadows across the polished marble. Vishakha inhaled deeply, steadying herself. She had spent months running, hiding, bleeding for this truth. And now, the moment of reckoning had arrived. She met Raza's sharp gaze.

"You're right, King Raza," she said. "None of this is a coincidence."

Saira tensed beside her brother, her fingers digging into the fabric of her dress. Raza remained still, but his eyes burned with something dangerous.

Vishakha continued, "I left Zahir because I saw through him. I was the only one who did. I was the only one who knew the extent of his cunning, his ruthlessness." She let out a breath. "I saw his darkness up close, and I knew—I had to get away before he swallowed me whole."

Raza's face tensed. "And yet, you stayed in the Mughal court."

Vishakha nodded. "Because I knew he wouldn't stop. When Malik was accused of treason, I was still working with Zahir. But I was kept in the dark. He never included me in his plan." Her voice grew sharp. "And yet, I always had my suspicions."

Raza narrowed his eyes.

"Even after I left him, I couldn't forget what happened to Malik," Vishakha continued. "So, I dug deeper. And what I found was exactly what I imagined." She locked eyes with Raza. "He framed Malik."

Saira gasped.

"I started digging," Vishakha continued. "I found evidence that Zahir had fabricated documents and bribed officers to give false testimonies. Malik was innocent, but Zahir needed him out of the way. He wanted Malik's Position. And once the charges were set, Malik was executed before he could even plead his case."

Raza's hands curled into fists. "And no one suspected?"

"No one did." Vishakha's voice was bitter. "He was too careful. Too convincing."

Raza exhaled sharply, but his expression remained stable.

Vishakha pressed on. "I was still piecing together the truth when I heard about his marriage to Amina. And just a few months later—Zain was dead."

Saira exhaled sharply.

"Prince Suleiman, the youngest, was sent to Bengal to take his place," Vishakha continued. "Emperor Qasim Khan was suddenly left with no sons in Dilli. And who stood beside him, whispering in his ear?"

Raza's voice was cold. "Zahir."

Vishakha nodded.

"Then King Imran Khan died in Allahabad. And Emperor Qasim, blinded by grief and blinded by Zahir's charm, made Zahir the ruler of Allahabad."

A muscle twitched in Raza's jaw.

"I knew Zahir was behind it all," Vishakha said, her voice steely. "But I needed proof." She took a breath before continuing. "Both Zain and Imran died from battle injuries, or so it was said. But both were treated by the same healer."

Raza narrowed his eyes. "Who?"

"A man named Moin."

Raza glanced at Saira before looking back at Vishakha. "Moin?"

Vishakha nodded. "A skilled healer, but more importantly, a man on Danish's payroll."

Saira inhaled sharply. "Danish… Zahir's personal spy?"

Vishakha's lips curled bitterly. "Yes."

Raza's fingers tapped against the armrest, his mind clearly racing.

"I had to find Moin," Vishakha said. "If I could get him to talk, I would have the proof I needed. I tracked him to a village between Allahabad and Devran."

"And?" Raza's voice was sharp.

Vishakha's lips quirked. "Moin was intelligent, but like all men who think themselves untouchable, he had two flaws—drinking and women."

Raza smirked slightly, but his eyes remained watchful.

"So, I sent a prostitute to his house," Vishakha continued. "Someone who could drink with him, make him feel powerful."

Saira looked at her, horrified. "You—"

"He spent the night with her," Vishakha said, cutting her off. "And under the heavy influence of alcohol and arrogance, he told her everything. How he was 'all-powerful.' How he had killed two kings." Her voice turned razor-sharp. "And I was standing outside, listening to every word."

Raza exhaled slowly, absorbing her words.

"I had my proof." Vishakha's voice softened, but only slightly. "I just needed to get to Dilli and tell Emperor Qasim."

"But Danish saw you," Raza guessed.

Vishakha's smile was grim. "Yes. I don't know if he suspected anything at first. He didn't stop me. But I know he must have gone straight to Moin." Her voice darkened. "And whatever Moin told him, it was enough to send Zahir's men after me."

Raza frowned. "That was your last interaction involving Moin?"

Vishakha shook her head. "Yes, I don't know what happened to him. I've been running ever since."

The silence in the room stretched.

Raza let out a long breath. Then, slowly, he turned toward Saira. "You were right," he said. "Zahir didn't just betray you. He betrayed our family. Our blood."

Saira's hands trembled. "I told you…" her voice was barely above a whisper. "I told you he couldn't be trusted."

Raza's gaze darkened. "I never trusted him." His fingers curled into fists. "But I didn't have proof." Now, he did.

A slow, dangerous smile crept onto his lips. "This changes everything."

Vishakha watched him carefully. She had seen many men burn with rage. But the fire in Raza's eyes was cold, calculated. He wasn't angry—he was ready.

He turned back to her. "My spies had suspicions too. They found traces of Moin's betrayal." He paused. "They tried to track him down."

Vishakha stilled. "And?"

Raza's voice was sharp as a blade. "Before they could reach him, he was found dead in his house."

Vishakha's stomach dropped.

Raza's next words were even colder. "The girl with him was dead too."

Saira gasped.

Vishakha closed her eyes for a brief moment. So that's what happened. Moin had confessed, and Zahir—or Danish—had tied up the loose ends.

"It's all coming together now," Raza said, his tone eerily calm. "I always suspected Zahir's rise to power wasn't a coincidence. Two of my brothers, dead within a year of his marriage to Amina?" His lips curled in disgust. "It was too convenient."

His voice turned lethal. "My father is blind. Amina is blind. But I am not." He exhaled. "And now, I have all the reasons to act."

Saira was still staring at him, wide-eyed. "You mean…"

"Yes." Raza's eyes gleamed. "Zahir will pay for his crimes."

The finality in his tone sent a chill down Vishakha's spine.

Then, Raza's expression shifted, something flickering in his gaze. "My spies tell me Zahir is in Agra," he said. "They've confirmed his arrival. But they lost his trail."

Vishakha's lips curled into a knowing smile. "If he's in Agra," she said, her voice steady, "I know where he is."

Raza's eyes locked onto hers. A slow, predatory smile spread across his face. "Then let's go find him."

Chapter 13

The moon hung high in the night sky as Rana and his group rode through the narrow, winding path leading to the city's underground market. The rhythmic sound of hooves against dry earth filled the silence between them, punctuated by the occasional rustling of leaves as the wind whispered through the trees.

Behind them, Aasif rode with a composed yet wary expression. He had seen much of this world—far too much. Amar and Chandan, however, were not as patient. Their curiosity burned through the silence.

"What kind of things are sold in this market?" Amar asked, adjusting his grip on the reins.

Aasif smirked slightly but did not turn his head. "On the surface, it looks like any other market," he said. "Grains, spices, silk, jewellery... the usual. But behind the curtains, a far darker trade takes place."

"Like what?" Chandan pressed, leaning slightly forward.

Aasif's eyes glinted under the moonlight. "Weapons. Afeem. Herbs that can make you lose your senses. Stolen gems and precious stones. And worst of all—women and children."

Amar and Chandan stiffened. A chill ran through the group.

"No one knows about this?" Amar asked, his voice laced with disbelief.

Aasif let out a hollow chuckle. "Only the right people know." He glanced at Rana, whose muscles were taut with restraint, his grip on the reins firm. "Rich men, foreigners, nobles with twisted desires. They pay hefty sums for what they want."

Rana's mind raced. The mere thought of Pari being dragged into such a fate sent a sharp, cold fear through his veins. Was she already sold? Was he too late?

Aasif continued, unaware of Rana's spiralling thoughts. "When women and children disappear from their villages, people don't ask too many questions. Some say the forest took them. Others believe a demon snatched them away. The traffickers rely on these superstitions. Fear keeps the villagers from searching too hard."

Chandan's fists clenched. "You're telling me no one tried to find the truth so far?"

"They have someone in the village feeding these fears," Aasif said darkly. "Someone who works for them. Encourages these stories. Ensures no one goes looking."

Rana's eyes burned with rage. "Someone from the village?" he asked, his voice low and dangerous.

Aasif met his gaze. "Always."

Silence fell between them. The truth of it all was suffocating.

Moments later, Aasif pointed ahead. "There," he said, nodding toward a looming structure.

In the distance, shrouded in darkness, stood a small fort. Its stone walls were weathered and cracked, overtaken by creeping vines. It had an eerie stillness to it, as if the air itself refused to move near it.

"Years ago, this belonged to a rich family," Aasif said. "But now, people believe it is haunted. No one dares to come here after dark. That makes it the perfect place to hide."

Rana inhaled deeply, steadying himself. His mind was set.

Aasif pulled his horse to a stop. "I have told you all I can. From here, you are on your own." His voice held a finality to it.

Rana met his gaze and gave a small nod. "Thank you."

The others echoed their gratitude, though their eyes remained locked on the ominous structure ahead.

Aasif turned his horse and disappeared into the night, leaving them standing before the place where the nightmare lived.

Rana exhaled sharply. "Let's move."

And with that, they tied their horses and prepared for what lay ahead.

The four men stood at a distance from the fort; their horses tethered to a tree several paces away. There was tension all around as their eyes locked on the looming fortress before them, its high walls casting ominous shadows in the dimming moonlight. The stone structure seemed impenetrable, a silent sentinel guarding whatever secrets lay within. Rana's mind raced as he scanned the fort from every angle, trying to find a way in. His gaze moved across the two floors of the building, the single entrance, the six windows—three on the ground floor, three on the first.

His hand rested on the hilt of his sword, the weight of the weapon grounding him. "The main entrance is out of the question," Rana muttered, his voice low but firm. "Too many guards. It's a trap waiting to happen. The ground-floor windows are probably guarded too—they're a potential escape route for whoever's inside. And the first-floor windows? Grilled. No point in wasting time there."

A heavy silence hung in the air as the others absorbed his words. The fort seemed to mock them, silent and impregnable. The night air was growing colder, the distant chirps of insects only adding to the oppressive atmosphere.

Suresh shifted uneasily. "Let's split up. Try to find a way in from different sides."

Amar's sharp laugh cut through the tension like a blade. "The stupidest idea I've ever heard. We're a group for a reason. Four heads are better than one. Splitting up will only get us caught."

Rana's gaze locked on Amar. For a moment, the two men stood face to face, the weight of their shared history simmering between them. But then Rana nodded in agreement, his voice steady. "Amar's right. We stay together. We've come this far—we don't split now."

His eyes moved over the landscape again, narrowing as they caught sight of something unexpected—a broken tree nearby. Its trunk had been hacked away, most likely for firewood, but its large, weathered log lay discarded, waiting. Something clicked in Rana's mind. He turned to the others, his voice low but decisive.

"We'll go up from the terrace."

Suresh raised an eyebrow. "And how do you suggest we get up there, Rana? Have you learned to fly when I wasn't looking?"

Rana didn't flinch; his focus unwavering. "We use that log." His eyes met each of theirs, the intensity of his words slicing through the doubt. "We position it against the south wall. There's no window there, and it'll be high enough to reach the terrace. We make sure it's quiet, and we move fast. But we have to be careful—if we make a sound, it's all over."

Chandan let out a soft whistle. "This is a deadly idea."

"But it's the best shot we have," Suresh replied, his voice steady despite the danger.

The four men moved quickly, lifting the log with surprising ease. It was light in their hands, the wood dried out from days of exposure to the sun. "Good for us," Amar remarked with a strained smile. "Less weight, more speed."

Together, they carried the log toward the south wall of the fort, their steps muffled by the lush grass beneath their feet. When they reached the wall, Rana nodded. "Place it here."

They stood the log slanting, the long length of it resting against the wall, just below the terrace. "Perfect," Chandan whispered, a grin tugging at his lips.

Rana moved to the base of the log. "I'll go first. Stay quiet and stay low."

With his half-spear and sword secured at his waist, Rana began to climb. The others held the log steady, their hands gripping the rough wood, hearts pounding in their chests. The quiet creak of the log under their weight felt too loud under those circumstances.

Rana reached the top of the wall, pulling himself onto the terrace with practiced ease. He signalled the others to follow. One by one, they climbed, each man silently taking his place behind Rana. Suresh was the second to reach the top, followed by Amar, and then Chandan. They stood together on the terrace, a silent victory in their eyes. But as quickly as the thrill of success flared, the weight of what lay ahead settled in.

Rana drew his sword, his half-spear at the ready. The soft clang of steel on steel was barely audible in the heavy silence. They moved cautiously toward the stairs leading down into the fort. Each step was premeditated. They had made it this far—but the real test had just begun.

Rana's hand brushed the edge of the terrace door, the faintest hint of a draft whispering through the cracks. He leaned forward, his eyes narrowing as he peeked around the corner.

His heart skipped a beat.

A lone guard sat by the door, his back to them. He was lounging, unaware of the danger looming just feet away. But his presence was a problem. A very real problem.

Rana signalled to the others to hold back, his heart hammering in his chest. They could take the guard—four against one would be easy enough. But there was something more pressing. The sound. If the guard made a noise, if his cries echoed through the fort, the rest would be on them in an instant. It would all be over before it had even begun.

"Stay quiet," Rana whispered, his voice a low hiss. "I'll take care of him." He secured the half-spear and sword at his waist.

His eyes flickered to Suresh. "Give me your knife."

Suresh hesitated for a moment, but then he nodded and drew the blade from his belt. He handed it over with a steady hand, his eyes meeting Rana's with silent understanding. The weight of what was to come pressed down on them all. There was no room for error.

Rana held the knife, feeling its cold steel against his palm. The guard was just a few paces away. His eyes flickered back to the others, who stood frozen in place. This was their only chance.

Rana moved, each step a whisper in the night – quiet, swift, deadly. His steps were steady, each one calculated. His breath was shallow, the rhythmic thud of his heart pounding in his ears, drowning out all other sounds. Every muscle in his body was taut, ready to spring into action at the slightest hint of danger.

The guard sat there, slouched against the wall, his back to them. The only sound was the soft rustle of his cloak as he shifted slightly, unaware of the danger creeping toward him. Rana's eyes narrowed. Why wasn't the guard moving at all? His mind raced, analysing the situation. The guard should have been more alert, more aware of the possibility of intruders. But there he was, motionless.

As Rana drew closer, a faint, unmistakable scent reached his nostrils—alcohol. The guard had been drinking, and heavily. His breath was fogged with it, a telltale sign that he was drunk. Rana's grip on the dagger tightened. A chance. He realised- the guard is asleep.

He signalled to the others, motioning them to move. The three men behind him followed in a line, moving with precision, their boots barely making a sound on the stone floor. They were shadows in the night, silent and deadly.

Rana reached the guard's side, standing motionless for a moment. He leaned close to Suresh and whispered, his voice barely audible. "The guard is fast asleep. Take his weapon, but be careful. Don't make a sound."

Suresh nodded, his expression hardening as he slowly crouched beside the guard. His hand reached for the weapon at the man's side, moving with the slow deliberation of a man who knew the slightest noise could ruin everything. The cold metal of the guard's sword slid from its sheath with a quiet hiss, and Suresh eased back, weapon in hand.

One by one, the three men passed the unconscious guard, moving toward the stairs, each one careful not to disturb the slumbering figure. The only sound now was the faint creaking of the floor beneath their feet.

But then, as they were nearly at the base of the stairs, disaster struck.

Chandan, his sword still tied at his waist, stepped too close to the guard, and in the silence, the unmistakable clink of steel on stone rang out. The sound shattered the quiet.

The guard's eyes snapped open. He groggily blinked, his hand instinctively reaching for his weapon. But before he could even utter a sound, Rana's reflexes kicked in.

In one fluid motion, he was on the guard, his hand clamping down on the man's mouth with terrifying speed. The guard's eyes widened in terror, his body thrashing as he tried to scream, but Rana's grip was iron-clad.

The blade in Rana's hand flashed as he pulled it across the guard's throat. Blood sprayed, a hot, crimson mist that splattered across the floor, the walls, and even Rana's face. The guard's body went rigid for a moment, a strangled gurgle rising in his throat before his life drained away. Rana held him tight, his hands steady, until the thrashing stopped and the guard's body went limp.

The silence that followed was deafening. Only the sound of their own breathing filled the space.

Chandan, wide-eyed with guilt, gave a subtle, apologetic gesture, his face pale in the dim light. Amar's gaze was cold, disappointment etched into his features as he shook his head. But Rana didn't look back. His focus remained unbroken; his eyes hard as steel.

"Keep moving," Rana whispered, his voice low, the edge of authority clear. "We're not finished yet."

The group moved swiftly down the stairs, adrenaline coursing through their veins. As they reached the first floor, they halted in front of three doors. The dim light barely illuminated the space, casting flickering shadows that seemed to stretch and twist with the shifting of their bodies.

One door was near the stairs, leading toward the north. The second was toward the west, and the third to the east. The tension in the air intensified, and Rana's mind raced as he weighed their options.

He glanced at the others. "Let's go together, one room at a time," he ordered, his voice steady despite the pounding of his heart.

The others nodded in agreement, their swords drawn and ready, their movements synchronized. There was no turning back now. Every step was a risk, every sound could be their last. But they had come too far to falter now.

With a final glance toward the door ahead, Rana pushed forward, his sword held high, his eyes locked on the path ahead. The true danger was just beginning.

Rana's eyes narrowed as he approached the eastern room. He paused, crouching low behind the stone archway. His breath was steady, but his heart raced, echoing in his chest. Slowly, he peered around the corner, scanning the room for any signs of danger. The space was eerily quiet, no movement, no guards in sight.

He glanced back at the others—Chandan, Amar, and Suresh—who were waiting with baited breath, each of them tense, ready for whatever was behind that door. Rana gave a subtle nod, signalling them to move forward.

They moved as one, slipping into the room with quiet precision. The air inside was filled with the smell of must and old straw. The flickering shadows from the narrow windows cast long, haunting figures across the stone floor. And then they saw them—children.

Dozens of small faces, their bodies huddled in every corner of the room, each one wrapped in tattered clothes, some sleeping, some wide-eyed, fearful. A cold dread gripped Rana's heart as he took in the sight.

Chandan, Amar, and Suresh spread out across the room, each of them searching with careful precision. Their hearts pounded in sync with the heavy weight of anticipation. The desperation was palpable—each of them wondering, is this where Pari is? They shuffled through the room, eyes scanning over each child, hoping, praying to find her.

But the children in front of them were not Pari. A sharp, sinking disappointment gripped Rana's chest as his gaze met Chandan's. Neither of them had found her.

Amar's face darkened, and Rana could feel the frustration in the air. Suresh, ever the pragmatic one, moved forward, gently lifting a small child's wrist to check the chain that bound them to the iron lock near the window. His fingers brushed the metal, a silent confirmation that this was where the children had been kept. All the children had different chains, but they all bounded them to a single lock on the grilled window.

"Do you know a girl named Pari?" Rana whispered urgently to one of the girls awake, his voice a quiet rasp of desperation. His breath caught as he looked into her wide, fearful eyes.

The girl shook her head, her lips trembling as she avoided his gaze. The others around her did the same. They didn't know Pari.

Rana felt his heart fall. Was it too late? The thought gnawed at him like a ravenous beast. Was she already gone? Had they failed her before they'd even had a chance?

Just as he began to rise, ready to give the signal to move on, the silence was shattered.

One of the younger children, a small girl no older than seven, tugged at Rana's sleeve with trembling hands. Her eyes were wide with tears, her voice barely audible. "Please, please save us," she whispered desperately. "Take us home... please."

Her voice was like a dagger to his chest, the weight of her pain settling on his shoulders like an unbearable burden. Other children began to stir, their tear-streaked faces turning toward him. Their small hands reached for him, desperate, pleading.

"We want to go home. Please..." they murmured in broken sobs, their voices a chorus of desperation.

Rana's heart twisted, the pain of their pleas nearly choking him. But he stayed calm. He had to stay focused. He shushed them gently, his voice low and steady despite the chaos inside him. "I promise you; I'll take you away," he whispered fiercely. "But you must stay quiet. I need to find Pari. Please, just a little longer."

The children wiped their tears, nodding, their tiny hands still clutching at his arms. Rana's gaze softened for a moment, but he quickly shook it off. He had to keep moving.

With a last lingering look at the children, he motioned to Chandan, Amar, and Suresh. They exchanged silent nods, the weight of their own disappointment evident on their faces. But they knew there was no time to waste.

They moved out of the room in a fluid motion, their footsteps nearly silent on the stone floor. There was suspense in the air, the walls closing in around them as they ventured deeper into the unknown. The children's voices echoed in his ears, their cries for help seared into his mind. How could he leave them?

As they moved down the corridor, the heavy silence hung between them. Each man carried his own doubts, his own fears. But Rana's resolve was unshakable. He would find Pari. He would bring her back.

Rana's heart pounded in his chest as he approached the west door, his senses razor-sharp. The tension was palpable, each step heavier than the last. He took a deep breath and peered through the crack in the door. The room was quiet, but something about the silence made his instincts scream.

He signalled the others to follow, his movements slow and conscious. The door creaked open just enough for them to slip inside. The room, like the others, was dimly lit, shadows creeping along the walls, curling into corners where the light couldn't reach. The sound of chains clinking echoed faintly—chains that bound these girls to the iron lock on the window grill. The same grim sight, but this time, it was girls, not children.

Rana's eyes scanned the room, finding only 2 or 3 awake, their gazes hollow with fear, their eyes darting to the door, waiting for any sign of movement. Rana's hand shot up instinctively—his fingers pressed to his lips, shushing them gently but firmly.

"We're here to save you," he whispered. His voice was calm, but there was a sharpness in it, an urgency that reverberated in the cold, stagnant air.

He moved further in, scanning the faces of the girls. Their eyes were wide, haunted, flickering between hope and despair. But none of them was Pari.

Rana turned to Chandan, Amar, and Suresh; his voice low. "This room doesn't have Pari."

They nodded in quiet understanding, but still, the weight of the failure loomed over them.

Rana's gaze fell on a girl, maybe sixteen, sitting near the back of the room. Her face was tear-streaked, her hands clutching the chains, eyes red from crying. Rana crouched down in front of her, his voice gentle, but no less determined. "Have you seen a girl named Pari?"

The girl's eyes filled with fresh tears, her body trembling. She glanced at her companions in the room, as if unsure whether to speak. Finally, her voice broke. "She was my friend," she whispered, barely audible.

Rana's breath caught in his chest. Was? His heart skipped a beat. Chandan, Amar, and Suresh froze, their faces pale as the girl's words sank in.

"What do you mean, 'was'?" Rana asked, his voice barely above a whisper, his pulse hammering in his ears.

The girl sniffled, her face a picture of sorrow. "They took her... they took her yesterday in the market. The others... the men... they gave money to the men who took us from our villages..." She choked on a sob, the weight of the memory crashing down on her.

Rana's heart shattered at the sound of her voice, the words like daggers in his chest. Pari is gone. She is gone. They were too late. The realization hit harder than any blow. He looked at Chandan, Amar, and Suresh, their faces a mirror of his own despair. They had come so far, fought so hard... and now, it seemed it was all for nothing.

The girl wiped her eyes, her voice trembling with grief. "She was my best friend... I knew her since my childhood."

Rana's expression froze, his mind racing. This girl... she knew her since childhood? But no, this wasn't possible. The girl was around sixteen, and she wasn't from Devran. If she had known Pari, he would've known about it. He clenched his fists, his breath coming faster now.

"You knew her since childhood?" Rana asked, his voice harsh, though his eyes were searching the girl's face for any sign of miscommunication.

The girl nodded, her head hanging low. "She was my neighbour," she whispered.

A surge of mixed emotions flooded Rana—relief, confusion, sorrow—all tangled together. She wasn't talking about his Pari. This girl was talking about someone else, someone with the same name. A small glimmer of hope flickered in his chest. Pari might still be here. She could still be here.

But the girl's sorrow still tore at him. She had lost her best friend, her childhood companion. Rana swallowed hard, swallowing the bitter taste of helplessness. He placed a hand on the girl's shoulder, his voice soft but firm. "I promise I'll take you away from here. But please, stay quiet. I need to find Pari first. I'll get you out. Stay safe."

The girl nodded, wiping her eyes with trembling hands, a faint, sad smile curving her lips. She couldn't say more, the pain too raw, but the gratitude in her eyes spoke volumes.

Rana gave her one last look before standing up, signalling to Chandan, Amar, and Suresh. They needed to move. He turned toward the door, his heart heavy but burning with new determination. Pari was still out there.

They had to keep looking. They couldn't stop. Not now. Not when they were so close.

The room, the weight of their mission, it all hung in the air. But they had no time to waste. There was still one more room. And in it, they prayed they would find the girl who had already lived a life too dark for her age.

The last door loomed before them, the final barrier standing between them and the end of their mission. Rana's heart thudded in his chest; each beat a heavy echo in his ears.

He couldn't let himself get distracted. He couldn't let hope overwhelm him now—there was still so much to do.

With a quiet breath, he peeked into the room, his eyes scanning the shadows. His gut twisted as he saw the sight he dreaded—the familiar chains, the same tragic scene as the other rooms. The room was filled with children, all of them asleep, chained like animals, bound by the same fate.

He stepped inside carefully, his every muscle tense, his eyes darting from one child to another. Chandan, Amar, and Suresh moved in behind him, each of them fighting their own emotions, knowing this was their last chance.

Rana's heart raced as he knelt down beside each child, searching, praying. Please let her be here. Please. His hands trembled as he gently moved aside the blankets, his eyes scouring the faces, one by one. His breath caught every time he saw a face that wasn't hers, the disappointment heavy in his chest.

But then—there.

His eyes locked onto the familiar, delicate face. His heart skipped a beat, and everything around him seemed to fade into the background. Pari.

He fell to his knees beside her, overwhelmed by a surge of emotions. His eyes blurred with tears as he stared at the girl who had been missing for so long. It was her; it was finally her. His Pari, the girl who had been his heart, his hope, his guiding light through all the darkness.

He reached out and gently shook her, the words barely forming on his lips. "Pari…"

She stirred, her brow furrowing as she awoke, her eyes flickering open. The moment Pari's eyes fluttered open, everything around her seemed to pause. Her gaze locked onto Rana, the man who had been her saviour in every whispered prayer, the light in her darkest hours. At first, her eyes were wide with confusion, clouded by the lingering effects of fear and exhaustion. Then, recognition struck her like a thunderbolt, and her lips parted, her breath catching in her throat.

For a split second, it seemed like she might scream, a desperate cry of terror, of helplessness. But before the sound could escape, Rana's hand was over her mouth—gentle yet firm, his touch soft but grounding.

"Shh, it's okay, Pari. It's me. I'm here. I'm here to save you," Rana whispered, his voice hoarse from holding back the flood of emotions threatening to drown him.

And then, as if a dam had burst, her eyes welled up with tears, her chest heaving with shallow breaths. The recognition, the relief, the weight of so many nights spent in terror—all of it broke through the fragile walls of her heart. Her body trembled as she reached for him, her small hands trembling like leaves in the wind, and she pulled him close, burying her face against his chest.

"I knew you would come..." she whispered, her voice barely audible, lost in the muffled sobs that tore through her. "I knew my Rana bhaiya would save me..."

The words sliced through Rana's heart, each syllable a jagged shard of truth. The simple, beautiful faith that Pari had held onto all this time, the unspoken belief that he would never abandon her, that somehow, he would find a way to rescue her from this nightmare—it shattered him. His heart swelled with a love so fierce, so overwhelming, that for a moment, he couldn't breathe.

His arms wrapped around her as if to shield her from the world, to hold her together, to never let her go again. Tears flooded his eyes; tears he had fought so hard to keep at bay. His fingers dug into her back, as if afraid that if he loosened his grip, she might vanish, might slip away like a dream. He buried his face in her hair, his tears falling freely now, his breath hitching as he whispered her name over and over again—Pari... Pari...

She trembled in his arms, and the sound of her cries, soft and broken, broke him further. The girl who had been lost to him, the girl who had been torn away from everything she loved—she was finally in his arms again. Safe. She was finally safe.

"I'm so sorry, Pari," Rana choked out, his voice cracking under the weight of the guilt he carried. "I'm so sorry it took me so long. I should've found you sooner. I should've—"

Pari pulled back just enough to look up at him, her tear-streaked face filled with a mixture of pain and love, of gratitude and relief. She cupped his face with her small hands, the touch gentle, but firm, as if grounding him in the moment.

"I knew you would find me, Rana bhaiya," she continued, her voice still shaking, but filled with a quiet strength. "You always find me. You always protect me. I knew you wouldn't give up."

Her words were simple, but they were everything. They were a testament of love, of trust, of bond that they shared, even in the darkest of times. And as they embraced again, as she clung to him with all the strength she had left, Rana's heart ached with the depth of her belief in him.

He held her tighter, as if trying to weave the moment into his soul, to hold onto this tiny sliver of peace before the chaos could take it all away again. The tears didn't stop. He let them fall, letting his grief and joy intertwine, because in this moment, everything else faded.

All that mattered was that she was in his arms, that the period of pain, of separation, had come to an end. She was alive. She was here. She was safe.

And as their tears mingled together, as they clung to one another, Rana whispered into her ear, his voice hoarse but determined, "I'll never leave you again. I swear it, Pari. I swear it."

And in that moment, the world outside ceased to exist. There were no chains, no enemies, no danger—only the two of them, together, in the silence of their bond. And in that silence, their hearts spoke a thousand words.

Chandan, Amar, and Suresh stepped forward, their faces softening as they watched the reunion unfold. Each of them had their own share of emotion, the weight of the journey lifting from their shoulders. One by one, they moved in to join the hug, their arms around both of them.

Tears flowed freely, unspoken, but understood—this was more than they had ever dreamed of. They had found her. They had saved her.

For a moment, they all just sat there, locked in an embrace, feeling the warmth of each other's presence, knowing that no matter what came next, they had done it. They had succeeded.

But the moment was fleeting. The escape was far from over.

Rana pulled back slightly, his hands still on Pari's shoulders as he looked into her eyes. His heart raced, a mixture of relief and something deeper in his chest. His fingers brushed against the ribbon he had carried with him throughout the journey—a token of the promise he made to himself. Without a word, he pulled the ribbon out of his tunic and gently, he fastened it into her hair, tying it with tender care.

The small act seemed to ground him, to bring a fleeting sense of peace, as if in that moment, everything was as it should be. But that peace didn't last long. His mind quickly shifted back to the situation at hand. They had found her, yes, but now they had to get out. The question was—How?

***

The night was deathly silent, save for the distant crackling of torches in the courtyard below. The stars above provided little comfort—this was no divine intervention, no blessing from the gods. This was a battle of wits, and every second mattered. To discuss the plan of how to escape, the four of them stood on the terrace, their minds racing as the weight of the situation bore down on them.

"We need to find a way to break Pari's chains without making noise," Chandan whispered urgently, his eyes darting between his companions.

Amar let out a frustrated sigh. "You're a blacksmith, aren't you?" Chandan asked, looking at him.

"I'm a blacksmith, not a magician," Amar snapped, rubbing his temples. "I can find a weak link in the chain, but even then, breaking it will make noise."

Suresh pinched the bridge of his nose, muttering under his breath. "And that noise is going to wake up all the kids. Even if the guards don't hear the chain breaking, they'll hear forty terrified children."

A heavy silence hung between them. The weight of reality was crushing.

"We take them all," Rana finally said.

Suresh's head snapped up. "Don't be ridiculous."

"We don't leave anyone behind," Rana said, his voice firm, unwavering. "I made a promise to those girls, and I intend to keep it."

Suresh let out a mocking laugh, his patience wearing thin. "A promise? Are you serious? Rana, you think you're a God? Like Sree Ram? Your promise can be broken, Rana. You don't have to play the noble warrior. This isn't a story. This is real life, and real life isn't fair. We can't save them all."

Rana turned to him slowly, his eyes burning with something fierce. "Can you live with yourself if we leave them behind?"

There was deadly silence, and for a moment, everything seemed still. Suresh clenched his jaw, looking away. His fingers curled into fists. "Yes." But his voice lacked conviction.

Rana didn't falter. He spoke with calm resolve. "Then go."

Suresh's eyes snapped back to him, his expression one of surprise.

Without a second thought, Rana gestured to the wooden log. "Climb down. Go back. Save yourself. I won't stop you. No one will blame you."

Suresh stood frozen, Rana's words ringing in his ears. Go back. Save yourself.

His fists clenched at his sides. His throat felt dry. He wanted to say something—argue, justify, curse—but nothing came out. His body felt heavy, as if the weight of the decision was pressing down on his chest.

His mind raced. Am I really the kind of man who would turn away? Leave behind children—girls—who have no one else?

But another thought fought against it. This isn't my fight. I didn't ask for this. I didn't sign up to play hero.

Tension flickered across his face as he glanced at Rana. There was no anger in Rana's face, no mockery—just quiet, unwavering resolve. The same expression he'd worn when they first set out on this madness of a rescue.

Suresh's heart pounded. If I leave now, I live. I walk away. I survive.

He inhaled sharply, trying to steady himself, but a sickening feeling churned in his stomach. The faces of the girls flashed in his mind. The ones who clutched Rana's hands, begging for help. The ones who whispered, please take us home.

Would they even have a home left to return to? Would they ever see their families again?

His feet felt like lead as Suresh took a step toward the log. The other three watched him, and he watched them back. His hands trembled slightly at his sides. His breathing was heavy.

Another step.

He swallowed hard. One step. Just one more.

And then—he stopped.

His fingers twitched. The thought of climbing down, escaping, vanishing into the night—it should have brought relief. But instead, it made his chest ache.

Would he ever be able to sleep again if he left them?

This is the nature of the world—right and wrong are often nothing more than perspectives shaped by circumstance. If Suresh had been joined by three others, the weight of his choice might have felt lighter. Surrounded by others making the same decision, he could have justified it, convinced himself that leaving was not betrayal but simply survival. But he stood alone. And in that solitude, doubt crept in. The absence of company made his choice heavier, pressing against his conscience in a way it wouldn't have if he had the comfort of shared guilt.

With a sharp inhale, he turned back, his eyes locking onto Rana's. His voice was hoarse, almost begrudging— "What's the plan then?"

Rana allowed the faintest of smirks to flicker across his lips. "I thought you could live with yourself."

Suresh glared at him. "Don't push your luck, Rana. Just tell me the damn plan."

Rana's smirk faded. His expression hardened. He stepped closer, lowering his voice to a whisper. "Listen carefully, because if we mess this up, no one survives."

Chandan, Amar, and Suresh leaned in; their faces set in grim determination. The risk was high. The odds were against them. But they had no choice. Because failure meant condemning forty innocent lives. And that was not an option.

Rana exhaled slowly, steadying himself before gripping the log and making his way down. The rough wood scraped against his palms, but he ignored the sting. The night was silent, apart for the distant rustling of leaves and the faint crackle of a dying torch somewhere beyond the fort walls. His feet touched the ground with barely a whisper.

Stay low. Move fast. The words echoed in his mind, a silent command he dared not ignore.

He crouched, pressing himself against the cold earth as he crawled toward the east window. The stone walls loomed over him like silent sentinels. He reached the edge of the window and carefully peeked inside. His breath slowed.

A single guard—asleep. He took note of it, committing the detail to memory.

Rana's fingers instinctively hovered over the hilt of his sword. "Not yet". He murmured under his breath before slinking away, keeping his movements controlled.

Keeping low, he moved toward the northern side, where the main entrance loomed like the gaping maw of a beast. The heavy wooden doors were closed. *Good.*

Flattening himself against the cold stone wall, he inched toward a narrow window slit. His breath slowed; muscles coiled tight as he peered inside.

Two guards—one awake, one asleep. He registered the detail, filing it away for what came next.

The awake guard sat slouched, his head dipping slightly before jerking back up. He was struggling, battling the weight of exhaustion as it clawed at him, dragging him toward sleep.

Rana pulled back, a faint smirk tugging at his lips. *Not for long.*

He moved again, careful to place each step with precision. The west window. He repeated the process.

Another guard—asleep. He took note of it, the final piece in the puzzle forming in his mind.

He moved quickly towards south side now, heart hammering against his ribs. Once he reached the log, he gripped it and climbed back up, his movements fluid despite the tension surging through his veins.

Reaching the terrace, he joined the others. He wiped the sweat from his brow before speaking.

"Four guards. Three asleep, one awake."

Chandan cursed under his breath. Suresh exhaled sharply.

"They're probably taking turns sleeping," Rana continued.

Suresh shook his head. "Idiots. They don't even know we're already inside."

"Which is why we need to strike together," Rana said, his voice firm. "The guards on the east and west sides are asleep. Suresh, Chandan, you take them out. Climb through the windows. Do it quick, do it clean."

Suresh nodded. Chandan rolled his shoulders, flexing his fingers. "They won't even have time to wake up."

"The north side has two. One asleep, one awake," Rana continued. "I'll take care of them."

Amar's eyes narrowed. "What about me?"

Rana looked at him. "The moment you hear the first sound of a fight downstairs, start breaking the locks."

Amar let out a slow breath. He knew it wouldn't be easy.

"One last adventure," Amar muttered, forcing a grin, though tension lined his face.

"Try not to get killed, guys," Chandan added dryly.

Rana let out a small chuckle. But beneath it, there was steel in his gaze.

They moved closer, their bodies pressing together as they formed a tight circle, their shoulders brushing in the shared weight of what was to come. There were unspoken words, unspoken fears that lingered in the space. Every breath felt drawn from the same place of resolve, a quiet understanding that there was no turning back. For a fleeting moment, they stood there, bound not just by necessity, but by the bond forged in this moment of silent defiance. Without warning, arms shot out in a fierce, brief embrace—strong, urgent, as if the world outside might come crashing in at any second. The hug lasted only a heartbeat, but it was enough.

Rana pulled back first. His eyes met each of theirs, one by one. "Whatever happens, we act together. We strike at the same time. If we don't, we lose our advantage."

Everyone nodded.

"The east and west windows are visible from the north," he reminded them. "Suresh, Chandan—you go in first. Kill them together when I give the signal."

There was tension all around. Then, without another word, they descended. The night stretched. Every second dragged like eternity.

Rana crouched low, pressing himself against the cold stone wall of the fort, his breath steady despite the storm of adrenaline surging through his veins. Chandan crept toward the east window, while Suresh moved toward the west. The three men exchanged glances—silent, sharp, unshaken. Amar climbed down the stairs, sitting at the top of the staircase, hands steadying his sword, waiting for the sound that would begin it all.

One chance. One mistake and everything would crumble.

Chandan and Suresh hoisted themselves through their respective windows, landing with the grace of seasoned predators. They moved like shadows, their swords gripped tightly, eyes locked onto the sleeping guards beside them.

Rana, reaching the north window, peered inside. The dim torchlight flickered across the rough stone walls. His eyes darted between his companions. Chandan was ready. Suresh was in position. The last guard—the only one awake—sat slouched in a chair, absently twirling a dagger between his fingers.

Rana's grip tightened around his half-spear. He raised it in his right hand, his muscles coiling like a drawn bowstring. With his left hand, he signalled—three… two… one.

A whisper of steel. A gasp that never became a scream.

Chandan and Suresh moved as one, their swords slicing through flesh with merciless precision. The guards beside them barely had time to stir before their throats split open, blood pooling silently around their twitching bodies.

At the same moment, Rana let the spear fly.

The weapon cut through the air in a deadly arc. The awake guard barely had time to widen his eyes before the iron tip pierced through his eye socket, lodging deep into his skull. He jerked violently, his body convulsing as he tumbled from his chair, landing with a sickening thud.

The sound shattered the silence.

The fourth guard stirred awake, his groggy confusion turning to panic as he scrambled toward his weapon.

Upstairs, Amar heard the noise. Without hesitation, he ran into the first room and brought his sword down on the first lock, shattering it. The chains rattled violently, the sound threatening to wake every captive inside.

Downstairs, the guard lunged toward his sword, but Chandan and Suresh pounced before he could reach it. He struggled, thrashing, a strangled yell forming in his throat.

Rana didn't hesitate.

He jumped into the room through the window and ran towards the last guard. One step. One strike. One kill. His sword sank into the guard's chest, piercing straight through the heart. The man's body stiffened; eyes frozen in shock before slumping lifelessly. Chandan and Suresh let go, breathing heavily.

There was sudden silence, broken only by the faint drip of blood pooling at their feet. The bodies lay still, lifeless, their final breaths stolen in the blink of an eye.

Chandan's chuckle broke the stillness, nervous and hollow, as he wiped the sweat from his brow. "Well... that was easy," he muttered, though his voice betrayed the tension still gripping him.

Rana shot him a sharp look. "Look for the keys."

They moved quickly, overturning tables and searching the fallen guards. Their hands were still bloodied when—A voice sliced through the air like a dagger.

"What do you think you are doing?"

Their bodies stiffened, hearts leaping into their throats. Rana's hand instinctively gripped the hilt of his sword, his muscles coiling with readiness.

From the black void of the south side of the fort—a side they had ignored, a place untouched by light—something moved. A figure emerged, its presence chilling the air.

It wasn't a man. It was a monster.

He was a giant, at least seven feet tall, his broad shoulders stretching like an iron gate. His arms were bulkier than most men's legs, his chest bare except for deep scars carved into his skin. He carried no weapons. He didn't need them.

Something about him made their blood run cold. A feeling deep in the gut, primal—unnatural. His voice rumbled through the air like distant thunder. "Run-away now... and I won't have to kill you."

For the first time in a long time, something unfamiliar gripped Rana—hesitation. It gnawed at him, a flicker of doubt he hadn't felt in years. But he didn't let it show. His gaze locked onto the figure, his grip tightening around the hilt of his sword, the cold steel grounding him. Every fibre of his being screamed for action, to strike, to fight, but the weight of his mission pressed down on him, relentless. His voice came out low and unwavering, the words heavy with purpose. "We aren't going anywhere without the girls."

The giant smirked. "Then I'll break you first."

Rana took a step forward. "We are three. You are one. Maybe you're the one who should worry."

The smirk widened. "We'll find out soon enough."

Rana didn't hesitate. He moved with practiced precision, instincts taking over. In one fluid motion, he yanked his half-spear from the body of a fallen soldier and hurled it straight at the giant's forehead. The throw was aimed to kill.

But it never reached its target.

With terrifying speed, the giant's hand shot up, catching the spear midair with a loud clap. The sound reverberated through the fort. Rana's breath stilled. His heart pounded in his chest. Without a second thought, the giant twisted his wrist and flung the spear back at them with ease, as if it weighed nothing.

THUNK!

Chandan let out a sharp, agonized scream. The spear had lodged deep into his right arm, pinning him to the ground. His body jerked violently, fingers clawing at the dirt in a desperate attempt to free himself.

Rana and Suresh stood frozen, their minds struggling to process what they had just witnessed.

The giant chuckled—a deep, bone-chilling sound. "Your turn."

Without thinking, Suresh and Rana charged, swords raised, adrenaline coursing through their veins. But the giant moved with an unnatural speed, his fist slamming into Suresh's chest before either of them could react. The impact sent Suresh flying backward, his body crashing to the stone floor with a sickening thud. His sword clattered away, his breath knocked from his lungs, leaving him gasping for air.

At the same time that the giant punched Suresh, Rana lunged, slashing at the giant's arm. The blade sank deep into the flesh, but the giant didn't flinch. His face contorted not in pain, but in fury.

Rana swung again, but this time, the giant dodged effortlessly. The speed with which he moved was impossible for someone of his size.

Rana swung once more. The giant's hand shot out, seizing his wrist in a grip like iron. With a brutal twist, his sword slipped from his grasp.

The giant's other hand reached out and clamped around Rana's throat. Before he could gasp for air, he was lifted off the ground, slammed hard against the stone wall. The pressure on his throat was suffocating, crushing his windpipe. His vision began to darken as his body fought for breath. He punched, clawed at the giant's arm, but it was futile. Nothing worked.

The world began to fade, and the giant's voice—low, guttural—was the last thing he heard. "I told you to run… you should have listened."

Then, something shifted.

A roar—loud and powerful—cut through the air, followed by a war cry. The giant's head snapped to the side just in time to see it. A mob of women and children stormed down the stairs, chains still wrapped around their wrists, their eyes burning with fury.

At the front of the mob, Amar led the charge, his sword raised high.

"NOW!" Amar shouted.

The women and children attacked with savage determination. Their chains lashed out like whips, striking the giant's back, his arms, his legs. Each blow was a release of all the pain, all the anger they had suffered.

CLANG! CRACK! THUD!

The giant staggered back under the force of the blows, his roar of fury filling the night. He released Rana, stumbling as the relentless assault continued.

Rana hit the ground hard, gasping for air. His vision cleared just in time to see the giant, disoriented, struggling to stay on his feet.

But the mob didn't stop. They kept striking him again and again, their chains crashing down on him with an almost rhythmic fury. The giant swayed, his body beginning to falter under the onslaught. He roared in defiance, but it was clear—the giant was falling.

Rana's eyes flicked to the ground, catching the glint of his sword. His one chance.

With a burst of strength, he lunged, grabbing the blade and slashing multiple times with all his remaining energy. The sword cut through the giant's legs, multiple deep and brutal cuts.

A final, deafening roar tore through the night as the giant collapsed, his massive body crashing to the stone floor with a sickening thud.

The mob fell back, breathing hard, their bodies trembling, but their eyes filled with relief. Silence descended, heavy and oppressive, as they watched the giant's chest rise and fall slowly, each breath weaker than the last.

Rana slowly got to his feet; his sword gripped tightly in his hand. He stepped forward, standing over the fallen giant, his gaze unwavering.

The giant's eyes flickered open. For the first time, there was something in them—not rage, not defiance, but fear.

Rana lifted his sword, the finality of the moment settling over him.

"I told you... We aren't going anywhere without the girls."

With a single, decisive thrust, he drove the blade straight through the giant's heart.

The body jerked once, then lay still.

The battle was over.

They had won.

They were free.

For the first time in a long time, the nightmare had ended.

Rana knelt beside Suresh and Chandan, his eyes scanning their wounds. Suresh's breathing was heavy, his chest rising and falling in strained gasps, but he was alive. Chandan winced as Amar yanked the spear from his arm, a fresh surge of blood spilling over his skin and staining the dirt beneath him. Gritting his teeth Chandan, swallowed the pain as Amar quickly pressed a cloth to the wound and tied it tightly.

"You good?" Rana asked, his voice low but firm.

Chandan gave a sharp nod. His face was pale, his arm useless for now, but his grip on his sword was unwavering.

Rana exhaled, steadying himself. It was over. Finally.

The first hints of dawn crept over the horizon, bathing the sky in streaks of deep blue and pale gold. The night had been long, filled with bloodshed and whispered prayers of survival, but they had made it through. Now, they just had to leave before the morning brought new threats.

"It's almost dawn. We need to move before more guards arrive," Rana said, his voice carrying the urgency of their escape. He turned toward Pari, kneeling beside her small frame, and lifted her gently into his arms. She curled into him without hesitation, her fingers gripping his tunic as if afraid he would disappear.

"We're safe now," he murmured.

The words felt strange, almost foreign, after everything they had endured. Yet, as they stepped away from the fort, a breath of freedom filled their lungs. The cold morning air brushed against their skin, and for the first time in what felt like ages, there was no immediate danger, no pressing fear. They had done it. They were leaving this nightmare behind.

But just as hope took root, the ground beneath them trembled. A distant rumble echoed through the trees, growing louder with each passing second. The realization struck them all at once—horses.

Before they could react, a wall of fifteen horsemen emerged from the thinning darkness, surrounding them like a noose tightening around their throats. They were dressed in jet-black cloaks, their swords already drawn, waiting for the order to strike.

At the front of the group sat a man with a commanding presence—Danish.

"Throw your weapons down," he ordered, his voice sharp, unyielding. "Unless you want to die right here."

No one moved.

Rana's grip on his sword tightened, his mind racing through their dwindling options. Danish, still seated atop his horse, regarded him with a knowing smirk.

"You're Rana, aren't you?" His tone was almost amused, as if he had been waiting for this moment.

Rana didn't answer.

Danish's gaze drifted over the group, his eyes scanning their faces like a predator toying with his prey. Then, his attention shifted to the girls. His expression darkened with cruel curiosity.

"Where is Vishakha?"

A cold shiver ran down Rana's spine.

"No answer?" Danish mused. "No problem." He turned to his men without hesitation. "Take them all."

The horsemen moved as one, their blades catching the light as they advanced. There was no time to run, no chance to fight—not when they were outnumbered and wounded, not with the girls to protect.

And then came the final blow.

"Zahir is waiting for you all" announced Danish.

A chilling silence fell over them.

It was only then that Rana fully understood. They weren't just being captured. They were being delivered—to him.

To Zahir. And there was no escape.

Chapter 14

The city of Agra sleeps under a blanket of oppressive silence, broken only by the occasional howl of a stray dog or the distant creak of a rusted gate swinging in the wind. The moon hangs low, casting a pale, ghostly light over the labyrinth of narrow streets and crumbling buildings

Above an abandoned shop, its windows boarded up and its sign long faded, stands a house that does not belong. It looms over the empty street, its tall walls imposing, its wrought-iron gates a masterpiece of intricate design. And yet, despite its grandeur, the air around it is shrouded—burdened, as if the very ground remembers the weight of its secrets.

The scent of jasmine lingers, delicate yet persistent. Perhaps it drifts from the vines that coil around the walls, their small white flowers blooming in defiance of the house's eerie stillness. Inside, the air grows heavier, steeped in silence and shadow. Carved nightingales perch on wooden panels, their frozen forms watching from every corner, their delicate wings forever poised as if caught in song.

The house is guarded. Men in dark uniforms patrol the perimeter, their faces shadowed by the brims of their caps. They move with mechanical precision, their eyes scanning the darkness for any sign of intrusion. But the real danger lies within the house, behind the towering walls and locked doors, where the night is anything but silent.

The air is filled with the scent of sweat and jasmine. The walls seem to close in, the shadows dancing like spectres watching the scene unfold. A woman lies on a large, ornate bed, her body trembling under the weight of the man above her. Zahir, his face a mask of cold determination, grips her neck with one hand, his fingers digging into her skin. His other hand pins her wrist to the bed, rendering her powerless. His breath is ragged, his movements rough and unrelenting.

The woman beneath him, stares at the ceiling with wide, unseeing eyes. Her lips part in silent cries, each moan escaping her throat like a plea for mercy. Her body aches, her muscles tense as she endures the pain. Her hands clutch the bedsheet, twisting it into knots, as if the fabric could somehow anchor her to a reality far removed from this nightmare. Tears stream down her cheeks, glistening in the dim light, but she makes no sound beyond the soft, broken whimpers that Zahir seems to relish.

"Call me your king," he growls, his voice low and commanding, almost a whisper but laced with menace.

The woman hesitates, her throat tightening under his grip. She forces the words out, her voice trembling. "M-my king…"

Zahir's lips curl into a cruel smile, and he leans closer, his breath hot against her ear. "Again."

"Y-you are my king," she repeats, her voice barely audible, each word a dagger to her soul.

He continues, his movements growing more forceful, more punishing. Her body jerks with each thrust, her mind retreating to a place far away, a place where she is free, where the weight of his body and the pain he inflicts cannot reach her. But the reality is inescapable. The room feels smaller, the air thinner, as if the walls themselves are conspiring to trap her in this moment forever.

As he finishes, Zahir collapses onto her, his body heavy and unyielding. He rests his head on her chest, his breathing slow and steady, as if he has no idea about her suffering. She lies motionless, her chest rising and falling in shallow, uneven breaths. Her tears continue to fall, silent and unending, as she stares at the ceiling, her mind a whirlwind of fear, anger, and despair.

"I really love you, Afsana," Zahir murmurs, his voice soft now, almost tender. He reaches up to brush a strand of hair from her face, but she flinches at his touch, her body recoiling instinctively. He doesn't seem to notice—or perhaps he doesn't care. He rolls onto his side, his arm draped possessively over her, and within moments, his breathing deepens as he drifts into sleep.

Afsana waits. She waits until his grip loosens, until his breathing becomes the steady rhythm of slumber. Then, slowly, carefully, she turns away from him, curling into herself as if to shield her body from the memory of his touch. Her shoulders shake with silent sobs, her face buried in the pillow to muffle the sound. The room is quiet now, save for the occasional creak of the bed. But inside Afsana, a storm rages—a storm of pain, of fear, of a desperate longing for escape.

Outside the room, moon is silver glow over the city. Somewhere in the distance, a dog barks, its voice echoing through the empty streets. The guards outside the house shift uneasily, their eyes darting toward the windows as if they, too, can feel the weight of the darkness within. But no one comes to Afsana's aid. No one hears her cries. She is alone, trapped in a world where love is a weapon and freedom is a distant dream.

And as the first light of dawn begins to creep over the horizon, Afsana closes her eyes, her tears drying on her cheeks. She knows this is not the end. Zahir will wake, and the cycle will begin again. But for now, in the quiet of the early morning, she allows herself to dream—of a life beyond these walls, of a day when she will no longer be a prisoner in her own skin.

***

The morning light filters through the heavy curtains of the living room, casting a golden hue over the lavish furnishings.

Zahir sits in an ornate armchair, his orientation relaxed but his eyes sharp, scanning the room as if expecting trouble. There was tension in the air, the kind that makes every breath feel like a struggle. Afsana stands at the small table nearby, her hands trembling as she slices apples and guavas with a silver knife. The rhythmic sound of the blade against the wooden board is the only noise in the room, a stark contrast to the storm brewing beneath the surface.

Zahir watches her intently, his gaze lingering on the way her hands shake, the way her shoulders slump under an invisible weight. He frowns, his patience wearing thin. With a wave of his hand, he dismisses the guards stationed at the doors and windows. "Leave us," he commands, his voice low but firm. The guards obey without question, their boots echoing against the marble floor as they exit the room. The door clicks shut behind them, leaving Zahir and Afsana alone.

For a moment, there is silence. Then Zahir rises from his chair, his movements calculated, almost predatory. He walks to the window, his back to Afsana, and stares out at the bustling streets below. The city is alive with activity, but to him, it feels distant, irrelevant. He turns to face her, his expression a mix of frustration and desperation.

"I don't understand," he begins, his voice tight with emotion. Zahir exhaled sharply, his frustration simmering just beneath the surface. He gestured around the room, his voice tight.

"Look around, Afsana. Look at this room—filled with the things I carved just for you. Every nightingale, every flower, every detail—crafted with my own hands. For you. Just like I did before you were taken from me"

His face stiffened as he took a step closer. "Do you remember what you once told me? When we were together, when everything still felt untouched by time? Sometimes I feel like this—us—is too good to be true. Like it's a dream I'll wake up from."

He let out a bitter chuckle, shaking his head. "And do you remember what I told you? It's not a dream, Afsana. And I won't let anyone take it away from us." His voice dropped lower, heavier. "I swore to you that we'd always find a way. That no matter what happened, you won't lose me. Not ever. And even if you do, I'll make sure to find you again."

His fingers curled into fists, the weight of his words pressing down on him. "And I did. The world tried to take me from you, but I found you again. I saved you, Afsana. I destroyed everyone who tried to come between us. I pulled you out of that miserable life, away from that pathetic husband of yours—a man who never deserved you, who never even knew what he had. I brought you back to where you belong. To your childhood home. To the streets who once filled your days with laughter."

Zahir's gaze searched hers, desperate for something—anything. "But you… you're not the Afsana I remember. You used to glow with life, with fire. With love. We were happy. We were whole. But now—" His voice caught for a fraction of a second before he forced himself to continue. "Now you look at me like I'm a stranger. Like none of it matters."

A heavy silence stretched between them, dense with unspoken words. Then, softer this time, almost a whisper, he asked, "Tell me, Afsana… what happened?"

His hands trembled slightly at his sides, his frustration no longer just frustration—it was something raw, something dangerously close to heartbreak. "What is it that I haven't given you? What is it that's still missing?"

His voice was barely above a whisper now, laced with something he wasn't ready to name. "Even after everything I've done for you… why are you still not happy?"

Afsana freezes, the knife hovering above the half-cut guava. Her breath catches in her throat, and she feels the weight of his gaze like a physical force. She wants to speak, to tell him the truth—that his love is suffocating, that his kindness is a denial—but the words stick in her throat. She knows what happens when she defies him. The memories of his rage, his violence, flash before her eyes, and she clenches the knife tighter, her knuckles turning white.

Tears well up in her eyes, spilling over and tracing silent paths down her cheeks. She keeps her head down, focusing on the fruit in front of her, as if the simple act of cutting it could shield her from his wrath. The room feels smaller, the walls closing in, and she wonders how much longer she can endure this.

Suddenly, the sound of commotion downstairs cut through the stillness.

Zahir froze.

The echoes of raised voices, hurried footsteps—it was happening again. His breath hitched, his body tensing as a wave of something cold and paralyzing gripped him. It was the same sound. The same chaos. The last time he had heard it; Afsana had been ripped away from him.

That morning came rushing back like a wound torn open. The shouts, the sound of horses, the desperate struggle. The feeling of helplessness as he was dragged back, held down, forced to watch as she was taken—her terrified eyes searching for him even as she was snatched away from him. He had been a nobody then, powerless to stop it. A forgotten man in a world that belonged to others.

But this time, he was not powerless.

This time, he had all the power in the world. Yet—his hands still trembled. His chest still tightened with that same, unbearable fear.

Because power meant nothing if he lost her again. It would all be for nothing. He has been through a lot, just to be where he is right now.

And for the first time in years, Zahir Khan—the man who had built himself into something unstoppable—felt exactly as he had that morning. Small. Helpless. *Terrified.*

Zahir's head snaps toward the door, his body tense, every muscle coiled like a spring. His hand instinctively reaches for the sword lying on the table across the room. He strides toward it, his movements quick and precise, and draws the blade from its sheath with a metallic hiss. The steel glints in the morning light, a deadly promise in his hands.

Afsana drops the knife, her heart pounding in her chest. She backs away from the table, her eyes darting between Zahir and the door. The noise grows louder, more chaotic, until the door bursts open with a crash. Soldiers flood into the room, their armour gleaming, their faces grim. They move with military precision, fanning out to line the walls, their weapons drawn and ready. Within moments, the room is filled with the sound of heavy breathing and the faint clink of chainmail.

Zahir's eyes narrow as he takes in the scene. These are not his men. The realization hits him like a blow, and his grip on the sword tightens. He steps back, positioning himself between Afsana and the intruders, his mind racing. How had they gotten past his guards? Who had betrayed him?

Then, a voice cuts through the tension, smooth and mocking, yet laced with an undercurrent of menace.

"Look what we have here," the man says, stepping into the room with an air of confidence. It's Raza Khan, his presence commanding, his eyes gleaming with triumph. Behind him, two women enter—Vishakha and Saira, their expressions triumphant and their eyes sharp with purpose.

Zahir's shoulders slump, the weight of the situation crashing down on him. His sword arm drops slightly, the blade now pointing toward the floor. He looks from Raza to the women, his mind piecing together the betrayal. "So, this is how it ends," he mutters, more to himself than to anyone else. His voice is heavy with resignation, but there's a flicker of defiance in his eyes.

Raza smirks, crossing his arms over his chest. "You had it coming, Zahir. You thought you could play god, but even gods fall eventually." He takes a step closer, his gaze flickering to Afsana, who stands frozen in the corner, her face pale and tear-streaked. "And you," he says, his tone softening slightly, "Who are you?"

Afsana doesn't respond. She can't. Her body is trembling, her mind struggling to process what's happening. She looks at Zahir, then at Raza, and finally at Vishakha and Saira. The room feels like it's spinning, the walls closing in, and she clutches the edge of the table to steady herself.

Zahir's gaze shifted to Afsana. She was still trembling, unable to meet his eyes. The look in her eyes—the tears that were never meant for him—cut deeper than any sword could. And for the first time, Zahir understood. But it was too late.

There was tension and suspense in the room, the air heavy with the weight of accusations and betrayal. Zahir stands in the centre, his once-confident demeanour crumbling under the weight of Raza's words. Raza's voice is sharp, commanding, each syllable dripping with venom as he lists Zahir's crimes.

"You are guilty, Zahir," he begins, his tone cold and unyielding. "How many treasons must I list for you? You killed Malik to take his position. You broke the heart of my little sister, Saira. You fooled my father, a man who trusted you like a son. You killed two of my brothers in cold blood.

And here, I find you in an affair while married to my sister Amina, whom you wed only for power. You have used and destroyed my family in every way imaginable. And I'm certain you had more plans, more schemes. But not anymore, Zahir. Not anymore."

Raza steps closer, his eyes blazing with fury. "I hate you enough to end you right here, right now. But I won't. I want to present you before my father in Dilli. I want you to look into the eyes of the man whose trust you betrayed and confess your crimes. Only then will justice be served." His voice rises, the anger palpable. "How could you do this? How could you live with yourself?"

Zahir's face is a mask of shock and panic. He stumbles back, his mind racing for a way out, for words to defend himself. His eyes dart to Vishakha, who stands silently beside Raza. Desperation claws at him as he points at her, his voice trembling. "Are you going to believe the words of this girl? She has no proof, only accusations! You're going to ruin me based on her lies?"

Raza smirks, a cold, knowing smile that sends a chill down Zahir's spine. But before he can respond, Saira steps forward, her eyes blazing with fury. "Am I lying too, Zahir?" she demands, her voice shaking with emotion. "Are you going to call me a liar as well? You used me. You made me believe you loved me, and then you plotted my marriage to another man. And after all that, you married my sister? How could you? How disgusting are you?"

Zahir's panic deepens. He raises his hands, as if to ward off her words. "It wasn't my plan!" he protests, his voice cracking. "It was your father, Qasim Khan. He made the decisions. How could I have disagreed? I had no choice!"

Saira's hand flew out, the sharp crack of her palm meeting Zahir's cheek echoing through the room. He stumbled back, his head snapping to the side, skin burning where she had struck him.

"At least once," she hissed, her voice trembling with rage, "you should tell the truth. You're the worst person I've ever met."

Her fingers throbbed. A sharp, stinging pain shot up her arm. She had never slapped anyone before. Not in her life. Not even in anger. The force of it had sent a jolt through her, but she refused to show it. She kept her poise regal, her expression fierce, as if the sting meant nothing.

Zahir barely had time to recover before he stumbled toward Vishakha. She stood unmoving, her eyes cold, unflinching. Not a hint of shock, not a flicker of sympathy. Just a silent, unwavering judgment.

"This is all because of you," Zahir snarls at Vishakha, his desperation turning to rage. He lunges at her, but before he can reach her, Raza's soldiers intercept him, wrenching his sword from his hand and pinning him to the ground. Zahir struggles against their grip, his face contorted with fury. "You ruined everything!" he shouts at Vishakha, his voice raw with desperation. "You ruined me!"

Raza raises a hand, signalling his soldiers to release Zahir. They step back, leaving him kneeling on the floor, dishevelled and defeated. "Where is he going to run?" Raza says with a cold smile. "This entire house, this entire street, is filled with my soldiers. He has nowhere to go." He gestures dismissively. "Let him talk. Let him beg. It's the last time he'll have the chance. And I enjoy seeing him like this."

Zahir scrambles to his feet, his eyes wild with desperation. He turns to Raza, his voice pleading. "Think about Amina and Sahiba. They'll be devastated if you do this. They love me. They'll never forgive you."

A shadow passed over Raza's face, his patience snapping, "I'll take care of my family," he growls. "If you mention their names one more time, I'll kill you here myself." His hand twitches toward the hilt of his sword, and Zahir flinches, his bravado crumbling.

Zahir turns to Saira, his voice trembling. "I loved you, Saira. Please, save me. You know I didn't mean to hurt you." Saira turns away, her face a mask of disgust, and Zahir's desperation turns to rage once more. He glares at Vishakha, his voice venomous. "You made me lose everything. But I'll make sure your Rana and his girl Pari suffer. You'll never see them again."

Vishakha's lips curl into a faint smile. "And what if I told you they're already safe?" she says softly. "What if I told you they're with me?"

Zahir's confusion is cut short as the door swings open. Akram strides into the room, dragging Danish behind him. Danish's head hangs low, his face pale with fear. Akram throws him to the ground at Zahir's feet. "He had them," Akram says, his voice cold. "But we attacked. All your soldiers are dead. Rana, Pari, and the others are safe. They're with us now."

Danish looks up at Zahir, his voice barely a whisper. "It's over. They're gone." Before Zahir can respond, Akram wiped his blade clean, with straight face—except for the faintest flicker of satisfaction in his eyes. He glanced at Raza, almost apologetic, though his voice carried no remorse.

"I've always hated him," he muttered. "I've been wanting to kill him for so long."

Raza met his gaze, unfazed. There was no shock, no reprimand—just quiet acceptance. He gave a small nod, his voice calm, measured.

"It's okay," he said. Then, without looking at Danish's lifeless body, he added, "Just keep the other two alive. We need to get a lot of information out of them."

Akram exhaled, rolling his shoulders. The tension in the room didn't dissipate, but the message was clear. Danish was dead.

Zahir stumbles back, his legs giving out as he collapses against the table. The fruits scatter to the floor, the knife clattering beside him. His face is a mask of despair, his once-proud demeanour shattered. Raza steps forward, his voice cold and final. "It's over, Zahir. Get ready for your final journey to Dilli. Once you confess your crimes to my father, I'll kill you myself. That's the end you deserve."

Zahir's world was crashing down. There was no escape. But then, just as the silence began to settle, a cold, sharp pain erupted in his back.

Afsana, standing in the shadows, had made her move. She had plunged a knife into his spine, and recoiled away from him. The soldiers tensed, ready to surge toward Zahir, but Raza raised a hand—silent, commanding. They halted at once, awaiting his word.

Zahir gasps, his eyes wide with shock, as he falls to the ground. He looked up at Afsana, his eyes wide with disbelief. "Why?" he whispered.

The room was silent, everyone was shocked, as Zahir lay on the ground, blood pooling beneath him. His breaths came in shallow gasps, his eyes wide with shock and disbelief as he stared up at Afsana. Blood spilled from the wound where she had plunged the knife, dark and unrelenting. She stood at a distance now, gripping the knife tightly. Tears streamed down her face, her chest heaving with the weight of years of pain and betrayal.

The room seemed to hold its breath. Raza, Saira, Vishakha, and the soldiers stood frozen, their eyes fixed on the scene unfolding before them. Afsana's voice broke the silence, trembling but filled with a fury that had been suppressed for far too long. "Why?" she echoed, the word dripping with venom. "You have the audacity to ask why?" Her voice quivered, but there was no question in her eyes. There was only hatred and a broken heart. "When I saw you for the first time in Dilli after my marriage, I was so happy to see you. I thought… I thought, my Nasir has made it in life. That even though we are not together, you are happy in your life. That maybe, you're back to fulfil your promise to never give up on us. But you… you were not the man I loved. The man I swore to always love was dead. The Zahir standing before me is a monster. A stranger. A killer."

She crumbled on her knees. Her voice cracked, but she continued, her words pouring out like a floodgate had been opened. "You killed my husband. You killed his entire family. You killed my father. You killed everyone I ever loved. And then… then you kept me in this house? This house, where you slaughtered my family? Where their memories still haunt me to this day? What kind of lunatic are you? Did you think I would be happy here? Did you think I could ever love you after what you've done?"

Zahir's face twisted in pain, both physical and emotional. He struggled to speak, his voice weak but defiant. "But… we loved each other. I removed everyone who ever came in our way. I did it for us."

Afsana's tears fell faster, her hands trembling as she gripped the knife tighter. "I loved Nasir," she said, her voice breaking. "The sweet boy who loved and cared. The boy who would never hurt anyone. But you… this Zahir you've become… you're a monster. I hated every minute in this house with you. I had nightmares of you when you were gone. You are the worst thing that has ever happened to me. Every night you raped me, I dreamt of killing you. And today… today I'll make that dream come true."

With a cry of anguish and rage, Afsana crawled toward Zahir's limp body, her breath ragged, her vision blurred with tears. Her fingers tightened around the hilt of the knife; her grip unyielding. With a raw, guttural cry, she drove the blade into his chest—again and again. Blood pooled beneath him, soaking into the cold stone floor, but she didn't stop. The room echoed with the wet, sickening sound of the knife tearing through flesh, with the unrelenting fury in her ragged breaths.

Even as the life drained from him, she kept going, lost in a frenzy of rage and anguish. A scream tore from her throat, wild and unhinged, a release of years of pain, betrayal, and vengeance. She was deaf to the world, blind to anything but the corpse beneath her, her arm rising and falling in a relentless rhythm.

It was only when Raza raised a hand that his men hesitated before moving forward. The soldiers rushed in, struggling to pry her away from the bloodied body. She fought them, thrashing, screaming, her fingers refusing to release the weapon. It took three of them to finally pull her back, wrenching the knife from her grasp.

And then, suddenly, it was over. The fight left her as swiftly as it had overtaken her. She collapsed against the wall, curling into herself. Her hands trembled, smeared with blood, as the weight of what she had done settled over her. The room was silent now—except for the ragged sound of her breathing, the distant echoes of her scream still lingering in the air.

The irony was undeniable.

Everything Zahir had done—every battle fought, every drop of blood spilled, every throne shaken—had been for Afsana. When she was taken from him, he had been nothing. A nobody. That loss had forged him into the Zahir Khan the world feared. The man who clawed his way to power, who destroyed anything that stood in his path, all in the name of never being powerless again. In his own twisted ways, he loved her and he did it all for Afsana.

And yet, tonight, it was Afsana who ended him.

The room remained silent for a long moment, the weight of what had just happened settling over everyone. The blood on the floor glistened under the dim light, the stillness of the body making the air feel heavier.

Saira's breath came in short, uneven gasps. Her hands trembled at her sides, and for a moment, she looked as though she might collapse. She had known violence, had lived surrounded by men who wielded power like a blade, but this—this was different. This was too close. Too real. A man she once loved, once hated, is now a mere corpse.

Raza noticed her shaking before she did. He stepped toward her, placing a firm hand on her arm. "Saira," he murmured. She didn't respond, her wide eyes fixed on the lifeless form at their feet.

"Saira," he said again, more firmly this time. He gently took her by the shoulders and turned her away from the scene. "You don't need to see this."

Still, she didn't move. Her body was rigid, her fingers curled into fists at her sides. He exhaled sharply, then reached for her hand, gripping it tightly. "Come," he urged. "Let's go."

She blinked, finally looking at him, her expression lost. Slowly, she let him lead her away from the body, away from the blood staining the floor. He guided her toward the door, where she hesitated, glancing back.

Raza squeezed her hand. "Take her outside," he told one of the guards standing nearby. "Make sure she gets some air."

As the guard moved to her side, Saira finally let go of his hand and walked away without a word. Only when she was gone did Raza let out a slow breath, rubbing a hand over his face before turning back to Akram.

His expression hardened once more as he looked down at Danish's body. The silence stretched for a few beats before he finally spoke.

"Send word to Father," he said, his voice quieter than before. Then, after a pause, he added, "I'll go meet him myself." His gaze flickered over the bloodied floor, his lips pressing into a thin line. "The position for the King of Allahabad is vacant again… and I suppose I should fill it soon."

He turned to Vishakha, his features softening. "Thank you," he said, his voice sincere. "For everything. The information you provided was invaluable. Without you, this wouldn't have been possible. If you ever need anything, let me know. You'll always have a place in my court."

Vishakha smiled, a quiet, contented smile. "This is it for me," she said. "My time in the court is over. I'll be going back to Devran. Someone is waiting for me there."

Raza nodded, a hint of a smile playing on his lips. "I understand. You have my permission, and my gratitude. But still, if you need anything ever, just know that you only have to ask!"

Vishakha hesitated, her gaze flickering to the floor before meeting his. "There is something," she said quietly, her voice carrying a weight that made Raza pause. "But I don't think you can grant me that."

Raza's demeanour shifted; his curiosity piqued. He stepped closer, his eyes narrowing slightly as he studied her. "Try me," he said, his tone firm but laced with intrigue. "You've earned the right to ask."

At last, Vishakha spoke, voicing her terms with calm resolve. Raza listened intently; his face betrayed nothing as she laid out her demands. When she finished, he gave a measured response, his tone neutral but firm. "I'll see what can be done," he said, before gesturing for his soldiers to exit the room.

As Raza turned to leave, the soldiers falling into step behind them, Vishakha turned to Akram, who had been standing silently by her side. "Thank you," she said, her voice warm. "For everything. I couldn't have done this without you."

Akram raised an eyebrow, a small smile tugging at the corner of his mouth. "Are you sure about going to Devran?" he asked. "It's a long way from here."

Vishakha's smile widened, her eyes shining with determination. "I've never been more sure of anything in my life," she said.

Akram nodded, his smile growing. "Then I wish you all the best. Take care of yourself, Vishakha."

As he turned to leave, Vishakha stood alone in the room, her gaze lingering on the scene before her. Zahir's lifeless body lay on the floor, Afsana still curled against the wall, her shoulders shaking with silent sobs.

The room fell silent once more, the only sound the faint rustle of the wind outside, carrying with it the promise of change—and the weight of the unknown. Vishakha's request lingered in the air, unspoken but palpable. Would Raza grant her wish, or had she asked too much of him? The answer remained shrouded in suspense, a question mark hanging over the future like a shadow. The weight of the past seemed to lift from Vishakha's shoulders as she took a deep breath, her heart lighter than it had been in years. She turned and walked out of the room, her steps steady and sure, ready to begin the next chapter of her life.

Chapter 15

The sun rose lazily over the village of Devran, its golden rays spilling across the banks of the Ganga. The river whispered its ancient secrets, as it always did, but today felt different. There was a lightness in the air, a sense of calm that hadn't been there in years. The villagers went about their daily routines, their laughter and chatter filling the narrow lanes. Life, for once, felt normal.

Amar stood at his forge, the rhythmic clang of his hammer against metal echoing through the village. Sweat dripped down his brow as he shaped a horseshoe, his hands steady and sure. The heat of the fire warmed his face, and he hummed a tune under his breath.

"Amar!" a voice called, breaking his concentration.

He looked up to see Chandan and Suresh approaching, their faces lit with mischief. Chandan, ever the joker, had a wide grin plastered across his face, while Suresh trailed behind, shaking his head in mock exasperation.

"What are you two clowns up to now?" Amar asked, setting down his hammer and wiping his hands on his cloth.

"Clowns?" Chandan feigned offense, placing a hand over his heart. "Is that any way to greet your dearest friends?"

"Friends?" Amar raised an eyebrow. "Last I checked, friends don't steal my last piece of jaggery and blame it on the dog."

Suresh burst out laughing, while Chandan shrugged innocently. "That dog looked guilty, Amar. I was just pointing out the obvious."

Amar rolled his eyes but couldn't suppress a smile. "What do you want?"

"We were thinking," Suresh said, leaning against the forge, "that we should go check on Rana. He's been sitting outside his hut all morning, staring at the forest like it's going to bite him."

"Again," Chandan added.

Amar sighed, his smile fading. "He's been like that ever since Vishakha left. I don't think he's slept properly in days."

"Which is why we're going to cheer him up," Chandan declared, slapping Amar on the back. "Come on, let's go. You can finish that horseshoe later."

Amar hesitated, then nodded. "Fine. But if you two start another one of your ridiculous arguments, I'm leaving."

The three friends made their way through the village, exchanging greetings with neighbours and teasing children who ran past. The atmosphere was lively, but Amar couldn't shake the feeling that something was about to happen. He glanced toward the forest, its dark canopy looming in the distance, and quickened his pace.

As they walked, they greeted Hari, who was playing with his children. But Hari barely acknowledged them, his expression tightening before he turned away and disappeared into his house. Amar sighed, shaking his head.

"How long do you think he'll try to avoid us?" he muttered.

Suresh shrugged. "Let him take his time. He's embarrassed. He'll come around."

They found Rana sitting outside his hut, his half spear resting across his lap. His eyes were fixed on the treeline, his face had a sense of worry.

"Rana!" Chandan called, waving enthusiastically. "We've come to rescue you from your brooding."

Rana turned, his lips twitching into a faint smile. "I wasn't brooding. I was thinking."

"Same thing," Suresh said, plopping down beside him. "You've been doing a lot of that lately."

Rana shrugged, his gaze drifting back to the forest. "There's a lot to think about."

Amar sat down on Rana's other side; his tone gentle. "We know you miss her, Rana. But Vishakha said she'd come back. You have to trust her."

"I do," Rana said quietly. "But trust doesn't make the waiting any easier."

Before anyone could respond, a sudden commotion erupted at the edge of the village. The distant sound of hooves pounding against the earth sent a ripple of panic through the air. Voices rose in alarm, a mixture of confusion and fear. Women pulled their children close; men abandoned their work to rush toward the source of the disturbance. The once peaceful hum of the village was now filled with sharp commands and the metallic clang of armour.

Rana was on his feet in an instant, his spear gripped tightly in his calloused hand, his stance firm. His pulse quickened as he exchanged a glance with Chandan and Amar. He could see the same wariness reflected in their eyes.

"What's going on?" Chandan muttered, squinting toward the dust cloud rising in the distance.

A procession of Mughal soldiers rode into the village, their polished armour glinting ominously under the afternoon sun. Their disciplined movements and unsmiling faces sent an uneasy hush through the crowd. At their head, seated tall on his horse, was Akram. His dark eyes swept over the villagers, noting the rigidity in their face. His face was carved from stone, unreadable, but there was something—just a flicker—hidden beneath that hardened gaze.

Behind him, dragging his feet through the dust, was a prisoner. The man was shackled, iron chains digging into his wrists and ankles, forcing him to stumble with every step. His clothes were torn, stained with dirt and blood. His head hung low, strands of matted hair falling over his face. The weight of his suffering was visible in every agonized movement.

The villagers pressed in closer, whispering amongst themselves, their voices rising into a wave of murmurs. Who was this man? Why had the soldiers come? Was this a new threat or an old enemy finally brought to justice?

Rana's grip on his spear tightened, his knuckles turning white as his gaze flickered between Akram and the captive. His instincts screamed at him to be ready.

And then—he saw her.

At the very back of the group, partially obscured by the imposing soldiers, stood a figure his eyes were searching all along.

Vishakha.

His breath caught in his throat.

She was dressed in traveling robes, dust clinging to the fabric, her hair tied loosely, strands escaping to frame her face. But none of that mattered. What mattered was the look in her eyes—tired, determined, and filled with something he hadn't dared hope for.

A heartbeat passed. Then another.

Chandan was the first to react, his mouth falling open in shock before he let out a strangled laugh. "No… it can't be—"

But it was.

Amar let out a joyous shout, his voice breaking through the stunned silence. Suresh clapped a hand to his mouth, as if afraid that speaking would break the spell. The tension shattered in an instant as the realization spread through the gathered crowd.

Vishakha had returned.

And at that moment, nothing else mattered.

Her eyes met Rana's, and she smiled—a small, emotional smile that spoke volumes.

He took a step forward, then another, until he was standing in front of her.

"You came back," he said, his voice barely above a whisper.

"I told you I would," Vishakha replied, her eyes glistening.

"But before I could, I had to find something."

Vishakha's voice was calm, but there was an underlying weight to her words that sent a chill through the air.

Rana frowned, his grip on his spear tightening. His gaze flickered toward the bloodied prisoner standing in chains. The man barely had the strength to hold his head up, his body swaying from exhaustion and pain. But there was something in his form—a tension, a guilt—that made Rana's stomach twist.

"Who is he?" Rana asked, his voice low, measured.

Vishakha's look darkened. "His name is Imran. He was one of Zahir's closest confidants."

At the mention of Zahir's name, a ripple of jitter moved through the gathered villagers. Some gasped, others murmured among themselves, exchanging glances heavy with fear. Zahir may have been dead, but his fear still loomed over them.

Rana's teeth ground together, his muscles tensing. "And?"

Vishakha inhaled deeply before meeting his eyes. "Before Zahir died, he swore he would make you and Pari suffer. That didn't make sense to me. How would he know about Pari? How would he know about this village?" She paused, allowing the weight of her words to settle. "Someone told him. Someone betrayed you."

A cold silence fell over the village, as if the air had been sucked from the space.

Rana's fists curled at his sides. "Who?" His voice was like a blade, sharp, dangerous.

Vishakha turned to Akram, who stepped forward, his presence commanding. His gaze swept over the gathered villagers; his tone grim.

"Imran has confessed that someone from this village was feeding information to Zahir." Akram let the words sink in, his eyes hard as steel. "We brought him here to identify the traitor."

The moment the words left his mouth, the village erupted. Shocked gasps, frantic whispers, cries of disbelief. Men turned to each other in suspicion, women clutched their children closer. The air grew seething with fear and anger.

"No one here would do that!" someone shouted from the crowd.

"This is a lie!" another voice protested.

But Akram remained unmoved. He raised a hand, silencing the chaos with a single gesture. Then, he turned to the prisoner.

"Imran," Akram commanded, his voice firm, unyielding. "Tell them the truth."

The shackled man shuddered, his body trembling. Blood dripped from his split lip, his eyes darting wildly across the sea of faces. The weight of the moment pressed down on him, suffocating. He swallowed hard, fear pooling in his gaze.

Then, slowly, he lifted a shaking hand.

The crowd held its breath.

Rana's heart pounded against his ribs as his eyes followed the trembling finger, tracing its path through the village until it landed—

On Dharamdas.

A stunned silence fell over the village. It was as if the world had stopped breathing.

Dharamdas.

The village headman. The man who had guided them for years. The man who had given shelter to Rana.

Rana's breath hitched, his chest tightening. His head shook slightly, as if rejecting what his eyes were seeing.

"No," came a choked voice—Dharamdas's son, stepping forward in disbelief. "No, this—this is a mistake!"

All eyes turned to Dharamdas.

For a long, agonizing moment, he said nothing. His weathered face was unreadable, his lips pressed into a thin line. But then—Rana saw it.

The flicker of guilt in his eyes.

Rana's blood ran cold.

"You…" The word barely left his lips, trembling with the force of restrained rage.

Dharamdas's nostrils flared. And then, as if something inside him snapped, his gaze hardened, his shoulders squared. He let out a bitter, humourless laugh.

"Yes," he spat, his voice turning sharp, venomous. "Yes, I told Zahir about you."

The villagers gasped in horror.

Rana took a step forward, his entire body trembling with fury. "Why?" His voice was low, but it carried the weight of a storm on the verge of breaking.

Dharamdas met his gaze, and this time, there was no remorse—only resentment. "Because I didn't want you to return."

The words hit Rana like a physical blow.

Dharamdas's voice rose, a twisted mix of anger and bitterness spilling forth. "I have spent my entire life serving this village! I am its leader! I gave everything fo0r these people, and yet, they look to you!" His eyes burned with years of hidden hatred. "You were nothing but an orphan—a boy I pitied and brought into my village. And still, they whisper your name like you're their saviour." He sneered. "I wanted you gone forever."

A deafening silence followed.

Rana's heart pounded, his mind reeling. He had trusted this man. Respected him. Looked up to him like a father.

And all this time… he had been the one holding the knife behind his back.

The villagers stood frozen; their breath caught in their throats. Shock rippled through the crowd like a wave, their disbelief lingering in the air. Mothers clutched their children tighter, men exchanged horrified glances, and the elderly murmured prayers under their breath, as if seeking divine intervention against the betrayal that had just been laid bare before them.

Akram stepped forward, his boots crunching against the dry earth, his stare was impenetrable, his voice when it came was sharp and unforgiving.

"If you are the leader of this village," he said, his words cutting through the stunned silence like a blade, "then you are guilty of another crime. It was you who has been selling the women and children of Devran."

A hush fell over the gathering, a breathless moment where the weight of the accusation settled over them like a suffocating fog. And then—

Chaos.

Gasps turned into outraged shouts. Cries of denial, of horror, of fury filled the air.

"Lies!" someone shouted.

"Our daughters, our sons—you sold them?" another voice shrieked, raw with grief.

"You monster!"

The crowd surged forward, their faces twisted with fury, their hands curled into fists. The air crackled with rage, with betrayal so deep it felt like the very ground beneath them had shattered.

But above them all, only one sound mattered to Rana.

The pounding of his own heart.

His vision blurred with fury, his body moved before his mind could catch up, and in the next breath, he was in front of Dharamdas. His fingers wrapped around the old man's collar, yanking him forward with such force that Dharamdas nearly stumbled.

"How could you?" Rana's roar split the air, his rage so fierce, so absolute, that even the most furious among the villagers paused. His grip tightened as he fought the urge to crush the man before him. "These people trusted you! I trusted you!"

Dharamdas did not flinch. Instead, a sneer twisted his face, his lips curling in contempt. And then he laughed. A low, bitter sound, void of remorse, void of shame.

"All village leaders do it." he spat, his eyes gleaming with something dark, something wretched. "Where do you think the money for weapons and festivals comes from? You think we survive on prayers and goodwill? No." His sneer deepened. "I did what was necessary for the betterment of this village."

A fresh wave of fury crashed through the crowd. Women wept in anguish, fathers cursed his name, young men clenched their weapons, aching to strike him down.

"Necessary?" Rana's voice was hoarse with disgust. He shoved Dharamdas back, his lip curled in revulsion. "You sold our own! Innocent children—our blood! What kind of man does that?"

Dharamdas straightened, brushing dust from his clothes as if Rana's grip had never shaken him. "A leader," he said, his voice filled with cold arrogance.

That was it.

The villagers could take no more.

They lunged forward; their fury boundless. A storm of rage and grief, a tide of vengeance about to crash.

But before they could reach him, Akram stepped between them, his voice a whip of authority.

"Enough!" he barked.

His soldiers moved swiftly, blocking the mob before they could tear Dharamdas apart. The villagers trembled with barely contained fury, but they did not challenge Akram. Not when his presence burned with the weight of justice.

Akram turned back to Dharamdas; his eyes dark with judgment. "You and the other village heads who took part in this vile trade will be taken to Dilli," he declared. His voice was final, absolute. "There, you will live out the remainder of your days as slaves to the emperor."

Dharamdas's eyes widened. His composure cracked, his sneer faltering.

"No," he rasped, stepping back. "You can't—"

Akram did not give him the dignity of a response. He gestured to his men. "Take him."

The soldiers seized Dharamdas, binding his hands in clunky iron shackles.

He struggled. He fought. He cursed, his voice rising in desperation as the weight of his fate settled over him. "I built this village! I saved you all! I protected you, you ungrateful—"

A sharp crack echoed through the air as a villager hurled a stone at him, striking him across the cheek. Another followed. Then another. The villagers, who had once revered him, now cast him out with their fury.

As Dharamdas was dragged away, his shouts grew weaker, swallowed by the sound of the people he had betrayed.

And Rana watched, his heart hammering, his soul heavy.

The storm had passed.

But the scars it left behind would remain forever.

As the soldiers dragged Dharamdas and Imran away, their chains clinking against the earth, the village remained frozen in a stunned, eerie silence. The weight of what had just transpired pressed down on every soul present. Eyes darted around, searching for something—reassurance, understanding, hope—but all they found was uncertainty.

A stunned silence settled over Devran, all-consuming and suffocating. The truth had landed like a thunderclap, leaving only chaos in its wake.

Then, the first shout rang out.

"Traitor!" someone screamed, hurling a stone that narrowly missed the young man.

"Your father sold our children!" another voice roared, and the crowd surged forward, their hands clawing at the air, their eyes burning with fury.

"How can we let his blood walk free?" another voice roared.

"He must have known what his father was up to," said another.

The villagers, lost in their rage, surged forward toward Dharamdas's son, their faces contorted with fury. His terrified eyes darted around, searching for an escape, but there was none. The people he had grown up with, the hands that had once lifted him as a child, now reached for him with violence in their hearts.

Just as the first villager lunged, a powerful voice cut through the madness.

"Enough!" Rana's voice cut through the chaos like a blade, sharp and commanding. He pushed through the crowd, his presence alone enough to make people step back. He stood between the mob and Dharamdas's son, his arms outstretched, his eyes blazing.

"A son should not suffer for the crimes of his father!" Rana declared, his voice ringing out with a power that silenced the crowd. "He is not Dharamdas. He is one of us. And if we turn on each other now, we are no better than the monsters we seek to condemn."

The villagers hesitated, their anger still simmering but held in check by Rana's words. He turned to the young man, placing a hand on his shoulder. "Go," he said quietly. "Take your family and go home. This is not your burden to bear."

Dharamdas's son nodded, tears streaming down his face, and hurried away, the crowd parting reluctantly to let him pass.

Rana turned back to the villagers, his chest heaving, his mind racing. The village was on the brink of collapse, its people lost and directionless. He knew what he had to do.

"Listen to me!" he called, his voice rising above the murmurs of the crowd. "I know you are angry. I know you are hurt. I know you have questions—questions that may never be answered. But this is not the time for vengeance. This is not the time for division. This is the time for unity."

He stepped forward, his eyes locking with those of the villagers, one by one. "For years, we lived in fear. Fear of the forest, fear of the unknown, fear of the monsters who walked among us. But today, that fear ends. Today, we take back our village. Today, we reclaim our future."

His voice grew stronger, each word resonating like a drumbeat in their hearts. "No longer will our women and children be stolen from us. No longer will we live under the shadow of betrayal. The chains that bound us have been broken, but our work is not done. We must rebuild. We must heal. And we must do it together."

He paused, his gaze sweeping over the crowd, his presence commanding their attention. "The head of this village has fallen, but Devran will not. We will choose a new leader, one who will guide us with honesty and strength. But remember—leadership is not the duty of one, but the responsibility of all. Together, we will protect this village. Together, we will thrive."

A spark ignited in the crowd. Where there was only grief moments ago, now there was something new—fire.

Rana took a step forward, his eyes burning with determination. "From this day forward, we forge a new path. A path where no man rules us through fear. A path where no family is forced to grieve their lost loved ones, wondering if they could have been saved. We will protect each other, as a village should, as a family should. And if any man dares to threaten our peace, let him know—Devran will not be silent again!"

A roar erupted from the villagers. It was not just a cheer—it was a battle cry.

They felt his words, felt the shift in the air, the change that had begun to take root.

Rana took a steadying breath, his voice gentler now, but no less firm. "As for the head of the village… Let us not be hasty. Let us choose wisely. On the night of the next full moon, we will decide who among us is worthy to lead—not through fear, not through greed, but through honour. Until then, let us go back to our homes, to our families, and cherish this new freedom. Because tonight, for the first time in a long time… we are truly safe."

A hushed silence followed. Then, slowly, one by one, the villagers began to nod. They had been confused, lost, afraid. But now, there was something else in their eyes—hope.

The tension in the air had finally lifted, replaced by a sense of relief and camaraderie. As the villagers dispersed, Rana, Vishakha, Amar, Chandan, and Suresh stood together, the weight of the day slowly giving way to lighter hearts. Amar, ever the joker, broke the silence with a grin.

"Damn, Rana," he said, nudging Rana with his elbow. "You had that speech ready to go, didn't you?"

Chandan burst out laughing, clapping Amar on the back. "Rana's probably been rehearsing that speech in his head every time he's sitting outside his hut, brooding in silence."

Rana shot them both a look but couldn't help the small smile tugging at his lips.

"Well, at least I know who I'm voting for," Suresh said, folding his arms.

The group erupted into laughter, the sound echoing through the village. Even Rana couldn't help but chuckle, the tension in his shoulders finally easing.

Amar turned to Vishakha, his grin widening. "You always bring action with you, don't you? Can't just show up with a basket of sweets or something. No, it's always 'Hey, here's a traitor, here's an army, here's a life-changing revelation.'"

Vishakha laughed, shaking her head. "Force of habit, at least I keep the life entertaining! However, I thought you'd be a businessman by now, Amar. What happened to that grand plan of yours?"

Before Amar could respond, Chandan jumped in, his tone teasing. "The only business Amar can run well is running his mouth. That's his true talent."

The group burst into laughter again, Amar playfully shoving Chandan as he protested. "Hey! I'll have you know I'm a very successful blacksmith. My horseshoes are legendary!"

"Legendarily crooked, maybe," Suresh muttered, earning another round of laughter.

Vishakha shook her head, her smile softening as she turned to Rana. "Leave all that and make me meet Pari. I'm dying to meet her after hearing about her a million times."

Rana's gaze grew gentle, a warmth spreading through his chest. "She's been asking about you too," he said. "Let's go find her."

The five of them began walking through the village, their steps light and unhurried. The sun was setting, casting a golden glow over Devran, and for the first time in what felt like forever, there was no stress, no fear—just happiness.

As they walked, Amar nudged Vishakha. "You know, this whole adventure thing? It's been exhausting, but I'm kind of going to miss it."

Chandan snorted. "Miss it? You? The guy who complained every time we had to walk more than five steps?"

"Hey, I'm allowed to have layers," Amar shot back, grinning. "Besides, who else was keeping you all entertained?"

Vishakha laughed, shaking her head. "You're impossible, Amar. But I'll admit, this journey... it's been something I'll never forget."

Rana glanced at her, then at the others, a quiet gratitude in his eyes. "We've been through a lot," he said. "But we made it. Together."

Suresh nodded; his tone uncharacteristically sincere. "And we're better for it. These are the times we'll look back on someday. The adventures that made us... well, us."

Chandan smirked. "We did become a great gang for what it is worth!"

The group laughed again; their bond stronger than ever. They might not have realized it yet, but these were the moments they would cherish forever—the times they would look back on with kinder eyes, the adventures that had forged them into a family.

As they continued their search for Pari once again, this time it was different. This time, there was no fear. No dread. They searched for her with a sense of joy, knowing that she was safe, that they were closer to reuniting with her than ever before. The weight that had once burdened their hearts had lifted, replaced by the lightness of hope.

The sun dipped below the horizon, painting the sky in breathtaking hues of orange and pink, like a canvas of possibilities. The long, gruelling period of hardship was finally over, its shadow receding with each step they took forward. They moved together, side by side, with hearts full of anticipation, each breath feeling like a new beginning.

And as the stars began to twinkle in the night sky, the five friends walked on, their hearts light and their futures bright, ready to face whatever came next—together.

Epilogue

The sun hung low in the sky, casting a golden glow over the banks of the Ganga. The river flowed gently, its waters shimmering like liquid amber under the fading light. The air was filled with the sound of laughter, the kind that comes from a place of pure joy and freedom. Pari darted across the grassy bank, her bare feet kicking up small clouds of dust as she ran. Her laughter rang out like a melody, bright and unrestrained, as Amar, Chandan, and Suresh chased after her, their exaggerated struggles to catch her only adding to her delight.

"You'll never catch me!" Pari squealed, her voice bubbling with glee as she zigzagged between them, her small frame quick and agile. Amar lunged dramatically, missing her by a mile, and Chandan stumbled comically, pretending to trip over his own feet. Suresh, ever the actor, clutched his chest as if out of breath, gasping, "She's too fast! We're no match for her!"

Pari's laughter grew louder as she sprinted toward Vishakha, who sat on the riverbank with Rana, watching the scene unfold. Vishakha opened her arms just in time, and Pari leapt into them, giggling uncontrollably. "Save me, Didi!" she cried, burying her face in Vishakha's shoulder.

Vishakha wrapped her arms around Pari, feigning seriousness. "Don't worry, little one. I'll protect you from these big, scary men."

Amar, Chandan, and Suresh approached, their faces mock-stern. "Hand her over, Vishakha," Amar said, crossing his arms. "She's ours."

"Never!" Vishakha declared, holding Pari tighter. "You'll have to go through me first."

Chandan smirked, stepping forward. "Careful, Amar. She's got that look in her eyes. She might just throw us into the river."

Suresh raised his hands in mock surrender. "I'm not risking it. I've seen her fight. She's terrifying."

Pari peeked out from Vishakha's embrace, her eyes sparkling with mischief. "Didi saved me from you all!" she declared, her voice triumphant.

The three men exchanged exaggerated looks of fear, and Pari burst into laughter again. Amar reached out and ruffled her hair. "Alright, little warrior," he said, his tone softening. "You win this round. But only because I'm feeling generous."

Suresh nodded in agreement, grinning. "Next time, I'll get her for sure."

Pari grinned mischievously and jumped down from Vishakha's arms, turning back to Amar and Chandan. "Sweets! I want sweets now!"

"I'm taking her," Amar said, lifting Pari onto his back. "I'll spoil her with as much sweets as she wants."

Chandan and Suresh joined in. "We'll spoil her too," they said in unison, both acting like protective older brothers, though they were anything but serious.

As the three men took Pari away, their teasing and laughter still ringing through the air, Vishakha and Rana remained by the river, sitting side by side in the growing quiet.

The light from the setting sun cast a warm, golden reflection on the river's surface, the ripples shimmering as the day gave way to night. The air was cool now, a gentle breeze rustling the trees, but the warmth between them felt more powerful than the fading daylight.

"She's really strong," Vishakha said softly, her eyes still following Pari as she disappeared around a bend with the others. "After losing her parents, and everything she went through being taken away... she still holds onto that joy. It's like nothing can break her."

Rana nodded; his gaze fixed on the horizon. "She is strong," he agreed. "But she's not unscathed. Sometimes, at night, she shakes in her sleep. She cries out, but when she wakes, she pretends everything's fine. She's still carrying that fear, that pain. She just doesn't show it."

Vishakha turned to him, her look softening. "She'll get through it, Rana. With time, and with love. Especially because she has you. You've given her a home, a family. That's more than most people ever get."

Rana glanced at her, a faint smile tugging at his lips. "She does. But even I'll need help raising her. It's not something I can do alone."

Vishakha's eyes sparkled with amusement, though she pretended not to catch his meaning. "Oh, you'll find someone," she said lightly, teasing him. "Just work on your humour first. No one wants to spend their life with someone who spends most of his time brooding."

Rana chuckled, a rare sound that made Vishakha's heart skip a beat. "I can work on that," he said. "I'll take some lessons from Amar and Chandan. They're full-time jokers, after all."

Vishakha laughed, the sound blending with the gentle rustle of the river. "Good luck with that. You might end up worse than you started."

They sat together in comfortable silence as the sun sank lower, the sky deepening into shades of purple and orange. There was no rush, no more uncertainty. Only the soft promise of a new beginning.

Vishakha leaned back on her hands, her gaze drifting to the river. "We've come a long way, haven't we?"

Rana nodded, his eyes reflecting the fading light. "We have. And we've lost a lot. But we've also gained something precious. This—this moment, this peace—it's worth everything."

Vishakha smiled, her heart swelling with a quiet joy. "Yes, it is."

They sat there, side by side, as the stars began to dot the sky. The river flowed steadily, mirroring the peace that had finally settled between them. For the first time in what felt like forever, they were happy. They were hopeful. In that moment, they knew they were right where they needed to be. Happy. Hopeful. At peace. They knew that they had found what they had been searching for all along—a place to belong, and the promise of a future filled with light.

And maybe, just maybe, that was all they needed.

Bio

This book began with a conversation. Somewhere in Chennai, two friends were deep in yet another debate over movie plots and missed opportunities in storytelling. Midway, one of them said, "If you're so full of ideas, why don't you write something on your own?" It wasn't said to inspire. It was said to provoke. It worked.

Abhijeet Singh, an engineer like countless others, had never called himself a writer. But stories had always lived in his head—shaped by films, shows, and quiet obsessions no one knew about. This time, instead of arguing, he sat down and wrote.

This is his first novel. It wasn't written to fulfill a dream or chase a trend. It was written because the story refused to stay quiet. Now that it's out, it's only the first of many.